Family Forever—Book One

just another Home

KIMBERLY BANET

Published by Scrivenings Press LLC
15 Lucky Lane
Morrilton, Arkansas 72110
https://ScriveningsPress.com

Printed in the United States of America

Paperback ISBN 978-1-64917-385-0
eBook ISBN 978-1-64917-386-7

Editors: Regina Rudd Merrick and Linda Fulkerson

Cover by Linda Fulkerson, www.bookmarketinggraphics.com

Scripture quotations marked (NIV) are taken from the Holy Bible, New International Version®, NIV®. Copyright © 1973, 1978, 1984 by Biblica, Inc.™ Used by permission of Zondervan. All rights reserved worldwide.

All characters are fictional, and any resemblance to real people, either factual or historical, is purely coincidental.

This book is dedicated to our Heavenly Father, from Whom every good thing comes.

And we know that in all things God works for the good of those who love him, who have been called according to his purpose.
~ Romans 8:28 (NIV)

one

A midnight phone call was the last thing Abbie Grayson expected at the end of this beautiful Tennessee spring day, even if the nighttime had turned stormy. She grabbed her cell phone from the nightstand while her husband John stirred beside her. A check of the caller ID made her heart pound. Could this be the call they'd been waiting for?

She held her breath and swiped her finger across the screen. "Jamie, hi," she whispered as she walked across their spacious bedroom and dropped to the reading chair in front of the bay window.

"Abbie, I'm so sorry to be calling you this late," the social worker said. "But I have a situation, and, well, it's not what you signed up for, but you came to mind anyway, and I just wanted to discuss it with you."

"Uh, okay, sure." Abbie twisted one of her long brown curls around her index finger.

John woke up and came around to sit on her side of the bed, facing her. "Who is it?" he whispered.

Abbie placed her hand over the phone. "It's Jamie Richards from the foster care agency."

"Well," Jamie began. "We have a boy who's been in and out of

1

foster care for many years. I've been his case manager for a long time and know him well." She sighed, and there was a palpable pause. "I know you and John said you didn't want to take any emergency placements or children over ten years old. But Abbie, my heart is telling me that the two of you could provide the perfect home for him right now."

John stared at her, and her head spun. "Okay, go on." It wouldn't hurt to hear her out, would it? She listened as Jamie told her about sixteen-year-old Sam, who'd been in and out of the system since his mother died when he was five. His father had custody of him on and off but was not a capable parent. Neglect and his father's drug use often resulted in the boy being returned to foster care. Earlier tonight, his father was arrested in a drug raid, in front of Sam.

"Like I said, I know this isn't the type of situation you had in mind. But it would only be for a few days until I can find another solution." Jamie paused again. "What are you thinking?"

John's intense gaze from just a few feet away bore into her. He looked both concerned and curious. "Let me discuss it with John and call you back in a few minutes," Abbie said.

"Of course," Jamie said. "And not to put extra pressure on you, but if you could let me know within the hour. He needs someplace to go tonight, if possible."

"I understand." The conversation ended, and Abbie stared at John, her knuckles white from clutching her phone. "Jamie has our first placement."

"Right now?" John asked as he turned his head toward the bedside clock and ran his hand through his hair.

"Yes." Abbie took a deep breath and paused. She'd have to tread lightly. "It's an emergency placement."

"Emergency placement?" John's voice rose. He was wide awake now. "I thought we agreed we wouldn't do those and would only take long-term placements."

"You're right, we did." Abbie nodded but averted his gaze. "Jamie is the case worker for this boy and knows him well. She thinks we'd be a good fit. He's in serious need of a place to go tonight. And there's something else." Abbie paused and bit her lower lip. "He's a teenager—he's sixteen," she said quietly.

"Abbie," John half-shouted, "when you talked me into this, we agreed we wouldn't foster teenagers, only young kids." He stared at her, his voice rising. "And no emergency placements. This situation is everything we agreed we wouldn't do."

Instead of responding, she stood and grabbed her satin robe from the back of her chair, slipped it on, and walked to the kitchen with John following her. He was right, of course. They had agreed to no emergency placements, but the call with the social worker had pulled at her heart.

She grabbed a glass from the cabinet, filled it with water, and stared straight into John's eyes as she leaned against the kitchen counter and took a sip. Any nervousness leftover from the phone call a moment ago was gone. Abbie noted gray streaks sneaking into her husband's hair—hair that once matched his dark brown eyes. After thirty-plus years of marriage, surely he realized she wouldn't back down without a fight. But she needed to measure her words with care as he was still trying to wrap his head around this whole foster-care situation.

John loved kids. They'd raised a son and a daughter, but once their children grew up and were out of the house, she and John had browsed stacks of travel brochures. They even talked about buying a vacation home in the Florida panhandle, not far from extended family. Then something deep in Abbie's soul changed, and she wanted to foster kids. After much discussion and prayer, John agreed, although he still had concerns.

John exhaled and broke the silence at last. "What else did she tell you about him?"

She smiled slightly. John would see her side.

"His name is Sam," she replied and repeated everything Jamie had just told her about the boy.

"I have to tell you, I feel a little ambushed right now," John huffed. "I thought we were on the same page about this. But I guess we're not." He pulled out one of the kitchen island stools and sat.

"Honey, what are you really afraid of?" Abbie put her hand on his shoulder and sat on the stool beside him. "I know there's more to your hesitation than just wanting to travel and retire in a few years. You're a college basketball coach. You work with teens and young men every day, and you love it. So, what is it?"

"You know what it is, or rather, *who* it is." He looked away from her before he continued, his shoulders slumped. "It's Andy Quinn. If I couldn't help a player under my watch, then why would I be able to help another troubled kid now?"

His answer didn't surprise her, and she hurt for him. So many years had passed, but John had never completely recovered from his perceived failure. "No. That situation was vastly different." Abbie shook her head. "Andy was nineteen years old and into drugs, alcohol, theft—you name it. You gave him every opportunity, but in the end, it was Andy who made the decisions that led to his downfall, not you." How could he still not believe the truth by now?

John nodded but didn't look convinced.

"I feel like God wants us to do this," Abbie reasoned. She caught herself twisting one of her long curls around her finger again and stopped. She wasn't as confident as she wanted her husband to believe. "I believe He placed this boy in our path for a reason. Please consider this, hon. I've prayed every day, asking that we get an opportunity to make a difference in a kid's life, even if he or she doesn't fit into the neat little boxes we've drawn."

John drew a deep breath and nodded. "Maybe you're right. Pastor Rob did just say in his sermon Sunday that God calls us out of our comfort zones. When do we have to let her know?"

"Now," Abbie uttered. "He needs a place to go tonight. I know we can provide stability and a safe place for him. Besides, it's only emergency placement, which means it's just for a short time. A few days, tops."

"Only emergency placement. Meaning the boy was just removed from a traumatic situation." John got up and paced their large, open kitchen and combined great room with his head down. Abbie recognized his process. He would weigh the pros and cons and silently pray, hoping to hear an answer from God.

She prayed her own silent prayer. *Please God, I believe You placed this boy in our path for a reason. Don't let this be more than we're equipped to handle, and for John's sake, please don't let it end up as another Andy Quinn situation.*

At that moment, John stopped pacing and turned to look at Abbie. "All right, as long as it's only for a few days."

Abbie was overjoyed, but at the same time, her intuition told her it might not be that simple.

two

S am Keller climbed into the car with his caseworker, Jamie, as his anger gave way to fear and panic, which had nothing to do with the thunder and lightning in the not-so-distant sky. His hands shook, and his heart raced as he fumbled with his seatbelt. How many more times would he have to endure a caseworker dropping him off at yet another foster home?

"You okay, Sam?" Jamie glanced over at him before she pulled out of the Department of Social Services parking lot onto the wet, dimly lit street.

"Yeah." The lie rolled off Sam's tongue, but he didn't care, and he certainly didn't want to talk. Instead, he stared out the window into the blackness of the night. Car lights and streetlights blurred together, partly from their reflection on the wet pavement but mostly from the tears of anger that burned his eyes. He refused to let them fall.

The light rain subsided as they made their way through the stoplights of Franklin on the southern outskirts of Nashville, but the respite was brief. Gigantic, random raindrops splattered the windshield, and then, without warning, the sky opened, and torrential rain poured. The huge drops pounded the car's roof as if the deluge desired to drown out his thoughts.

This is fitting. The perfect backdrop for this dismal night. If his life were a book, the first line would read *it was a dark and stormy night*. Thunder rumbled, low and constant, and lightning lit up the sky to provide glimpses of the black clouds that were otherwise unseen under the night sky.

Much like himself. Unseen and unnoticed in his dark world until abuse or neglect lit up his existence and allowed cops and social workers a small window into his bleak life as they whisked him away. But that small window only allowed them a glimpse—Sam never allowed anyone access to his entire story.

"I hope this heavy rain stops before we have to get out of the car." Jamie increased the speed of the windshield wipers and slowed the car to navigate the downpour. "We're almost there."

Almost there. The knots in his stomach tightened their grip. *Don't think about it. Just breathe.* He focused his thoughts on pleasant things, like his best friend, Lauren—the only one who befriended him when he was the new kid in junior high—or the classic books he devoured or the country music he loved to listen to, but it was no use. He couldn't concentrate on anything except the situation that lay before him and the memories of every horrendous thing he'd gone through in his sixteen years. It all flashed through his mind like scenes in a bad movie.

Out of nowhere, his stomach dropped, and panic of a different kind hit him. Where had the picture of his mom gone? He snatched his frayed backpack from the floorboard beneath his feet and ransacked it, the only light coming from the car's dashboard. Oh, no, it must be here! Did he pack it before leaving his father's apartment?

"Is something wrong?" Jamie asked.

Her eyes were on him, and he didn't blame her. At that moment, he probably looked like a madman. "Just looking for something," he mumbled.

His heartbeat thudded in his ears, and panic threatened to overtake him as he grabbed his tattered journal, opened it, and the worn, creased picture of his mom fell out. He let out a huge sigh and positioned the picture carefully and tightly into the middle of his journal, closed it, and returned it to his backpack.

Of course, he'd grabbed it. He packed without thinking. Packing was second nature to him since he'd moved so many times. He always grabbed his backpack, his journal, his only picture of his mom, and whatever book he was reading at the time. Those were the only objects that even mattered.

Sam ran his hands through his longish hair out of habit and laid his head back against the headrest as he thought of his mother. How different would his life be if she hadn't died? Perhaps he wouldn't have had to move from one foster home to another because his dad—

"Here we are." Jamie interrupted his thoughts before the simmering anger toward his father boiled to the surface. "And thankfully, the rain stopped."

Even in the darkness, he could see the home was at least three times the size of any other he'd been in. He was awestruck for a moment until he realized he'd have to stay in it with the people who lived here.

Sweat broke out on his forehead as he imagined walking into another unfamiliar home to live with people he didn't know. The fear he'd been suppressing took over. He couldn't catch his breath, and he grew lightheaded.

"I can't... I can't do this again," he uttered, his voice barely above a whisper. How could he? He'd seldom lived in a foster home that turned out okay. In the best-case scenario, the foster family left him alone, and he merely survived day to day, with no plans, no dreams, no real life of his own. He simply existed on the fringes of someone else's life. He quickly shut down thoughts of the worst-case scenario.

"It's okay. Try to relax." His long-time caseworker put the car in park and looked at him. "I know this is hard, but I came to know this couple well during their training, and they are genuine, good people, who just want to help."

Sam fought the urge to yell at her and ask her if that's what she believed about all the foster parents she'd worked with, even the ones who proved abusive or neglectful. More than anything, he wanted to ask her if she realized this was his 3,304th day in foster care. Without warning, the tears of anger he'd held in all night escaped and slid down his face.

"I'm sorry," he said, more to himself than to her. He quickly swiped the tears away with the back of his hand and took several deep breaths.

"You have nothing to be sorry about, Sam. You're exhausted, and once you get a shower and a good night's sleep, you'll feel better," Jamie said gently.

Yeah, then tomorrow morning I'll wake up in a strange house with people I don't know. He needed to get a grip. None of this was her fault, and she couldn't comprehend what his life was like. His gut told him Jamie tried her best and cared about what happened to him.

They sat in the car for a few minutes so he could compose himself. The lightning and thunder had moved beyond them, and the rain had dwindled to a light drizzle. He had no choice but to go into the house, so he drew one more big breath to prepare himself for whatever was to come.

"Okay, I guess I'm ready."

He was certain Jamie had no idea what number today was.

three

Abbie went to the kitchen to make some herbal tea while John paced the floor of their great room. She'd tried to sit patiently and wait for Jamie to arrive with Sam, but anxiousness got the best of her. She hoped the tea would help calm their nerves.

The kettle whistled, and she poured the hot water over the tea bags. Her mind couldn't shake the things John had just told her about research he'd done when they went through foster care training. He'd read teenage boys like Sam, who'd been in the child welfare system for years, were almost impossible to place in foster homes because they likely had endured trauma that negatively affected their behavior.

She walked carefully from the kitchen with the two steaming mugs of tea and set them on the coffee table in front of the sofa. "I was just thinking about what you said. About the trauma these kids go through. I feel like this is where we can help and really make a difference, hon."

John sighed and stared into his wife's eyes. "It's just there are so many assumptions and "what if" scenarios surrounding these boys. Many times, they turn aggressive or even violent by the time they're Sam's age. I know it isn't fair to make blanket assumptions, but I'm worried, especially where you're concerned."

She understood where he was coming from, and maybe she was naïve, but she didn't share his concerns. "I can't imagine what his life is like." Abbie veered the conversation in a slightly different direction. "How awful would it feel to be dropped off at a home with people you don't know, over and over again?"

John sipped his tea and sank back into the large, brown leather sectional sofa. "I can't begin to fathom it. Look at how nervous we are, and we're in our own home and have each other. How must he feel right now?"

Abbie shivered at the thought, and then the doorbell rang. Their eyes met, and Abbie summoned all the determination she could muster and prayed silently that she conveyed more confidence than she possessed.

"Here we go." Her husband extended his hand to her as she got up from the sofa. They walked to the front door together, and John opened it. There stood Jamie, and on the step below her was a blond-haired teenager with his head down, a backpack on his shoulder, and a trash bag in his hand.

"Hi, thanks for having us so late." Jamie's pleasant voice cut through the awkwardness as she smiled and made the introductions. "This is Sam Keller. Sam, this is Mr. and Mrs. Grayson."

Sam cast his eyes to the ground. The child was pale and thin, with dark circles under his eyes, and Abbie was struck by his boyish looks. He appeared much younger than sixteen. His disheveled, stringy hair fell just to his shoulders and hung in his eyes. He wore a faded flannel shirt and dingy jeans with a hole in the knee.

"Welcome, Sam. You can call me John, and this is Abbie." John smiled and ushered them into the house from their covered front porch. "Come in out of the damp air."

Again, Sam didn't smile or attempt to make eye contact with them, but he mumbled something that sort of sounded like

"Hello." Abbie offered to take the trash bag from him, which she assumed held his clothes and belongings. *What must it be like to carry all your belongings in a trash bag?* Sam let go of the bag but held on to the worn, brown backpack like it contained treasure, so Abbie didn't attempt to take it. She ached for him.

While John led them all through the foyer to the great room to get comfortable, Abbie came to the unnerving realization that their foster-care training hadn't truly prepared them for this moment.

"Would either of you like something to drink?" Abbie asked, and John smiled at her, which immediately put her at ease. *Okay, together they could do this.*

"No, thanks, Abbie," Jamie said.

Sam shook his head without looking up, his face without expression. Once they exchanged pleasantries, Jamie told them basic, practical things, such as prescription medication that Sam took for anxiety, and that he had contact lenses as well as glasses with him.

Of course, she'd be in touch when she found a home for Sam to go to for the longer term. They signed paperwork, including privacy notices and medical forms that allowed her and John to seek medical treatment for Sam if needed.

Not long ago, they'd completed more paperwork to buy a car than they had to complete to foster a child, which didn't seem right. Once they signed the documents, Jamie gave them an envelope. Abbie had learned from their training that the envelope held additional information about Sam for them to look over later.

During the meeting, Abbie nodded in all the proper places, but she found herself only half listening. She watched Sam, who sat on the large sofa at the farthest point away from everyone else, his eyes cast down. To her, he didn't look like the brooding, angry teen she'd expected, but more like a broken boy who wanted to disappear. *What could this poor kid be thinking?*

She'd never seen her own kids, Kyle and Hannah, look like

this, and for the first time, she seriously doubted their ability to handle this situation. *This is gonna be hard, Lord. Please guide us.*

"Abbie?" Jamie's voice startled her back to the conversation, and she realized all eyes were on her.

"I'm so sorry, what did you say?" Abbie asked.

"It's usually me who gets in trouble for not listening," John quipped.

The heat rose in her cheeks, and she chided herself for letting her thoughts wander.

"I asked if you had any other questions for me right now," Jamie offered politely.

"I don't think I do," Abbie said, and John echoed her sentiment.

"I'll be in touch tomorrow, but in the meantime, you know how to reach me." Jamie picked up the signed paperwork and her purse and stood to leave.

Abbie and John stood also, but Sam remained seated.

"That goes for you too, Sam," Jamie said.

Sam mumbled "okay" but still didn't glance up. He seemed lost as he sat with his arms crossed and stared at the floor.

The couple walked Jamie out, and she paused at the front door. Abbie had learned during training that Jamie was in her late thirties, but tonight her weariness showed, and she looked older.

"The first night is always hard," Jamie said with a weary smile. "Give him some space tonight. It's incredibly tough on kids when they're dropped off at an unfamiliar home, even for the ones who've done it as many times as Sam has."

Something about that statement overwhelmed Abbie, but she nodded. John told Jamie, "Thank you" and closed the door behind her. They paused, John blew out a long breath, and his eyes told her he was as anxious as she was.

The two of them headed back to the great room where Sam sat, arms still crossed with his backpack on his lap. With Jamie gone, he appeared even more lost than before. Only minutes ago, Abbie wouldn't have thought that was possible.

"Well, uh, Sam," John stumbled over his words and then cleared his throat, his nervousness clearly showing. "Abbie and I are glad you're here. We'll show you your room and help you settle in."

The boy nodded but again didn't say anything. His face was a blank slate, holding no clue as to what he was thinking.

As an afterthought, Abbie spoke up. "Are you hungry? I'd be glad to fix you a sandwich."

Sam's "No, thank you" was barely audible.

"Okay, well, it's late, and you must be tired, so let's get you settled in your room," Abbie said.

He stood and slung his backpack over his shoulder. Abbie led the way past the kitchen and the smaller family room to the bedroom she'd transformed for their foster child. She'd painted the room a neutral light gray with white trim, and the furniture and bedding were also white and light gray so it would be appropriate for a boy or girl. It was a large bedroom, bright and inviting, filled with books and school supplies and a TV mounted on the wall.

"Here's your room. It has its own bathroom, so you don't have to share. There's a big, walk-in closet for you, and a desk, dresser, and bookshelf," Abbie said. "And our bedroom is across the hall if you need us."

Sam nodded but his eyes were vacant. She wondered if any of this was even registering with him.

"C'mon, I'll help you put your things away," Abbie said with as much cheer as she could muster in an effort to act as if she hadn't noticed the boy's lack of response.

He simply looked exhausted. Besides the weariness though, there was something else she hadn't picked up on earlier—fear. His timid demeanor and the careful, seemingly intentional way he left plenty of space between himself and her and John revealed the boy was terrified beneath the surface.

Abbie fought to keep her composure. What had he been through? A shiver went up her spine, and for the first time tonight, a certainty overwhelmed her. They were absolutely doing the right thing by offering him an emergency place to stay, no matter how hard or awkward it might be for her or John. If nothing else, they could keep him safe.

Abbie put away the clothing he'd brought with him in the trash bag, and Sam quietly followed her lead. She offered to wash the things he didn't need right away and showed him a big basket of toiletries in the matching gray and white bathroom that contained soap, toothbrushes, toothpaste, and anything else he might need. Then she and John left him to take a shower and go to bed while they retreated to their room across the hall.

Once in their own bedroom with the door closed, Abbie and John both sat on the bed. Her eyes filled with tears, the cheeriness in her voice from earlier completely absent. "I've never seen a child so broken, have you?"

The confidence John had exuded earlier in the presence of Sam was also completely gone, and he simply shook his head. "And to think all his belongings are in that trash bag and backpack. It's beyond sad."

This situation tore at Abbie's heart much more than she'd prepared for. "Maybe you were right, John." Panic rose within her once again. "What if we can't do this?" This rollercoaster of emotions was nothing like she'd experienced before.

"We can do this, honey," John said with a new determination. "I know we can," he said as he put his arm around her shoulders.

Abbie's eyes filled with tears. That's exactly what she needed to hear. John was with her in this one hundred percent, the way he'd always been in anything they did, and with God present at the center of it all, they wouldn't fail.

* * *

John stretched out on their huge, king-size bed, lost in thought, while his wife brushed her teeth and got ready for bed. In their affluent existence, they'd never given much consideration to the way some kids lived. Even though they discussed this in their foster parenting classes, the reality of it never registered until tonight.

Once Abbie came to bed, they talked for a few minutes before she drifted off, but John's mind refused to shut down. He lay in the quiet darkness and stared at the ceiling, replaying the events of the night, and thinking how strange it was to have someone in their home they didn't know who was probably scared and confused.

With that thought, John got up out of bed and decided to go check on Sam to see if he was asleep, but once he crossed the hallway, he paused before going in. Should he even go in? He was unsure.

The bedroom door was half open and the light still on, and he decided to take a couple of steps in. Sam appeared to be asleep with the comforter pulled up above his chin, so John turned to walk out and switched the light off, but as soon as he did, he heard Sam stir.

"Can I please keep the light on?" Sam's quiet voice cut into the darkness.

"Of course, that's no problem." John flipped the light switch back on. "Sleep in as long as you want tomorrow. We'll be in the family room or kitchen when you get up. Until then, we'll be across the hall if you need anything," John reminded him.

"Thanks," the boy said sleepily.

John turned and left Sam's room, and it was no longer a question in his mind. He was positive Sam had gone through something horrible.

* * *

Drew sat in his jail cell and plotted his next move. He'd played it cool and pleaded his drug trafficking sentence down to possession by turning in a couple of low-level dealers. The police had busted him on a tip from someone in their apartment complex, and he figured they had no idea the magnitude of what he was doing, because if they did, he wouldn't have a future to plan for.

His pro bono lawyer had just left, and Drew thought about the details of the meeting. The attorney said with good behavior, Drew's release could come as early as October. Just five months from now. The lawyer had also talked about the steps Drew would need to take to get his kid back.

Drew chuckled just thinking about it. Frankly, he cared nothing about the kid, but being a father had always been a good cover for his drug business. Besides that, he was also able to get food stamps and public assistance he wouldn't otherwise get. And now, his developing plan included more lucrative reasons to keep the kid around.

"Hey, man, you been thinkin' about what I told ya?" Right on cue, the low-level meth-head-turned-dealer in the next cell was awake.

Ironically, Drew didn't have much patience for druggies. He didn't do drugs anymore—he was in the drug business solely for the money. No way would he live the rest of his life the way his parents had. His old man had overdosed and died when Drew was ten, and his mother was a raging alcoholic. As a result, Drew spent a good part of his childhood homeless. Now his one and only priority in life was money. Nothing, and no one else, mattered.

He would put up with the addict in the next cell because the guy intrigued him with his money-making ideas. Drew sucked in a breath. A couple of years ago, he wouldn't have dared go down this path, but now with this most recent arrest, he realized he needed to branch out to more than just drugs.

"Yeah, man," Drew answered as he walked to the front of his

cell so he could talk with the guy more easily. "You got some good ideas. I never knew so much money could be made in trafficking people."

"I'm tellin' ya, man, that kid of yours can really help you out too. You said he's got the looks to lure the girls in. Somethin' else to think about if you want to go another way, you can just sell him and keep all the profit yourself," the dopehead said, matter-of-factly.

Drew winced. His kid didn't mean anything to him, but he didn't want to go that route. That went too far, even for him.

"Now tell me exactly how I would use him to lure the girls in." Drew ignored the man's last remark.

"First thing, man," the guy said excitedly, "you have to threaten him good, or he won't do it. Threaten to kill his girlfriend or somethin'. That usually does gets 'em to cooperate. Then you have to follow him to make sure he does what he's supposed to and beat him up if he don't do it. And get a second dude you can trust to go with him to keep him on track. They both gotta be good lookin' to attract the young girls, ya know. And the girls gotta be twelve or thirteen, no older." This was obviously his wheelhouse.

Drew made a mental note of the ages while the man kept talking.

"Then just send 'em out, have 'em hit on girls and invite them back to their room, or even a drink, coffee, or somethin'. Anything to get in a position where you and your crew can swoop in and grab the girls."

Drew scratched his scruffy-bearded chin as he thought about the setup. They would go to a beach in southern Alabama that he and his associates had already scoped out for drug dealing. But this was a better idea, or maybe they could even do both.

"Huge bucks, man. Huge bucks. You do it for a year, and you'll be set. You won't never have to do nothin' else again."

The man rambled on, but Drew quit paying attention and sat back down on his cot. Could he pull this off? Could he use the kid to lure girls in so he and his associates could auction them off to wealthy men all over the world?

Now he had something productive to do while behind bars. For the next five months, he would continue to work on his brilliant plan. Drew would be a model prisoner in order to get out of jail in October, and then he'd do whatever it took to appear to be a model parent and get that kid back.

four

Sam bolted upright in bed, his heart pounding hard in his chest. Where was he? He scanned the room and tried to catch his breath. He had no idea where he was or how long he'd slept. Everything smelled clean and new, unlike the stale, smoky air he'd become accustomed to. Sunlight streamed through the window above the desk, and it all came back to him. Yesterday had been a nightmare, and today that nightmare continued—at a new foster home.

What are their names? Panic rose again when he couldn't remember the foster parents' names.

The couple had been nice enough, but this was emergency placement only, and that all-too-familiar panic and anxiety rose within him as he contemplated moving again very soon. He tried his best to push those feelings down and steady himself. He remembered what the man had told him last night, to come find them when he got up.

As he got out of bed, he glanced at the clock on the dresser, and his heart pounded once more. It was approaching noon. How could he have slept that long? The couple was bound to be angry or annoyed, so he dressed as fast as he could, fumbled through the big basket of toiletries in the bathroom, and then brushed his teeth and ran his hands through his shoulder-length hair. It looked a mess but at least he'd showered last night, and it was clean.

After a last check in the mirror, he took a deep breath and headed down the hallway to find the couple. For a brief moment, he wished he still believed in God so he could offer a silent prayer asking for relief from the rising anxiety that threatened to overcome him, but he dismissed the thought. There was no god who would help him.

He walked gingerly toward the sound of a TV and approached the doorway to the family room where the sound came from. The couple sat watching a news station. It had struck him last night how big this house appeared. This was supposed to be a second, smaller family room, but it was bigger than any family room he'd ever seen. It had two large sofas, a couple of recliners, and a fireplace with a gigantic TV above it. On both sides of the fireplace were windows overlooking the deck and backyard. It seemed like a peaceful place to hang out, and he relaxed a little.

Unexpectedly, the man's name popped into his head—John. But should he call him that or something else? He figured he wouldn't call them anything until he found out for sure. He studied them for a moment before they realized he was standing in the doorway.

John sat in a recliner scrolling through his cell phone, and the lady sat on the sofa flipping through a magazine. They were older than most of the couples Sam had been placed with, but they didn't seem terribly old. The man's hair was a little gray, and the woman had light brown, curly hair just past her shoulders. They both looked tanned like they'd been to a beach or something.

Sam didn't know what to do so he coughed, and they both looked up at the same time and smiled warmly at him as he took a small step into the room. He was relieved that they didn't appear mad or annoyed.

"Sorry I slept so late," he apologized sheepishly.

"That's okay, Sam," the lady with no name said. "I'm sure you were exhausted. Did you sleep well?"

"Yes, ma'am," he replied.

In fact, it was the most comfortable bed he'd ever slept in, but he didn't feel quite chatty enough to tell them that. He sat at the other end of the long sofa, careful not to get too close to either one of them. Unsure of what to do with himself, he hated the awkwardness of getting to know new families. If it were up to him, he'd just hide away in his assigned room and only come out for food.

"You're bound to be hungry, so I'll go make us some lunch." The lady hopped up from the sofa and disappeared in an instant.

He nodded at the lady just as John said, "Thanks, Abbie."

Abbie. At least he had both their names now. But when he realized he and John were alone in the room, sweat broke out on his forehead. The man didn't give off any weird vibes or anything, but Sam's past had taught him he couldn't trust adults, especially men. He would have to keep his guard up.

John leaned forward in his chair and smiled. Not a weird, creepy smile, but a normal, friendly one. He seemed comfortable, and Sam wondered if John could sense Sam was anything but comfortable.

Although Sam distrusted most adults, he had to admit there was something different about this guy. His smile and the way he spoke both seemed genuine, and Abbie appeared to be cheery and friendly. But Sam's hardened heart wouldn't allow him to let his guard down. Not yet—maybe not ever. He decided a long time ago not to trust anyone because people eventually revealed their true nature and motives.

A familiar, overwhelming weariness came over him, like a suffocating weight, making it difficult to breathe, difficult to put one foot in front of the other, and difficult to face each new day. Memories flooded his mind of the times he'd been handed over to new foster parents who acted nice at first but turned into anything but nice.

Or even worse were the families who were actually nice and treated him well, but turned around and gave him up without warning, for any reason or no reason at all. He'd written about them all in his journal to try to make sense of his anger and sadness.

"Tell me a little about yourself, Sam."

John's voice snapped Sam's attention back to the present, and for a split second, he was glad until he realized it was the "let's get to know each other" part Sam hated. *Ugh.* It all seemed for nothing because his social worker had told him he'd only be here a few days. He wished he could just hide away in the guestroom until she came to move him again, but he would play along with the game because that's what everyone expected.

"What do you need to know?" Sam heard the frustration and annoyance in his voice. He hated it because John had acted nice toward him so far. But if John took offense to Sam's tone, he didn't let on. *Cut the attitude, Sam.* He didn't need to be labeled as difficult and land back in a group home.

"Why don't we start with school? What grade are you in, and what's your favorite subject?" John asked.

He hated school but that had nothing to do with academics. Reading and learning were great—he hated how the other kids treated him. They always saw him as the new kid, the foster kid, or the weird, quiet kid. He had a best friend, Lauren, but other than her and just a couple of other kids he'd met in a group home, he'd never made friends easily.

"I was in tenth grade. And I like English best, I guess," Sam replied without emotion.

"What do you like best about English—reading or writing?" John continued the questioning.

Sam rolled his eyes and shook his head just a little. If he were in a better mood, he would've laughed at how enthralled John was with this boring conversation. The man leaned forward in his chair, focused on Sam as if the continuation of humanity relied on his answer.

"*Um*, I guess both." Sam shrugged.

"Follow me, I think you're going to like this room." John smiled as he rose and motioned for Sam to follow. "We didn't go in there last night, but I want you to see it now."

After hesitating for a moment, Sam followed. He didn't know where they were heading. A twinge of fear hit for a split second, but he had a gut feeling it would be okay. John seemed harmless, and Sam hoped his intuition was right.

John led him around the kitchen, through the gigantic room where they'd all sat last night, and then down another hallway to the other side of the house Sam hadn't seen yet. These people must be rich. Not only was this the biggest house he'd ever seen, but everything appeared nice, new, and smelled clean. The huge windows everywhere made the house bright and cheery, and for some reason the brightness and openness made him feel a little safer.

They stopped in the hallway, where John pointed out his office, then he directed Sam's attention to the room across the hall, behind big, wooden double doors. John smiled and stepped through those doors. Sam followed him in and immediately stopped and stared, his eyes wide. It was a library. A library inside a house. Sam had never seen anything like it.

Bookshelves from floor to ceiling lined all four walls of this huge room, and in the middle of the room stood a large, heavy-looking table with big thick legs. On the back wall between bookshelves, cushioned window seats in front of huge windows gave way to a view of the lush landscape. The walls were a deep shade of blue.

"*Whoa*." Sam wanted to hide his excitement, but he couldn't. This was the coolest thing he'd ever seen.

John smiled as if he understood. "When you said you liked to read and write, I thought you'd like this room. When our kids lived at home, they came in here to do their homework or read, and they'd have their friends over to work on projects or study together."

"You can use this room whenever you want," John continued on. "I'm not quite the avid reader my wife and kids are, but according to them, any kind of book you would want to read is in here, so help yourself. In fact, why don't you go ahead and look around? Make yourself at home, and I'll see if I can help Abbie with lunch."

"Thanks," Sam said without looking at John. He walked around the room with his mouth open in awe of all the books. One wall held all the classics, and on another wall the books were arranged by color. It even smelled like a library. Not that musty, old smell, but the smell of paper and leather together, kind of a woodsy scent, and Sam breathed it in.

Books had always been an escape from his mixed-up, unfair world. He could completely lose himself in a story that made him forget his own miserable life and everyone in it. Except for Lauren, of course. A twinge of sadness overcame him knowing she probably wasn't even aware of what had happened to him. He needed to contact her soon.

As Sam browsed the library and thumbed through some of the books, he briefly forgot his fear and the awkwardness from earlier. John had been nice and then left him alone. Now his favorite things in the world surrounded him—books.

For the first time, he decided he might like it here if he gave it a chance. He sat at one of the window seats and gazed out at the sprawling backyard full of trees and flowers. It was peaceful here. This house was insane, and John and Abbie acted nice, but based on his experience, he couldn't let his guard down.

His thoughts drifted to the families he'd lived with that weren't necessarily good or bad. They provided shelter and nothing more. But he'd also lived in some bad places. Really bad. When he turned twelve and his father disappeared after what had been a traumatic time, he lived with a foster family who inflicted further trauma, complete with both physical and emotional scars.

After that, social services shuffled him from one home to another, including a couple of group homes he ended up in when he'd gotten in trouble for skipping school and drinking, and no foster family would take him. The group homes had their own problems because they were full of kids no one wanted. Kids just as messed up as him.

Then, six months ago, he ended up with the Steins. They were nice enough. He didn't have to worry about having enough food, and no one in the house bothered him. They took him to all his counseling appointments, and in their home, healing began.

But a couple of months after Sam had been placed with them, Mrs. Stein found out she was pregnant, with twins. Since they had two children already, they said they couldn't handle Sam once the babies were born.

Sam understood. It wasn't their fault, but that didn't make it any easier. And the timing coincided with his father coming back into the picture which made it even worse. Sam didn't even want to think about it right now. He did his best to bury what had happened during the past few months.

No one had ever wanted him except for his mom, and she died eleven years ago. In the journal he wrote in every day, he drew emojis next to each day's date, and he suspected he'd have to flip back a whole lot of days to find one with a happy emoji next to it. After what he'd been through, being wanted or happy didn't even matter anymore. Being safe was most important now. The rest was unattainable.

five

Abbie stood in the kitchen tossing a salad for lunch, while John leaned against the counter next to her. "Honey, I don't think talking to Sam alone was the best idea," he said. "He stiffened up immediately, and his body language changed as soon as you left the room. Not only that, but he sat as far away from me as he could and still remain in the same room."

Her husband wasn't at all accustomed to this. In John's career as a college basketball coach, new recruits acted a bit nervous when they first met him, but they relaxed as soon as they started talking about basketball. This situation differed tremendously. She knew he'd have to make an extra effort to carefully measure his words and actions to make Sam comfortable. For a moment Abbie was thankful this was only short-term, but that wasn't fair, and she brushed the feeling aside.

The day proved to be a little rough. Sam had clearly put up walls, which Abbie expected, but that didn't make it any easier or less awkward. The three of them ate lunch outdoors on the deck, and Abbie did most all the talking, with John occasionally asking questions. They asked Sam questions to get to know him better, but he answered them as briefly as possible. He'd been trying to be polite, although the politeness came off as a little forced.

"Do you like sports, Sam?" John asked.

"Not really." Sam shrugged without even a glance up from his plate.

"What kinds of things do you like to do?" Abbie asked.

"I mainly like reading and music," Sam replied.

At last, they had something they could latch onto in an attempt to connect with him. "Do you play any instruments?" Abbie asked hopefully.

"I play piano a little. I had a foster mom who was a retired music teacher, and she taught me to play," Sam replied. That was the longest sentence he'd spoken since he'd been here.

"Did you see the piano in the basement?" John asked. "You can play it any time you want. It would be great to hear music in the house again. No one has played it since our daughter, Hannah, lived at home."

Sam didn't say anything but nodded, and he ate a little more than he did before. Maybe the ice had started to break.

But for some reason, the icebreakers never lasted long before Sam distanced himself. By the time they finished lunch, he had become quiet again. *This is going to be harder than I imagined.* When the three of them went inside to take their lunch dishes to the dishwasher, John decided to show Sam his office, and Abbie followed along.

"Wow, there are three TVs in here," Sam's voice was filled with awe.

John laughed. "Yes, this is where I sometimes watch game tapes with my coaching staff."

Sam squinted his eyes and glanced around the room. "Wait— you're a coach?"

John laughed again. Most people around here recognized him anywhere he went, but Sam had said he wasn't into sports, so he must not recognize John.

"Yes, I coach the Tennessee University men's basketball team." John smiled proudly.

Sam stared at him without saying anything for a long moment, but then he nodded slowly, an apparent 'light bulb' moment.

"Oh yeah ... I thought you looked familiar," Sam replied. If he was impressed, he definitely didn't show it as he glanced at all the awards and back at John. "I've seen you on TV. Y'all just won the national championship, didn't you?"

"Yes, we did!" John answered. This might finally be the icebreaker they'd prayed for. "Did you watch the game?"

"No," Sam replied flatly, crossed his arms, and looked around the room as if trying to see if anything else in the office besides basketball interested him. And that marked the end of that conversation.

Abbie covered her mouth to stifle a giggle over the way John hung his head as though his pride was hurt. Sam definitely wasn't impressed, although he was awestruck by the three TVs.

After they toured John's office, Sam went to the basement to check out the piano. His attitude had softened somewhat, which Abbie counted as progress, even if he still didn't say much. They'd pressed him enough for now, and he needed time to himself.

Besides, she and John needed to read over the information in the envelope Jamie had given them last night. The emotion from last night and the late hour had left them exhausted, so they'd decided to leave it for today.

Abbie retrieved the envelope from a kitchen drawer, went to find John in his office, and closed the door behind her. She sat on the black leather sofa next to John, and they opened it. Inside was a four-page printed document, with handwritten notes from Jamie on the last page.

Skimming the document, she read portions aloud, "medical history, no medication allergies." She nodded along as she read but paused and frowned as she came to the next part. "Alcohol abuse at age fourteen." But the next sentence took her breath away. "Overdose of pills at age fifteen, although patient said it was accidental, and cutting to deal with anxiety."

"What?" The alarm sounded in John's voice.

"I thought there were cut marks on his arm earlier, but I wasn't sure," Abbie said quietly.

"You did? Why didn't you tell me?" John demanded.

"I noticed it when we were eating lunch." Abbie's said in a soft voice. "He saw me look and quickly pulled his sleeve down."

John took a deep breath and shook his head. "What have we gotten ourselves into? We are without a doubt in over our heads."

Abbie was panicked also, but she certainly didn't want him to know that, so she directed her focus back to the letter and continued to read. Once she got to Jamie's handwritten notes at the end, it got worse. "Suspected abuse from a foster home and possibly someone connected with Sam's father, although Sam never admitted to it."

"You're right, we're in over our heads," Abbie said, her eyes wide. "We don't know how to deal with anything like this."

"Which is the reason I didn't want a teenager in the first place," John lashed out sharper and louder than he ever had before. He got up and paced the office, his arms flailing. "You talked me into this. I told you from the beginning I didn't want a teenager, and now here we are."

"Don't put this all on me, John. In the end, you agreed." Abbie's defensiveness took over as she crossed her arms and bit her lower lip, willing herself not to cry.

After a moment, the fight left him. John sat back down on the sofa, laid his head back against the headrest, and stared at the ceiling. "You're right, I'm sorry I snapped like that. I agreed, even though I still feel a little ambushed by this emergency placement. But there's no sense arguing about it now. We need to stick together and be a team, the way we always have with everything we've faced." John sighed and reached for Abbie's hand.

Abbie took a deep breath, still trying hard to keep the tears at bay. "You're right, I'm sorry, too, hon."

"I know, it's okay." John locked eyes with Abbie. "This is only for a couple of days, right? We'll get through it, and the next time they call us we'll stick to our original plan of no emergency placements and no child over eight years old. And I can promise you, I won't give in next time."

As if on cue, Abbie's cell phone rang. She checked the caller ID—Jamie Richards.

"Jamie, I'm so glad you called," Abbie said, hearing the desperation in her own voice.

"How are things with Sam going so far?" Jamie asked.

She needed to be honest with the social worker, and she put the phone on speaker so John could participate. "Well, to be honest, we're panicking a little bit," Abbie said, as she got up and paced the room. "We finished reading the info you gave us last night, and I have to tell you, I don't think we're equipped for this."

"I understand completely," Jamie said, empathy in her voice. "I know this is overwhelming, especially since it's your first placement, but let me reassure you both, I've known Sam for eight years now, and in the time I've gotten to know the two of you, I think you're a great match for each other. He's definitely gone through a lot, but he's a good kid who's in dire need of stability. I feel like the two of you have so much to offer him."

To Abbie's relief, Jamie's tone was empathetic and not the least bit judgmental. She nodded at John. He was stronger and more reassured than he had been moments earlier. They'd talked last night and agreed they trusted Jamie. If she thought they were good for Sam and could handle the situation, they'd continue with the emergency placement with her support.

"Rest assured, I'm working hard on a more permanent placement for him," Jamie offered. "I should have something in a couple of days. Do you think you can continue for just a day or two?"

Abbie paused for a few seconds then answered with more confidence than she possessed. "Yes, we'll continue."

"It'll be okay," Jamie reassured them. "Just remember your training and call if you need me."

* * *

Sam came up from the basement to grab a notebook and pen from a cabinet in the library John had shown him. He started to head back downstairs, but as he left the library, Jamie's voice on speakerphone coming from John's office caught his attention, so he pressed his ear to the door to try to listen. They were talking about the information Jamie had given them about him.

This part of the process was painfully familiar to Sam—the part where the foster parents find out just how tarnished their new foster kid is. But they wouldn't find out everything, because he'd never told anyone all the horrendous things he'd endured over the years.

In any case, Abbie and John would be a little more reserved toward him. It always happened. Sam made decent grades and never got in any real trouble anymore since he quit drinking and skipping school, but when foster parents found out about his past, they acted cooler toward him. That signaled he was on his way out.

But that's okay, he never allowed himself to get too attached to a family. Especially a temporary emergency placement. He wouldn't be here long, so he'd act nice enough not to make any trouble for himself, and he'd be sure not to let his guard down enough for them to get close.

He listened at the door as they finished the conversation. Abbie hung up the phone, and as he walked away, he overheard something that took him by surprise. John and Abbie prayed out loud that God would help them with Sam, and that he would be comfortable in their home and find peace and rest.

He went back downstairs so they wouldn't catch him eavesdropping, but he replayed their prayer in his head and wasn't quite sure what to make of it. He'd never heard anyone pray for him, and he was confused by it.

He shook his head as he flopped onto the basement sofa. The prayer sounded nice and all, but he wouldn't let them force their beliefs on him. At one time he had believed in God, but not anymore. Not after everything he'd been through.

six

One week had passed by since Sam had come to stay with the Graysons, and until today, it had gone better than he'd expected. After the phone call he'd overheard when John and Abbie talked to Jamie about his background, Sam braced himself for the coolness, the backing away he'd always experienced from foster families. Surprisingly, none of that came. If anything, the Graysons acted even nicer toward him, and they went out of their way to make him comfortable in their home.

Until this morning.

When he went to the kitchen for breakfast, Abbie told him Jamie would be coming over to talk to him. He understood exactly what that meant—she'd found another home.

He wasn't hungry anymore. Abbie chatted cheerfully about something, but Sam couldn't concentrate on her words. He stirred his cereal without eating any of it and then excused himself to his room. As he packed his stuff up, anxiety set in when he thought about where he might end up next.

The thought of leaving the Graysons made him sad. They'd been nice to him, and he'd even begun to feel comfortable here. Possibly even safe. He wished he could stay here for a while longer, but this was supposed to be an emergency placement only, normally a couple of days at the most, and he'd already been here a week.

"Sam?" Abbie stuck her head in his room. She tilted her head and paused when she realized he was placing his things in a trash bag. "Jamie's here, I'll send her in, if that's okay."

"Sure." He shrugged and noted that Abbie's voice was even cheerier than normal this morning. She was obviously glad he was leaving. He listened and waited for the inevitable as Abbie went back out to the kitchen and then returned with Jamie.

"Hey, Sam, how are ya?" Jamie smiled. It irked him that everyone was so happy this morning when once again his life spun out of control.

"Fine," he said without emotion, without looking at her. *How does she think I am?* He wadded up the last shirt, stuffed it into the trash bag, and tied the top of it in a knot as Jamie watched, then he sat on the bed.

He chastised himself whenever he wasn't nice to her. She'd been his caseworker for a long time now and had always been nice to him, even if most of the time he didn't like the news she delivered. Especially times like this when she showed up without warning.

"How are things going here with the Graysons?" She walked to the desk near his bed, pulled out the chair, and sat.

Sam wondered why it mattered at this point, but he figured he'd better answer her. "It's good. They're nice. I wish I could stay here." It was true, but he winced because he'd only said it to make her feel guilty about moving him. He had to keep reminding himself it wasn't her fault.

"You'd like to stay here?" Jamie leaned forward in her chair with her elbows on her knees and smiled at Sam.

She waited for him to answer, so he shrugged and nodded.

"That's good to know because that's the reason I'm here. I called John and Abbie last night, and they said things were going well, too, and ... well ... they would be happy to have you stay longer. But only if you want to. When I came in and saw you packing, I wasn't certain."

He stared at her with his mouth open, allowing her words to sink in. "They want me to stay?" Disbelief rang in his voice, and even though he tried to stop himself, he smiled just a little. This never happened. Foster parents were normally ready to pass him on to someone else at the first opportunity. "I only packed because I thought you were coming to move me."

Jamie's smile disappeared. She didn't say anything for a moment but then slowly shook her head. "I'm so sorry we gave you that idea, Sam," she said softly. "But yes, they want you to stay. I just needed to come talk to you to make sure things here were okay, because the Graysons said they couldn't tell whether you liked it here or not."

The comment stung a little. John and Abbie were genuinely nice to him, and he hadn't been particularly nice to them. It wasn't until today, with the prospect of having to leave, that he realized John and Abbie were different from most adults, and they were by far the best family he'd ever lived with.

"Yeah, I really do. How long can I stay?" he asked cautiously.

"We didn't put a timeframe on it. They said they don't want to uproot you again if they don't have to. We talked a little about school, so they're thinking longer term." He'd been in the system long enough to know Jamie couldn't make him any promises. But if they were talking about sending him to school, they must be thinking he'd be here for a few months at least.

"I'll let them know you want to stay," Jamie said as she stood up, pushed the chair back under the desk, and headed toward the door. "But you know how to reach me if you need me."

Sam nodded, his head still spinning with this news, as Jamie walked out of the room.

"Oh." Jamie poked her head back in the doorway. "In the meantime, you can unpack that trash bag." She winked at Sam as she left the room.

* * *

John walked Jamie out while Abbie took the coffee cups to the kitchen sink and washed them, and when he came back in he picked up a towel to dry. Jamie had called last night and told them she was having a hard time finding a placement for Sam, but she found a group home that could take him by the end of next week. She and John had discussed it, and the idea of Sam going to a group home didn't sit well with either of them.

"I know this will shock you," John had told her. "But I'm fine with him staying with us for a while."

"Well, I am shocked." Abbie had laughed. "It's going well, don't you think? I mean, I know he isn't real talkative, but there are times when I can tell he wants to talk but stops himself, like he's afraid of something. I think, in time, he'll open up to us. That's what I've been praying for, anyway."

They'd called Jamie back last night to tell her they wanted Sam to stay. They weren't sure for how long, but they just couldn't let him go to a group home.

Sam walked into the kitchen as Abbie put up the coffee mugs. "Hey, Sam, pull up a seat," Abbie said, and he followed John's lead in pulling up a barstool to the large kitchen island that separated the eat-in kitchen from the great room.

"Thanks for letting me stay here longer," Sam said as Abbie set out some chocolate chip cookies she'd made last night.

"We're glad you're here." Abbie smiled her warm smile. "And please come to us if you have any questions or if you just want to talk, okay? We want you to be comfortable here."

Sam nodded and said, "Thank you," as he took two cookies.

"We do need to talk about school, since it's almost June and school starts in August." Abbie walked to the refrigerator and poured a glass of milk as she talked. "We ran two options past Jamie, and she said either one was fine, but we want to get your input on it as well before we make a decision." Abbie went on to tell him about the school in their town, Franklin High School.

"I went there before," Sam said, and he didn't sound at all enthusiastic about it. Jamie warned them he might feel that way. The communities of Franklin and Brentwood consisted of a lot of people in the music business, since both communities were near Nashville. There were large rolling hills and farmland, and it was a great place to raise a family. But Jamie told them Sam had a hard time fitting in there. He said other kids thought less of him because, in a small town, everyone knew everyone else, and he was always known as the foster kid. An outsider.

"Well, Abbie came up with another option you might like better," John interjected. "Abbie homeschooled our daughter Hannah for a couple of years. She can homeschool you, if you'd like to try that. The curriculum is already approved by the state."

Even though Abbie worked a few hours a week at their church, they agreed she could still homeschool Sam.

Sam perked up. "How would that work?" he asked, seemingly interested in that idea.

Abbie jumped in. "You and I would work here together three days a week, doing courses in English, history, social sciences, and a couple of electives. Then, two days a week, you would go to what's called a home school academy with about twenty other homeschooled kids, where you'd have classes in math, science, and foreign language."

He nodded along, his eyes intent on Abbie.

"That way you get some interaction with other kids, but you don't have the pressure you'd have going to a big high school every day. Hannah completed her first two years of high school this way. She loved it and made some good friends along the way."

Sam listened, but the way he bit his lower lip told Abbie he wasn't totally sold on the idea of the homeschool academy.

"If you want," she offered, "we can try the academy for a while and see how it goes. If it doesn't work, we can always go back to one hundred percent homeschooling."

"Okay, that sounds good to me." Sam's answer was decisive.

"Good, we have a plan then," John said. He then hesitated and looked at Abbie. As usual, they read each other's minds. She nodded, urging him to continue, so John turned toward Sam. "We hate to throw too much at you at one time, but since you'll be staying here awhile, we need to set some ground rules since we haven't done that yet."

"Sure." Sam gave them his full attention.

John went on to explain the curfews they set for him, which were the same their own two kids had to abide by. They were fairly strict, but she and John had always agreed that's what had been best for their kids' well-being.

"Okay, fine by me." Sam seemed sincere and didn't try to negotiate anything different, which was a relief. They hadn't been sure what to expect.

"For us to be able to stay in communication when you're out, we got you a cellphone. Like we told our kids when they were in high school, there should be no expectation of privacy with your phone. We will ask to look through your phone from time to time. Visiting inappropriate websites will result in losing phone privileges."

Sam laughed for the first time since they'd met him. "Once you get to know me better, you'll find out I stay far away from all that stuff."

John smiled. "That's good to know, Sam. And just so you know, we are anxious to get to know you better."

They'd made monumental progress today. This was the longest conversation they'd had with Sam since he'd been here. He'd even made eye contact and given them his full attention.

Although they were still treading unknown waters, at least now they had a few ground rules and somewhat of a plan for the near future. Abbie was optimistic. For the first time, she was in control of this foster-care thing.

bbie opened her sunroof on this beautiful Franklin morning and turned up the radio when the new Chris Tomlin song, "Holy Forever," came on K-Love. The sun shone brightly, and she had a few hours to herself—a rarity since Sam had come into their lives. John stayed home today, recognizing her need to get away for a little bit, so she took him up on it.

She drove around the town square, pulled up to her favorite coffee shop, and searched for her friend's car. Wendy waved at her from a corner table as Abbie entered. Her heart soared as she hurried toward her friend.

"I'm so glad to see you," Abbie exclaimed as her best friend got up and hugged her. "I know it's only been a few weeks, but it seems like forever." Abbie sat opposite Wendy and reached for the coffee. "You even got iced coffee for me."

"Well, of course," Wendy laughed. "I'll never know how you drink that stuff black. But anyway, tell me everything. How is Sam? Have things gotten better?"

Abbie smiled. This is what she loved most about her friend. They'd been friends since elementary school and had gone through every phase of life together. They had similar upbringings, and each had escaped the entrapments of the high society lifestyle their parents lived. She could talk about anything with Wendy.

"So much better. That first week was rocky. But once Sam found out we weren't handing him off, apparently like foster parents in the past have done, he opened up a little. He really is a good kid." Abbie sipped her iced coffee.

"*Hmm*, that's amazing, especially after how tough the first week sounded. And John is still good with everything? I can't believe the way he's come around." Wendy smiled and tucked her light brown hair behind her ear.

"Oh, my. Compared to when I first told him I'd like to foster, you mean?" Abbie laughed along with her friend. No, John definitely hadn't been on board in the beginning. "He is so good with Sam, and he admitted he's missed having a kid around. At first, we were both nervous, but now that we've settled into a routine, it's been good for both of us. And Sam too."

When Abbie had first told John she wanted to foster a child, he'd brushed her off. He said he couldn't imagine doing that now that their kids were grown and out of the house. But then a funny thing happened. After the discussion about it had been dropped, their church hosted an adoption weekend. Pastor Rob featured testimonies from several foster and adoptive couples. When they went home that night, John told her he understood why she had wanted to foster, and his heart had opened up to the idea as well.

"That adoption weekend at church was no coincidence," Abbie said.

"No, it sure wasn't. But of course, with God, there are no coincidences." Wendy shrugged. "What do Hannah and Kyle think?"

Abbie put her drink down and settled back into the chair. "I don't know," she admitted. "Kyle is studying for the bar exam, and Hannah is still in that intensive class to get her master's degree, so they haven't been home to meet Sam yet. Hannah asks about him, and it seems she likes to hear about him, but not Kyle."

"Oh, what do you mean?" Wendy frowned.

"Well, John had lunch with Kyle last week on campus, and he said Kyle didn't even ask about Sam. John brought him up, but Kyle barely said anything and then changed the subject. And when I've texted Kyle or talked to him on the phone, it's been the same way. I don't know what to think." Abbie sighed.

"Well ... he is studying for the bar exam. I can't imagine how intense that must be. Maybe he's just preoccupied." Wendy took a sip of her coffee and waited for Abbie's response.

"Maybe." Abbie wasn't convinced. "I guess I just expected more, especially from Kyle with him being the oldest. He's always been so mature about everything."

Wendy nodded and let that sink in. "Are you going to introduce them soon?"

"Yes, definitely. We're just trying to find the right time."

"Maybe the sooner you do that, the better you'll feel about the situation with them. Especially where Kyle is concerned," Wendy said.

Her friend was right, of course. The longer they put it off, the more awkward and difficult it might be.

Abbie stayed for another half hour and talked about Wendy's husband, Roger, their daughter Isabella, Abbie's part-time job at church that she'd be going back to soon, and Wendy's job as office manager for an adult care service. Time with her best friend always went by too fast, and Abbie was grateful for every single second.

* * *

Sam stared out the car window at the blue skies and smiled. He'd never been as at ease and comfortable living with a foster family before. Of course, all that could change next week when his homeschool classes started. College classes would start soon after, and from what he understood, John would be gone more then. But Abbie assured him she would be home and not traveling, and John would be home as much as possible until basketball season started in November.

This morning, John and Sam were on their way to the TU campus for a visit. Although Sam didn't show it, he was excited to go. He'd never been to Tennessee University. Even though it was located just on the outskirts of Nashville, he was surprised by the enormity of the campus, with beautiful brick and stone buildings, two huge libraries, a clock tower in the center of campus, and tons of huge shade trees on the sprawling, green grounds.

He and John got out of the car and walked to the athletic center where John's office was, taking in the sunshine and the breezy, warm day. A few college kids were milling about, but John said it was nothing in comparison to when school started. Most of the kids here today were going through orientation or registering for classes, John told him.

Sam took it all in as they walked into the basketball arena. "Wow, this place is huge." He was astonished and impressed.

"Yes, it is. It seems bigger when it's empty." John chuckled as he pointed to various areas of the arena. "This area over here is packed with students during games, and up there is our adult booster section. The entire place is filled to the top for every game. There's nothing better than when the home team is so loud that I have to yell when I'm in a huddle with the team just for the guys to hear me. The support we get here is amazing," John said with pride. "Well, you'll see for yourself once the season starts."

"I can't wait." Sam had never attended a college basketball game and couldn't imagine watching the team play in person.

"The seats for family and friends are right back here, not far behind where I sit with the team." John acted happy that Sam wanted to come to the games. "And don't forget, you'll be able to bring a friend, if you want."

The prospect of going to a basketball game was exciting, especially since he could bring Lauren. He didn't have many other friends since he moved around so much, but lately he found himself looking forward to the homeschool academy. He hoped to make a friend or two there.

As they walked through the sports complex, John introduced him to a couple of the upperclassman on his team who'd stayed in Nashville all summer. They saw John's best friend and assistant coach, Wes. Then John and Sam went to lunch, just the two of them.

Sam's favorite food was tacos, so John took him to a little Mexican place right off campus. They ordered tacos with tortilla chips and salsa. While they ate, John didn't pry or ask many questions, and Sam was thankful. Although he liked the Graysons, he still didn't want to reveal too much about his personal life. John talked about different things, like sports, and asked Sam's thoughts on his upcoming school. The conversation rolled along easily.

They arrived home around 3:00. John had some recruiting calls to make, and Abbie had gone to work at church for a few hours, so Sam went into the library. He sat his backpack on the big center table, pulled out his journal, and went to his favorite window seat.

Maybe he would write about today. It had been fun, and he'd rarely experienced fun in his life. Conversation with the Graysons became easier, and Sam even let himself begin to trust John and Abbie a little. Up until now, Sam hadn't truly trusted any adults. Never. So, this was a big deal.

What would it have been like to have John and Abbie as parents? How different would his life have been?

The opposite of life with his father, that's for sure.

So far, all he knew about his father's situation was that he faced some drug charges and was in jail for a while. According to Jamie, his father would have to complete rehab and parenting classes before he could even petition the court to get Sam back.

Sam hoped the process would stretch out another year plus a couple of months. Then he would be eighteen and would never have to go back to his father again. That was probably wishful thinking, though. He hoped his father wouldn't want him back so he could stay with the Graysons.

Sam had resumed therapy while staying with John and Abbie. His sessions focused on his feelings toward his father. Mostly feelings of hate. Hate because the man had abandoned him repeatedly and hate for the things he had not protected Sam from. He had a foster mother one time who told him it was wrong to hate, and he even had a counselor tell him he should forgive his father. She was crazy. No way he could ever forgive his father. Not ever.

He sighed and glanced at the blank page in his journal and the picture of his mother that held the page. Writing used to be therapeutic for him. He'd write down his feelings, and it helped. But lately, he hadn't been able to write anything. He'd become numb, or possibly afraid that if he put the words on the paper, they'd become more real.

Instead, he'd drawn an emoji next to the dates in his journal when he couldn't connect with that place deep inside his soul that allowed him to write. Today would be a smiley face.

He stared out the window again at the green landscape dotted with bursts of color from the blooming flowers. This view always gave him peace. He allowed his mind to drift to his younger years. As a small child, he thought what he and his father had was normal. But as he grew older and met the biological children of his foster parents, and even classmates and their fathers, he realized his relationship with the man was anything but normal. In fact, it was outright dysfunctional.

It became apparent to Sam that other kids didn't have bruises all the time like he did, and no one ever talked about being taken away from their home and going to live with a strange family. At around twelve years old, he realized other kids his age didn't talk about drug deals they'd witnessed or strangers traipsing in and out of their homes throughout the day and night. He understood his life was far different from other kids' lives.

Sam's father had never loved. He only did whatever necessary to get Sam when it was convenient, when he could use him to get what he wanted. Then he'd throw him away, abandon him. That cycle played out over and over. His father never wanted him, and neither did relatives of his mother or father. No one ever wanted him—no one except his mom. The only person who'd ever wanted or loved him was dead.

He'd been thinking a lot about her lately, especially since he met Abbie Grayson. He didn't know much about his mom or have much memory of her, but he liked to think she'd been a lot like Abbie—a caring and loving mother.

He picked up his mom's picture and stared at it intently. How had he managed not to lose it over the years with all his shuffling from home to home? He always kept it inside his journal, in his backpack, so he wouldn't have to hunt for it if he had to move to another home abruptly.

Sam ran his fingers over the tattered edges of the four-by-five picture. The colors were fading, but her blonde hair and blue eyes still stood out. She wore a green dress and held Sam on her lap in front of a Christmas tree. He held a small car, and his mom was smiling. Not at the camera, but at him. The way she gazed at him in that picture made him think she'd genuinely loved and wanted him.

He guessed he was about five years old in the photo, probably not long before his mom died. She appeared incredibly young, and for the first time, it dawned on Sam that she probably wasn't much older than he was right now when she had him. How difficult her life must have been. She and his father had never married, and he couldn't imagine his father had done much to support them.

He liked to think she had loved him, but he suspected there were a lot of things he didn't know about. He'd overheard his father tell someone that she'd once overdosed on drugs and ended up in the hospital. Someday, he hoped to learn more about her, but he didn't know how. He asked his father once, and he told Sam to never ask about her again. And Sam had no idea how to contact any other relatives.

As for now, he would keep on going, day to day, holding on to the photo of his mom and the possibility that she had loved him. And that someone had once wanted him.

Abbie was happy that John went to play golf with his buddies in an attempt to wash away the stress and uncertainty of the last couple of months. He returned home a few hours later happy, saying it was exactly what he'd needed. Saturdays during his off-season had always been golf days, but he hadn't played in a couple of months because he'd put that on pause when Sam arrived.

One of the things she loved most about her husband was that he tried his best to always put his family first. Sometimes all the traveling during the basketball season and cross-country trips during off-season recruiting periods made it nearly impossible, but he made it up to them every moment he was home.

She only wished she could tame her own anxiousness and nervousness about this evening. Instead, she ran around the kitchen trying to get everything perfect for dinner. Although John tried to help, both of them in the kitchen just made her more anxious.

"What's wrong, honey?" John asked.

"I'm sorry. I just have a bad feeling about Hannah and Kyle coming to meet Sam today." She bit her lip and paused to look at John momentarily, then continued her frantic pace.

"Why on earth would you feel that way? We've delayed this meeting as long as we could, until Sam settled in. Kyle and Hannah are good kids. What could go wrong?" John seemed oblivious to all the scenarios that had taken hostage of her mind today.

"A lot could go wrong." Abbie stopped and blew a stray curl that had escaped her ponytail away from her face. "Whenever we've talk to Kyle on the phone and mentioned Sam, he changes the subject. Even back when we first talked to the kids about fostering, he didn't want to talk about it." It had been on her mind a while, and now she reconsidered whether or not this dinner was a good idea at all. She finished mixing up the fruit salad and moved over to the other counter to put the finishing touches on a cake.

"I promise, it'll all be fine. Our kids are great, Abb, and I think they'll be very receptive to Sam."

She knew John was trying his best to reassure her. Abbie was usually the optimistic one, and although she appreciated John's take on things, she didn't feel any better.

Time had gotten away from them. Sam had been here almost eight weeks, and they hadn't yet introduced him to their kids. Kyle's bar exam and Hannah's intensive summer session were part of the reason, but not the whole reason.

At first, Abbie and John didn't think Sam would be here long, so they waited to make the introductions, but in all truthfulness, they missed their kids. This had been the longest they'd gone without seeing them. Although the kids were really busy, was it possible Kyle and Hannah stayed away because of Sam? Abbie didn't want to think that way, so she'd kept the idea to herself.

She wasn't worried about Hannah at all. Hannah was a social person with a bubbly, vibrant personality who never met a stranger, much like both of her parents, but especially John. Hannah engaged in church activities and even went on a few overseas mission trips. Most involved teaching young children.

She'd just landed a job at a Christian elementary school about thirty miles away, teaching second grade, and she loved her new career.

Kyle, on the other hand, remained more reserved and serious. His mind was always in problem-solving mode, which had suited him well in law school. Abbie had no doubt he would excel in his career as an attorney. He could be blunt at times, and he hadn't been thrilled the last few weeks during their phone and FaceTime conversations when the subject of Sam came up. Perhaps Kyle was jealous, but Abbie couldn't figure out why their son would feel that way. John and Kyle had always been close, although John admitted his only regret was being gone more than he would've liked when the kids were still at home.

No matter the reason, the time had come for them to meet. Abbie prayed that their kids, *both* their kids, would step up and welcome Sam with open arms.

* * *

Sam's stomach churned, and he wished he could find his lip balm. When his anxiety level rose, his lips and throat dried out. He was about to meet the Graysons' two kids. Their biological kids. What if they didn't like him? Could they influence their parents to drop him as a foster kid? He liked the Graysons, and he was safer here than he'd ever been anywhere. He didn't want anything to jeopardize that.

To make matters worse, Sam had never told anyone he'd suffered abuse at the hands of an older biological son of one of his foster families several years ago. But that couldn't happen here, right? After all, Kyle didn't even live with them, and he was a lawyer, so—

"Sam, Hannah's here!" Abbie's voice rang through the hallway to Sam's room.

For some odd reason, the thought popped into Sam's head

that he should pray, but he brushed it off immediately. Even if God did exist, He wouldn't help someone like him.

A long time ago, he'd believed in God, back when he lived with the older couple who had taught him to play the piano. They'd taken him to church every Sunday, and it had been easier back then for him to believe. He was a little kid and hadn't been through as much or seen so many bad things. But he didn't believe anymore. Too much had happened. So much had gone wrong.

How could God let terrible things happen to kids? Not only himself, but horrible things had happened to other kids Sam knew. He couldn't understand how a supposedly loving God could let those things happen.

"Sam?" Abbie yelled again.

"Coming!" He took a swig from the water bottle on his desk to keep his throat from closing. *Deep breaths, stay calm,* he told himself as he walked toward the kitchen.

He entered the kitchen, and before he could even say hello, a slender young woman with long, straight, dark hair and a big smile came out of nowhere and had her arms around him in a huge hug.

"I'm so happy to meet you, Sam." Hannah beamed as she squeezed him hard, startling Sam. Although he didn't mean to, he automatically took a step back from her.

Hannah stepped back also, apparently realizing she'd made him uncomfortable. "Oh, my. I'm sorry. I shouldn't have rushed at you like that, but I'm a hugger." She laughed. "And I've been dying to meet you!"

Sam smiled at how talkative and friendly she seemed. She reminded him a lot of his friend Lauren.

"It's okay." Sam laughed, too, and some of his nervousness fell away at Hannah's friendly demeanor. John and Abbie's eyes were on him, probably afraid Hannah had scared him to death with her dramatic greeting.

"I'm glad to meet you too," he said shyly. He hoped they'd get along well. Maybe Kyle would be a lot like her. If so, today would go better than he'd dared to hope.

They normally sat on the stools at the enormous kitchen island, but today, they all sat around the dining room table. It was larger than the island, and Sam figured at least a dozen people could fit around this table.

Hannah didn't waste any time before she asked him a ton of questions, mostly about school and friends. None were too personal, though, and she was easy to talk to. They were discussing homeschool when Kyle walked in, and Sam's stomach dropped once again.

Kyle was about the same height as his dad, probably around six feet tall. He looked and carried himself like an athlete, his dark hair cut short with a close, scruffy beard. Sam imagined John must've looked a lot like him at that age. He also imagined Kyle was intimidating in a courtroom because he definitely intimidated Sam now.

He'd entered the room more quietly than Hannah had, but his presence loomed large in the room even though he hadn't approached Sam yet. Kyle greeted his mom and dad with a hug. Hannah jumped up and gave him a hug. Then he approached the table, made eye contact with Sam, and extended his hand for a handshake.

"Well, you must be Sam. I'm Kyle. Nice to meet you," he said. They shook hands, and Kyle took a seat at the table. The greeting had been rigid and cold. Kyle didn't smile at all, but what made Sam most nervous and uncomfortable was the way he stared at Sam while the others talked. The weight of that stare bore right through him.

Abbie jumped up to get drinks for everyone, and Kyle began peppering Sam with questions. They weren't the easy questions Hannah had asked. In fact, these questions were downright calculated and mean.

"So, Sam, why are you in foster care? Why aren't you with your parents?" Kyle asked without emotion.

Sam winced. *Just like the stupid kids at school.*

"Kyle, that's a little too personal don't you think?"

Sam hadn't heard that kind of sternness in Abbie's voice before.

"It's okay," Sam replied, but he wasn't happy about it. Maybe the jerk would feel bad if he just spilled out all the horrific details of his sorry life right here and now. That would show him. But Sam wouldn't do that to the others.

"My mom died when I was five, and my father is in jail right now." Sam didn't look up from the table. He wanted to stare Kyle down, but he certainly didn't have the confidence to do that. Instead, he did what he always did in situations like this. He shut down.

In the meantime, Kyle continued to stare at Sam and he scratched his chin. Not an ounce of empathy to be found.

"What did your dad do to land in jail?" Kyle continued. This guy was plain rude.

"Kyle, that's not any of our business." John spoke firmly "You don't have to answer that, Sam."

"Well, Dad, I think it should be your business since his kid is staying with you." Kyle wasn't about to let it go. This guy must be a really aggressive lawyer. Sam hated arguments and confrontation so maybe if he answered, things would settle down.

"If you must know, he's in jail for drug and illegal gun possession." Sam's answer came out louder and ruder than he intended, but at that point, he didn't care.

"Kyle—enough. Now, please, let's just eat." Abbie's voice was even more stern this time and her cheeks were bright red. Sam hadn't seen her flustered like this before. She sat at the table, passed a large salad bowl around, and they each put salad on their plates.

What little appetite he had before disappeared, so he didn't even put any food on his plate. Kyle's judgmental stares bore through him, and Sam stared at the floor, trying to will this meal to be over.

"Hey Sam, what kind of things do you like to do?" Hannah asked. It was obvious she wanted to lighten the tension in the room. She was nice and down to earth—sweet like her mom.

But before he could open his mouth to answer her, Kyle started up again. "How many foster homes have you lived in?"

"All right, that's enough." John tossed his napkin onto his plate as he pushed back from the table. He stood up, then motioned to Kyle. "Outside for a minute. We need to talk."

Kyle sighed and shook his head, got up from the table, and followed his dad out onto the deck.

Sam was thankful John broke in when he did. He didn't like to talk about all this stuff with anyone, let alone some jerk he just met. It made Sam extremely uncomfortable, and he could tell they all noticed. Sweat had beaded his forehead and his mind raced. He considered bolting. He'd run away for less in the past.

He wished he could hear what John said to Kyle outside. They were only gone for a couple of minutes, but when they returned, things were different. Sam appeared to be off the hook. Not only did Kyle not speak to him after that, but he barely looked his way, which was fine. Hannah tried to make up for it and talked to Sam more. Even though Kyle didn't engage in the conversation, the tension from earlier remained in the air. Sam hated drama, and this was about as dramatic a dinner as he'd ever been to.

John took over the conversation so the spotlight wasn't on Sam anymore. He was grateful. John talked about the basketball season ahead and involved the whole family in the conversation. The discussion stayed light and friendly.

Abbie served the roasted chicken and baked potatoes, and this time Sam put some food on his plate. Kyle remained quiet, so the rest of dinner stayed pleasant enough.

When they finished eating, John got up from the table to get dessert, but Kyle said he needed to skip dessert and head back to Nashville.

Sam let out an audible sigh. He hoped no one noticed.

Kyle hugged Hannah goodbye but didn't say anything to Sam as John and Abbie got up to walk him out.

"Sam, I'm so sorry." Hannah leaned over the table toward him as soon as the others were out of earshot. Her eyes were serious. "I have no idea why my brother acted that way. Kyle is really a great person and one of the nicest people I know. Honestly, I don't know what was wrong with him today."

"It's okay," Sam said, but it bothered him much more than he let on to Hannah.

"Well, you don't deserve to be treated that way at all," Hannah replied softly.

Sam was glad Hannah acknowledged that Kyle acted out of line and affirmed it wasn't simply him being sensitive. "Thank you." He stared at his plate.

"You don't have to talk about anything that makes you uncomfortable. If I ever ask anything that makes you feel that way, tell me to mind my own business. I'm serious," Hannah insisted.

Sam laughed at the way she said it, and he doubted Hannah would ask him anything that made him uncomfortable. At least not on purpose.

He was glad he got along with at least one of the siblings.

* * *

Abbie hung up the phone from the latest of a string of frustrating conversations with Kyle over the past week in an attempt to get to the bottom of his behavior at dinner last weekend. "I still don't understand it." She shook her head as she glanced at John. "He's always so kind and laid back around us. I've never seen him act like this."

They both were shocked at the way Kyle had acted, and

they'd told him as much when they walked him to his car after dinner that night. Kyle wasn't happy about the discussion, and he'd left mad.

"I don't get it either." John scratched his head. "He finally said he was sorry, but when I suggested we try again, he balked at the idea."

"*Hmm*, do you think he's jealous?" Abbie wondered out loud.

"I thought of that. Especially after last year and our conversation about how he wished I'd been around more." John winced.

He and Kyle had gotten into an argument last year, and Kyle had made the "if you'd been around more" comment. John and Kyle's relationship had always been good, but that comment came up in the heat of an argument, and he and Kyle had discussed it at length later. Kyle said he made the comment in anger, and he understood for all the traveling John had to do with his job, he'd done the best he could.

But Abbie suspected Kyle sincerely felt that way deep down or it wouldn't have bubbled to the surface. Plus, there was truth to it. Though he'd tried his best, John had missed many things that were important to his son—ball games, father-son events, and just being there when his son had needed him.

Abbie understood. It was part of their life, and they had discussed it before he'd taken the job with TU. His travel and commitment to the team and university made it impossible for him to attend every sports event, dance recital, and school activity like a lot of the other dads did. Abbie tried to step up and be both mom and dad when John was away, but she couldn't possibly take his place.

She and John had talked to Sam and apologized for Kyle's behavior. He told them it was okay, but that didn't make either of them feel any better. At least things between their daughter and Sam had gone well.

Hannah had even come back a few nights later with some books the two of them had talked about. She seemed almost protective of him, probably because of the way Kyle had acted, but no matter the reason, she and John were thrilled they were getting along. Hannah would be a great role model for Sam.

Abbie could only pray that things would improve where Kyle was concerned.

nine

Sam's best friend Lauren was coming to visit, and it'd been months since they'd seen each other. Thanks to his new cell phone, he could call and text her now, and they'd arranged for her to come over to the Graysons' home for a cookout.

Abbie had called Lauren's mom and told her Sam and Lauren would be supervised, and her parents agreed to drop her off for a few hours. He was so happy to get to see her and have an easy, familiar conversation with his best friend.

He helped Abbie cut veggies for the salad, but when the doorbell rang, he dropped the knife into the sink and ran to the door.

"Hi, Lauren. Hi, Mrs. Asher," he said. Lauren's mom smiled and said hi to Sam. Lauren grinned from ear to ear. Abbie came to greet them and invited Mrs. Asher in for coffee while Sam showed Lauren around the house.

"I've missed you sooooo much," Lauren squealed.

He hadn't realized until now how much he'd missed seeing her. And he missed the familiarity of someone who'd known him for several years.

"Wow, this house!" Lauren gushed as Sam showed her around. "Do you like it here?" she asked tentatively, and she wasn't referring to the house itself. In the past, he'd confided in her about some of the hard times he'd endured in foster care.

"Yeah, I seriously do. They're nice people, and the house is great—wait till you see the library." He grinned. They made their way through the house, and he saved the library for last.

"Wow ... this is so cool!" Lauren looked around the room in awe.

Sam smiled to himself. One of the reasons they were friends was because she loved books as much as he did.

"I would be in this room all the time if I lived here." Lauren walked around the edge of the room browsing the bookcases full of books and running her fingertips along them, exactly as he had done the first time he had entered this room.

Sam laughed. "Yeah, I spend a ton of time here. The window seat is so cool. It's a peaceful place to sit and read."

Lauren tilted her head and stared at him for a moment. "You really do seem happy. I've worried about you a lot. How long do you get to stay here?"

"I hope for a long time." Sam shrugged, his hands in his pockets. That's why he loved talking to Lauren. Although she didn't know the very worst parts, she realized his life in foster care had been difficult and traumatic. "And get this—they're planning on homeschooling me, so no more Franklin or Brentwood High Schools."

"That's awesome, Sam, really," she said. "You won't have to deal with all the stupid kids at school." She paused as if she wanted to say something else. "What about your dad? When does he get out, and what happens when he does?" Lauren asked, her voice quiet.

He shrugged again, but a sense of dread washed over him. "I don't know that either. I'm hoping he stays in jail until I turn eighteen, so I never have to go back to him. But I probably won't get that lucky." He stared at the floor.

He'd told her once, in confidence, some things his father had done, so she recognized he was a bad person. But again, she didn't know everything the man was involved in. Sam considered telling her once, but he didn't for fear of what his father and his associates might do to Lauren if they found out she knew things. So, he kept the worst parts to himself. It was safer for her.

As they headed outside, Sam couldn't help but notice how beautiful and grown-up Lauren looked now. Her long blonde hair fell in big ringlets halfway down her back. She wore shorts but was dressed modestly and tastefully, unlike a lot of girls their age.

He pushed those thoughts aside. Lauren remained his friend, his absolute best friend in the world, and he would never do anything to jeopardize their friendship. He didn't have anything to offer anyone in terms of a relationship anyway.

They made their way outside to the deck where they found John starting the grill. Sam introduced them.

"Thank you for having me over, Coach Grayson," Lauren said with her warmest, brightest smile. "I'm a big fan by the way."

"You are?" Sam was surprised. "I didn't even know who he was."

"Sam! Are you serious?" Lauren laughed and playfully punched his arm. "Oh, that's right, you don't watch sports much."

"Well, thank you, Lauren." John smiled and laughed at Sam. "I hope you can come with Sam to some games this season."

She laughed and jumped up and down. "Oh, wow, I would love to!"

"That's hilarious." Sam laughed. "I didn't know whether I would even ask you or not because I didn't think you liked basketball. I guess I was wrong."

Conversation came easy with Lauren, and she caught him up on all the gossip concerning the kids he knew from his old high school. John and Abbie were in and out the whole time, but Sam didn't seem to notice. It always seemed that way when he and Lauren were together—he never noticed much else around him.

John cooked hamburgers on the grill while Abbie fixed a big

salad and macaroni and cheese. Lauren had offered to help, but Abbie told her to relax, sit back, and catch up with Sam.

The conversation between the four of them over dinner outside on the deck was light and fun. Until the subject of church crept in. Lauren had asked him to come to the church in Brentwood, where she lived, but he didn't want to go back there where a lot of people knew him and his background. The church was small and cliquish in Sam's opinion. He grew tired of being known as the foster kid. And besides, he didn't see any need for church.

The Graysons had also brought up church before. John and Abbie attended every Sunday, but as a foster kid he had a say in the matter, and he chose not to go. So far, the Graysons hadn't pushed the issue, although Abbie jumped on the subject now that it was out in the open.

"Lauren, we go to Franklin Community Church, and we've wanted Sam to go with us. Maybe you'd like to go sometime so we can get him to give it a try," Abbie said, but John shot Abbie a look and shook his head.

"I don't think my mom and dad would mind. I'll ask," Lauren replied.

Maybe she'd forget all about it, but if she didn't and her parents said she could go, he'd go only this once. If Lauren was with him, he'd be more comfortable. But he wouldn't make it a habit, that's for sure.

The talk then turned to school. Come next week, Lauren would start her junior year at the high school she and Sam had attended together, and Sam would also be a junior—homeschooled by Abbie three days a week. He'd attend the academy for homeschooled kids like him the other two days a week.

He'd missed the last few weeks of his sophomore year due to the drama in his life, but his social worker, Jamie, had met with the principal, who'd agreed to promote Sam to the next grade level based on the work and standardized tests he'd completed.

He never had trouble with his schoolwork—it was mainly his attendance that caused him problems.

Abbie had told him some friends of hers ran the school. They were teachers who left the workforce to raise their children and founded the academy for homeschooled kids. She and John said it would give Sam a fresh start and a chance to meet other kids. The thought of it made him nervous, but as hard as that would be, it sounded better than going back to his old school. But he'd miss Lauren, for sure.

The evening wound down and Lauren's parents arrived to pick her up. She hugged Sam and then John and Abbie and thanked them for having her over. As she left, he realized he was happy for once. He was in a good home, cared for and safe, and his best friend was back in his life. What more could he ask for?

ten

One week of homeschooling done. For maybe the first time ever, Sam didn't mind school. He liked Abbie's teaching style. They planned for him to study English, psychology, and history with her, along with an elective he'd chosen—music theory.

But today, he'd attend the academy for the first time, and he didn't sleep last night. He took one last look in the mirror, grabbed the new backpack Abbie had bought him, and thought positive thoughts as he headed to the kitchen for breakfast. He focused on the good things he had going for him now. This was the best foster home he could imagine being in, and John and Abbie were wonderful to him. Life got a little easier each day, and he was grateful.

The thought of school, though, locked him in a state of dread and forced his anxiety to the surface. He'd always loved books and learning, but he hated the social aspects of school because he differed too much from the other kids. Everyone referred to him as the foster kid. Even during the times he lived with his father, he perceived himself as different. Certainly, none of them went home to the same things he did or were subjected to the things he was when in his father's custody.

"Good morning." John looked up from the news feed on his phone and set it aside as Sam entered the kitchen. Sam was startled to see him there.

"Oh, I figured you'd already be gone," he said as he set his new backpack on the counter.

"Well, I wanted to be here to see you off on your first day at school. Pretty corny, *huh*?" John laughed.

Sam didn't know what to say. No one had ever cared about his first day of school before.

"Are you nervous?" John asked.

He sat opposite John at the kitchen counter. "Yeah, super nervous," he admitted. Abbie set a plate of scrambled eggs and toast in front of him, and he poured himself some juice. He picked at his eggs and forced himself to eat a couple of bites since Abbie had gone to all the trouble of making them, but his nervous stomach wouldn't allow him to eat very much.

"Oh, hon," Abbie chimed in as she sat to eat with them. "You'll be fine. The teachers and other kids will love you. Most of the kids go to our church, so you'll be able to see them on the weekend, too, if you decide to go to church."

Sam wasn't so sure. Abbie meant well, but school was never easy for him. He ignored the church comment. He wished she'd quit bringing it up.

John told him to take one day at a time. "Be yourself, focus on your classes, and you'll be fine. But if it doesn't work out, nothing is set in stone. We can always change things up."

Relief washed over Sam until Abbie said again that everything would be fine. She was an optimistic and positive person. "Sunshine and rainbows," John always teased her, but her comment pressured him even more to say school was good even if it wasn't. He preferred John's way of thinking.

They finished breakfast, Sam loaded the dishwasher, and they all headed to the garage at the same time. John wished him good luck once again and got in his car for his drive to campus, and Abbie and Sam got into her car. The drive to school lasted less than ten minutes but seemed to take forever. His stomach churned, and he regretted eating the eggs. The last time he remembered being this nervous was the night his social worker had dropped him off at the Graysons' house.

Sam was amazed that they arrived at school without him getting sick. They were about twenty minutes early, and as he stared at the building, he was not impressed. It looked like regular retail space on the corner of a strip mall. When they walked in, however, it was much more spacious than it appeared from the outside. The area contained an office in the front area, a hallway down the middle with two classrooms on one side of the hall and another classroom and a lunchroom on the other side.

Abbie had given him some money and told him he could go grab something for lunch today at one of the places in the strip mall or the ice cream shop next door that also served food. Great. He'd be sitting by himself for sure. He especially missed Lauren today.

Just as anxiety tightened its grip, a lady about Abbie's age came out of the office area, hugged Abbie, and then turned her attention to Sam.

"Sam, welcome! We're so happy you're joining us. I'm your teacher, Mrs. King," she exclaimed.

He reached out to shake her hand but was immediately sorry because his hands were hot and sweaty. If Mrs. King noticed, she didn't show it. She was very bubbly and friendly, much like Abbie, and Sam breathed a tiny bit easier.

Mrs. King explained that there were a total of twenty kids here in grades ten through twelve, and he would be one of six kids in the eleventh grade. He would get to know the tenth and twelfth graders as well as the kids in his own grade level because they often did activities and even field trips together.

Abbie gave him a quick hug and told him she'd pick him up

at 2:30. And just like that, she vanished. Awkward and exposed, Sam turned toward Mrs. King as she grabbed some files. "Come on with me Sam. I'll show you our classroom."

He drew a deep breath as he entered the classroom. It was different from any schoolroom Sam had ever seen. He didn't know what to think of it since it had no desks. Instead, a large, round table anchored the center of the room. Some smaller, square tables and bookcases stood along the sides of the room. There wasn't even a teacher's desk.

While Mrs. King showed him where the books he needed were located, he glanced around the room, relieved to see all of the other kids weren't there yet. So far there were only two—a pretty brunette and a boy sitting next to her. When they spotted Sam, they both got up from their seats and walked toward him.

"Hi, what's your name?" the girl asked in a happy tone as she approached Sam.

"Sam," he meekly replied.

"Hi, Sam. I'm Tara, and this is Nathan. C'mon, I'll help you get your books."

Sam hesitated.

"You'll be in good hands with Tara," Mrs. King laughed.

Nathan said hi and smiled. He was reserved like Sam, but Tara talked enough for all three of them. Sam was relieved not to have to talk much and hoped they were truly this friendly and wouldn't ditch him when they found out he was a foster kid. He tried not to think about it while he followed Tara around getting the books he needed.

When he had all his books, Tara led him back to the round table, and he took a seat next to her and Nathan just as another kid walked in. He introduced himself as Michael, and he sat on the other side of Sam. Then two girls, who Michael told him were Kelsey and Ashley, walked in, took their seats at the table, and talked to each other the whole time without seeming to notice him, which was perfectly fine.

At 9:00 a.m., Mrs. King came back into the room and sat at the big round table with them. She welcomed the class of six to their junior year and then proceeded to introduce Sam. Kelsey and Ashley were at full attention now and noticed Sam for the first time, and they both smiled and said hi. Everyone acted nice so far, which calmed his nerves somewhat. Things might be okay here after all. As long as they didn't find out he was a foster kid.

Mrs. King explained the classroom rules and talked about always showing respect to one another. Then they opened their English literature book and had a general discussion about who had read what.

Of the five books Mrs. King asked about, Sam had read them all. He didn't want to offer that, though, and appear to be a know-it-all. He'd only read so much because no matter where he lived or what went on in his life, he could always get his hands on a book. Reading had always been his escape from his often-nightmarish world. When things at home got bad, he'd lose himself in a book for hours and forget everything going on around him.

The morning went by faster than he imagined it would. Soon lunchtime rolled around, and those familiar nerves crept back in. Lunchtime had always been the worst. He rarely had anyone to sit with and became self-conscious about it. Usually, he sat by himself and read.

Mrs. King announced they would eat as a group at the Mexican restaurant next door. An even worse scenario—eating alone at a restaurant. A knot formed in the pit of his stomach. As the group walked along the sidewalk, panic rose inside him, then someone from behind grabbed his arm. He spun around.

"Oh, sorry. I didn't mean to startle you," Tara said as she got in stride with Sam. Nathan came to her side and shook his head and laughed, as if apologizing for Tara. "Sit with Nate and me," Tara offered.

"Oh, okay, thanks," he muttered. Someone wanted to sit with

him? Shock and relief came over him at the same time. The only person he'd ever sat with at lunch had been Lauren. Tara was a little bossy, but in a good way. He liked her. If Lauren met her, he was certain they'd be friends.

They were able to get a table for six, so it turned out they all sat together. That solved one of Sam's problems. The other problem was conversation, as he wasn't entirely confident in his social skills. Once the server placed the chips, salsa, and drinks on the table and they each ordered, the general chatter died down, and Michael directed the attention toward him.

"So, Sam, where do you live?" Michael asked.

Sam's face grew hot. He hated being the center of attention and talking about himself when it could drive people away. But all eyes were on him, so he had no choice but to speak.

"Well, I live with John and Abbie Grayson right now." Sam kept it as vague as he could.

"Oh, the basketball coach?" Kelsey asked, half surprised and half impressed.

He nodded and hoped that was the end of it, but, of course, he wasn't that lucky.

"That's so cool, are you related to them or something?" Michael asked.

Sam bit his lower lip. Tara and Nathan kept their eyes on their chips and salsa, and he wondered if they already knew.

"No." Sam took a sip of his Coke. "They're actually my foster parents. I've lived with them since May." There it was. The table of six became quiet as if no one could figure out what to say, least of all Sam. He wished he could simply disappear.

Finally, Nate broke the silence. "Well, we're glad you're here," he said. "I prayed the new student would be a boy so Michael and I wouldn't be outnumbered by the girls anymore. Now, we're even."

"I'll drink to that!" Michael laughed and raised his glass of soda in victory.

Everyone laughed, and they all talked at once and told Sam how glad they were he was here. For the first time he could ever remember, other kids accepted him. When their food came and Ashley volunteered to pray, for once, he didn't mind.

eleven

"Okay, Sam, you ready for this?" Abbie asked, maybe with a bit too much enthusiasm.

"*Um*, no, but I guess I don't have a choice," he muttered, making it apparent he didn't share her enthusiasm over this math test.

Abbie was pleased with how Sam's homeschooling had gone so far. He enjoyed reading and writing and did extremely well in all his classes. If she had to point out a weakness in his academics, it would be math, but then again, high-school level math wasn't Abbie's strong suit either, so he'd receive most of his math instruction from the homeschool academy.

Today, she worked with Sam on a practice math placement test, just like the one he'd take next week at the academy so Mrs. King would know what level to place him in.

"You have thirty minutes, starting now. Good luck, hon." Abbie sat at the opposite end of the big table in the center of their home library. She watched Sam and smiled. He'd come a long way and was doing so well. So far, their plan for his education was succeeding.

Abbie wanted to teach the Bible but couldn't. Since they fostered through a public social services agency and not a church or faith-based one, she was limited to only answering biblical questions if Sam asked. And they couldn't make him go to church. So, for now, Abbie would have to shelve her plans and keep praying an opportunity to share the Bible with Sam would present itself.

As Abbie kept an eye on the timer for Sam's test, she thought about her own education. She'd grown up attending private Christian schools, but not necessarily because her parents wanted her to have a Christian education. It was more because of the prestige of a specific private school. That's what her affluent parents wanted most for her—prestige. Abbie graduated high school and learned what the teachers taught in religion classes, but she never gave God too much consideration outside of class, and she certainly never developed a relationship with Jesus.

After high school, much to her parents' dismay, she decided against Vanderbilt and went to TU instead. That's where she began attending college worship gatherings with her roommate, and in time, she developed a relationship with Jesus that continued to grow stronger every day.

"Can I use a calculator?" Sam asked, interrupting Abbie's trip down memory lane.

"Yes, on this part, you're allowed to use your calculator," Abbie replied and got up to get it for him.

"Thanks," he said, relieved.

Abbie glanced at his paper and then checked her watch as she sat back down. "You're doing great on time," she said.

He nodded without looking up.

Her thoughts drifted once more to her days at Tennessee University, because it was also at TU that she'd met John during their sophomore year. Again, disappointing her parents.

She came from a family of means, and John came from a family of Appalachian coal miners. Not people of means or affluence, but blue-collar laborers who barely lived above the poverty line. Abbie's mother did not refer to them in a kind way.

To further horrify her mother, John majored in education, not pre-med or pre-law. That was another huge strike against him as far as her parents were concerned. As an only child, she had a complicated relationship with her parents. She loved them, and underneath their sophisticated façade, they loved her, too, but they'd never agreed on things. They'd considered her relationship with John nothing but a rebellious stage.

That's not at all what it was to Abbie. From the time she'd turned sixteen, she'd been fixed up with the sons of her parents' friends. Boys who were all predestined for Ivy League schools followed by high-profile careers in high finance, law, or medicine.

Abbie had found all those boys boring. She wanted someone real, and once she started college and developed a love for Jesus, she intended to find a young man who shared that love. Someone who, if they were to get married, would put Jesus first in the marriage, front and center.

She met John at a worship gathering. He was a devout Christian, and she liked him at once. It became apparent from his good grades, his athletic scholarship to play basketball, and his multiple jobs during the summer, that he worked hard for everything he had and hadn't been handed anything. He was easy to talk to, had a great sense of humor, and was unusually humble for someone his age who excelled in athletics. And being tall, dark, and handsome didn't hurt.

Although he played college basketball, he wasn't the star of the team. Not by far. In fact, he only got to play if his team was ahead by quite a few points, and a win was all but in the books. He wouldn't go on to play in the NBA like a couple of other players on the team.

But that was okay with John because he had a plan. He wanted to teach high school and coach. Neither of those things would make him wealthy, but that's what he wanted to do. Abbie respected him and supported him wholly. In time, they got married, and a few years into their marriage, they had their two kids.

The couple credited their relationship with God for keeping them aligned with each other through the tough times over the years, and even more so, when success and money started coming fast. They found out quickly that those things came with complications and temptations they'd never dreamed of.

Abbie glanced at her watch. "Five minutes left, Sam."

He nodded and worked fast and furiously.

Abbie returned to her thoughts about the early years of their marriage. They struggled financially for years, but once John got his division one head coaching job with Tennessee University, he brought home more money than they'd ever need.

Then there were the fans. John had been in his late thirties by then, and women hit on him everywhere he went. It infuriated Abbie to know there were women out there who would tempt another women's husband just because he had money or happened to be well known.

Thankfully, John walked the walk and never strayed, and he had Abbie proudly by his side whenever possible. After a few years, all the nonsense subsided when it became clear to all who knew him or knew anything about him, that through his actions and his words, John Grayson put God and family first.

"Finished!" Sam lifted his test booklet into the air, a mix of relief and pride in the gesture.

Abbie smiled at Sam. She prayed every day he would accept Jesus as his Savior one day. Right now, it seemed impossible, but nothing was impossible for God. He could take even the worst of circumstances and turn them around for His glory, so she continued to pray.

twelve

Much to his surprise, Sam loved school, he loved his time with Abbie and all she taught him, and he even looked forward to the days at the academy. If any of the kids thought it was weird he was a foster kid, he sure never sensed it from anyone. They were all nice to him, and they quickly became his friends, especially Tara and Nate. He was grateful for all five of his classmates, but those two in particular.

They both loved reading, writing, and music as much as he did. They were mainly interested in church music, or contemporary Christian music, as they called it. The idea of it sounded weird to him at first until they gave him a couple of CDs to listen to, and he liked it. It was unlike any church music he had ever heard and sounded more like something you'd hear on the radio. In fact, he found out there were radio stations that played it.

In part because of their coaxing, and also to make Abbie happy, Sam reluctantly agreed to go to church. Lauren's parents allowed her to join him and the Graysons for church and lunch afterward. They'd picked her up at her house. Sam was thrilled to see his best friend, but not about the rest of it. Maybe if he went this once, both his friends and Abbie would drop it and not ask him to go again.

He'd made plans with Tara and Nate to meet in the back of the sanctuary so they could all sit together, since this was also their home church.

To make things even weirder, last night Abbie gave Sam a Bible and told him he could keep it so he could highlight it or write in it if he wanted. He couldn't imagine what he would ever want to write in a Bible, or why, but to make her happy, he grabbed a pen and notebook like Abbie suggested and took it with him along with his Bible.

When they pulled into the church parking lot, his hands grew sweaty when he saw how big the building was. There were a ton of kids his age there, all headed toward the same building. He still wasn't certain he was up for this, and without Lauren here, he wouldn't be.

John dropped Sam and Lauren off in front of the building and made plans to meet up later. The two walked into the huge building where the high school services were held and found Tara and Nate exactly where they said they'd be. He introduced his new friends to Lauren, and as he'd predicted, Lauren and Tara were already laughing about something and hit it off right away.

They all headed together toward the front and sat a few rows back from the stage. Sam's nervousness eased up as the worship band came out. He was blown away by the quality of the contemporary worship music. But as Tara and Nate worshiped with hands raised and eyes closed, Sam was a little weirded out. He couldn't imagine ever doing that.

A young pastor named Matt gave a sermon about serving others, and Sam was intrigued by the number of different ways a kid like himself could help others. He'd never considered anything like that before because he was always consumed with simply surviving. But now, since he didn't have to focus on survival these days, maybe he could serve in some small way. It would be amazing to do something to help kids like himself. Foster kids who had gone through some of the same things.

On the way out of the service, Tara and Nathan talked about signing up for a service project, and they asked Sam and Lauren if they'd like to join them. He figured John and Abbie would not only allow it, they'd encourage it. Lauren acted excited about it also and said she'd ask her parents. This was all foreign to him, but it made him feel good to think about helping someone else instead of focusing solely on his own survival for once.

* * *

"You know, truthfully, I can't believe the changes in him in the last month," John marveled while inching the car forward in the pickup line, waiting for Sam and Lauren. "He seems to be doing so well right now. I mean, compared to when he came to us."

"He really is," Abbie agreed. Her heart soared every time John made a comment about how well Sam was doing—a testament to how far they'd all come. "He's doing well in school too. Sheila King said the same thing—not only is he performing exceedingly well in academics, but he's also getting along great with the other kids."

"I hope things stay this way." John sighed wearily. She understood and nodded while she stared out the window. She always remained positive for the family, no matter what the situation. But the meeting she and John had with Sam's social worker, Jamie, nagged at her soul and threatened her positive outlook.

They hadn't told Sam about the meeting yet. Jamie had told them his father could be released from jail in a few weeks, and he'd indicated his intention to petition the court to regain custody. Jamie didn't know how serious he was, so she suggested they not say anything to Sam yet.

The man would have to go through rehab first, followed by the petitioning process, so it could take several months. Abbie and John hoped that was the case, because neither could imagine reuniting Sam with his father was in his best interest.

"I'm praying hard it doesn't happen." John sighed. "It feels like Andy Quinn all over again."

Abbie shook her head. "Honey, you did everything you could for Andy, and more. Plus, you can't compare the two situations. Andy was one of your basketball players, not our foster child, and he didn't want a different life. You gave him every chance, but he threw it all away when he chose drugs over everything else. After several 'second' chances. You know that."

It was the truth. Until now Abbie had never thoroughly understood John's perceived failure surrounding Andy Quinn, but with everything at stake with Sam, she began to understand.

John let out a long breath. "I know, you're right. But even though it happened a lot of years ago, I still think about it. I did all I could think of to try to keep him on the right path, but I guess the pull of drugs and that world was too strong. I wonder all the time what happened to him."

"With the path he was on, my guess is he's dead." Abbie winced at her own harsh choice of wording. "Or at the very least, in prison. He was dealing heroin back then, so he was probably using it too. But John, you know the situation with Sam is nothing like that. He's living in our home, so we have influence over him right now, and we can try to lead him to God and teach him to make good decisions." She said the words as much for herself as for John.

"You're right. Sam's on a good path right now," John said. "Let's pray things stay this way, for his sake."

thirteen

Sam enjoyed his new friends, but John and Abbie had agreed to let him hang out with a couple of old friends from a group home he'd lived in, and he couldn't wait to see them. They both lived in the vicinity, and the three planned to meet up tonight to hang out for a while.

Tyler, Justin, and Sam had all lived together for a time in their early teens and became close. They were "in the trenches together" as they used to say. But as often happens in the world of foster kids, they were split up and hadn't seen each other since those days in the group home. Until last week, that is, when Sam ran into Tyler at the coffee shop across the street from church.

He'd gone there with Abbie to help her pick up some muffins and coffee cake she'd ordered for a church meeting, and Tyler was there. They sat for a few minutes and caught up a little over hot chocolate while Abbie chatted with a couple of her friends from church. Tyler had been adopted and was doing well, and he'd recently run into Justin, who still lived in a group home and was not doing as well.

"You know what would be great?" Tyler had asked excitedly. "What if the three of us got together again? Me, you, and Justin.

Man, last time I talked to him he seemed down and out. Maybe getting the three of us together would cheer him up.”

“That’s a great idea,” Sam agreed. “It would be cool to see him again.”

So, a plan formed. Sam asked John and Abbie if he could hang out with Tyler, and they said yes. But for a reason he couldn’t quite explain, he didn’t mention they’d be meeting up with Justin too.

Sam hated that he’d lied to the Graysons. Tyler had told him some stuff about Justin, like he drank a lot and occasionally did drugs, and he’d been in and out of juvie for some petty theft stuff. Thinking about it now, a pang of guilt hit him, but he didn’t want to take a chance they’d keep him from seeing his old friends, so he didn’t mention Justin.

The three had agreed to meet at a park shelter house where they could hang out and talk, so he made the fifteen-minute drive from the Graysons’ house to Community Park in Cool Springs. Cooler, autumn air began to filter in, and the fall leaves were changing colors. He enjoyed the drive with the windows down and sunroof open in Abbie’s car. As he pulled in, he spotted Tyler and Justin sitting on the picnic table. As soon as he parked, they jumped up and came running before Sam could even get out of the car.

“Sam! I can’t believe it bro. How long’s it been? I hear you’re livin’ the life of luxury,” Justin exclaimed. The comment bothered him a little, but he brushed it off. He didn’t want anything to take away from the thrill of meeting up with his old friends.

“It’s so great to see you guys!” Sam bear-hugged both his friends, and the trio headed over to the pavilion, but as he approached the picnic table, he studied the cooler and the beer cans sitting on the table. He’d hoped Tyler and Justin had quit drinking, but apparently, they hadn’t.

He cringed when he remembered the haze from the days when his own drinking had gotten him into some trouble. Now the guilt crept in once again because John and Abbie knew nothing about that part of his life, and he was certain they wouldn't approve of him drinking now.

They sat at the picnic table and Justin tossed him a beer, but Sam put it aside.

"No, thanks, man. I'm driving tonight," he said.

"Ah, c'mon, Sam. One for old time's sake won't hurt. It'll wear off before we leave," Justin said.

Sam looked to Tyler for backup, but Tyler shrugged his shoulders and took a swig from his own beer can. He pushed thoughts of what John and Abbie would say out of his head, picked up the beer, and popped it open.

What harm would one beer do?

* * *

John had scheduled a lengthy phone call with a recruit, so Abbie decided to straighten up the house a bit. She prided herself on keeping their house organized, although sometimes, when their schedules got busy, it became more difficult.

Sam did a good job straightening up his room and even doing laundry, but Abbie walked into his room anyway to see if there was anything in there that needed done. It all seemed to be in good shape except for four half-empty water glasses sitting on his desk. Abbie laughed to herself and shook her head. Sam had a habit of leaving his water glasses sitting around the house, and it had become a joke between them.

As she picked up one of the glasses from his desk, she noticed his open journal, and she glanced at it but then backed away. No, she couldn't invade Sam's privacy like that. She reached for the trash can under his desk and emptied it into a trash bag she was carrying, and when she did, she glanced at the journal again and something in it caught her eye. He'd drawn a smiley face.

Despite the pang of guilt, she decided to take a peek anyway, just to see what the smiley face pertained to. She picked up the journal, and next to today's date was a number—3402—and that's where the smiley face was, right next to the 3402.

She hesitated, but her curiosity took over so she thumbed through the journal, even though she knew she shouldn't. It was filled with dates and numbers. Consecutive dates, and all had either a smiley face, frown face or something in between.

Lately, most were smiles or at least half smiles, but as she thumbed farther back, there were a lot of frowns, and then even farther back, there were no faces, just some single teardrop shapes. Then she read one of the dates and had to sit.

Next to the number 3304 Sam had written "new foster family," and it was the date he came to stay with her and John. He'd drawn a single teardrop next to that date. Her breath caught, and it became clear—the numbers represented the number of days he had spent in foster care.

The room shifted, and she was glad she'd been sitting. She still had the journal in her hand, and her eyes filled with tears as she sat on Sam's bed. *He has counted every single day he's been in foster care.* It was inconceivable, and the heaviness of it hit her hard. Just when she thought she understood a little about foster kids and what they endured, this journal staring her in the face served as a reminder of how much she didn't know.

"Honey, what are you doing?" John asked from the hallway, and as he entered the room the curiosity in his voice turned to concern. "Abbie, are you crying? What's wrong?"

"You need to see Sam's journal," she said as she handed it to John. "He's counted every single day he's been in foster care. And he's labeled them with emojis. Look at this, the day he came here. A teardrop."

Abbie rambled on, and she sensed from the way John stared at her that he didn't comprehend at first. He scanned through the journal, and she recognized the moment he caught on. He shook his head and dropped beside her on the bed.

"This is ... sad. I mean, I can't imagine keeping track of this, and in this way. And the teardrop. Wait—is that the day he came here?" John struggled to get the words out as the realization hit.

Abbie nodded her head and brushed the tears from her face. "It breaks my heart, hon, it truly does. If we ever question again whether we're doing the right thing by fostering, we need to remember this," Abbie said with a renewed resolve, and she closed the journal and put it back on his desk. "He'll be home soon. I don't want him to know we were in here snooping."

"We?" John laughed half-heartedly. They walked out of Sam's room and closed the door behind them.

"Speaking of Sam, what time did you tell him to be home?" John asked as he glanced extra-long at his watch. "It's almost 10:00 now."

"It is? I told him 9:00." Abbie couldn't believe it was that late already. She'd become engrossed in the journal and had lost track of time.

"Well," John sighed, "we may need to remember that journal tonight."

fourteen

Four beers in—or had it been five, or maybe even six? Sam lost count. He laughed at everything his friends said and had trouble getting his words to come out correctly, but he still had the presence of mind to realize he hadn't paid attention to the time. It'd been dark for a long time now, and the air was chillier than what he'd dressed for, so he figured it was past his curfew. Maybe way past. But he couldn't drive in his current state.

He attempted to focus his mind on a solution when out of the blackness, headlights approached. Sam and his friends were at the backside of the park and hadn't seen a car since well before dark, and he vaguely wondered who would be driving around the park this late. They were off the beaten path, so it probably wasn't someone cruising. He hoped it wasn't trouble.

Then, unexpectedly, red and blue lights flashed and made his breath catch and his head throb.

"Cops!" Justin yelled, and he took off running for the woods. For a second Sam considered running, too, but then he remembered he'd driven Abbie's car here. Tyler had also driven, so running wasn't an option for either of them. Whatever was about to happen, Sam still had the sense to realize it wouldn't be good.

* * *

John replayed the phone call in his head as he drove to the park to pick up Sam, and he considered whether he should notify Jamie. He would rather handle this himself if possible, so he decided to wait until tomorrow to decide whether to call the social worker.

He couldn't comprehend that Sam had not only violated his curfew, he'd also been drinking in the park with two other boys. Which brought up a whole other issue—he only asked to hang out with one boy, Tyler, so John didn't have a clue who the other boy even was.

He'd been told Tyler's parents were on their way to pick him up, and the other, unknown boy, had run off. John was grateful the officer decided to handle this by calling him, because he could have taken Sam to juvenile detention, which wouldn't have been good for any of them. As it turned out, the police officer was off duty but performed security for the park at night to deter crime there.

John drove the winding road to the back of the park near the woods, where the shelter house was located. He glanced at the clock on his dashboard and shook his head. Nearly 11:30 p.m.—a full two and a half hours past Sam's curfew.

Not only had he and Abbie been worried, but when that phone call came, they were scared. He hadn't decided yet what he'd say to Sam or what his punishment would be. A lot would depend on Sam's attitude about the whole incident, and John could picture things going a couple of different ways.

He pulled up to the shelter house and immediately spotted Sam sitting at the picnic table, slumped over, with his head in his hands. The other boy, Tyler, was getting into a car on the other side of the shelter with a man John guessed was his father. John got out of the car and walked toward the policeman, but Sam never looked up.

"Hi, I'm John Grayson, I'm here for Sam." John extended his hand to the officer.

The man's eyes grew wide, and his mouth fell open. It was the look of recognition John had become accustomed to when out in public in the state of Tennessee.

Great. What a time to be recognized.

"Well, what do you know." The officer smiled as he shook John's hand, and then laughed. "Coach Grayson, I never dreamed you were *the* John Grayson when Sam gave me your information. I'm a huge fan of you and your teams."

"Thank you, I appreciate that." John didn't know what to say in this situation. "Sam's our foster child. Thank you for contacting us." John was indeed grateful he didn't have to go to the police station tonight.

"No problem, Coach. These boys weren't causing any real trouble, other than the underage drinking of course. But they'd have to leave here eventually, and neither was in any shape to drive. I only wanted to prevent something tragic from happening."

"Oh, absolutely. This is the first time we've had this problem with Sam, and I can assure you, it'll be the last." John gave the officer a knowing look. Discipline would unquestionably be in the boy's future.

"Do you have any idea if I need to let social services know? I'm not sure how any of that works. My wife and I are still pretty new to this world." John felt very lost. He was glad the officer was friendly and obviously a fan, and more than grateful for any assistance the man could offer.

"I checked their IDs against our system, and they haven't been in any serious trouble before, so that's when I decided to call you and the other boy's father instead of taking them in. To answer your question, I won't be filing a report, so whether or not you notify social services is up to you," the officer explained.

While they talked, Sam got up and walked away from the picnic table, in the opposite direction of him and the officer and threw up in the bushes. *This night just keeps getting better and better.* He hadn't thought about Sam being sick from the alcohol. This would not be a fun trip home. John and the officer both shook their heads, and John took a deep breath and let it out.

"Thanks again, Officer, for calling me. I appreciate all you did. Do you happen to know who the other boy was, the one who ran? Sam only told us about Tyler," John asked.

"Sure don't." The officer shrugged. "He ran as soon as I pulled in, and he made it into the woods over there before I could even park the car. Neither boy would say who he was. My guess is the kid has a record and couldn't afford to get caught."

The officer then pointed toward Abbie's car. "I'll tag it 'do not tow' so you can come get it here in the morning."

John once again shook the officer's hand and thanked him. Then he looked over at Sam. He was sitting at the picnic table again and still hadn't acknowledged John since he'd arrived. It was clearly time to get him home.

"Let's go, Sam," John shouted. Sam got up and walked toward John's car with his head down.

"Hold on, let me get you a plastic bag in case you need it for the car ride home," the officer said as an afterthought.

John nodded and took the bag from the officer, grateful the man had offered it. Sam reeked of alcohol and even in the dark, the boy looked a little green. John slid into the driver's seat and handed the bag to him. "Here, in case you get sick again."

"I think I'm okay," he replied as he tried unsuccessfully to fasten his seatbelt into place.

From the way he bungled his attempt with the seatbelt, John doubted he was anywhere close to okay. "Let me get that." John reached over and buckled him in. "All right, let's get you home."

John decided to save the lecture for tomorrow when the boy would actually remember it. The ride home was quiet as Sam fell asleep with his head against the window. John pulled into the garage and was relieved Sam didn't get sick in the car, but he was still upset about the situation.

"Go on to bed and we'll talk in the morning," John said gruffly as he pulled into the garage and Sam woke up.

Sam squinted at John in the bright white light of the garage. "I'm sorry. I know I messed up."

John's heart, as well as his tone, softened a bit. "I know. We'll discuss it in the morning, okay? Get some sleep. And take a shower."

fifteen

Sam woke up but didn't want to open his eyes in case the sunshine streamed in. His pounding, throbbing head couldn't handle that. His tongue stuck to the roof of his mouth, and his stomach did somersaults. Memories of the night before were hazy, but he remembered enough.

How many beers had he consumed? Four or five? More? Then the cop showed up, and Sam had thought for sure he'd take them all to juvie, but instead, the cop said he'd call their parents to pick them up. Of course, Justin ran. He'd been in and out of juvie too many times to count and was even on probation, which Sam had just found out last night.

He'd used terrible judgment, and now he'd have to pay the price. Jamie would be here to pick him up today for sure. He was angry at himself for messing this up so badly. Finally, he'd found a family he liked, where the parents were nice and caring, and he destroyed all of it in one night.

He managed to drag himself out of bed but the instant he stood, his stomach jumped to his throat, and he ran to the bathroom. Nothing came up, just dry heaves that left his head pounding even worse than before. He sat on the bathroom floor to give his stomach a chance to settle down.

As soon as he could get up without getting sick, he'd get dressed, pack his things, and then face the music with John and Abbie. Jamie might already be here waiting for him.

"Sam, you up?" John yelled.

He shuddered. Yep, he sounded annoyed. Jamie must be here, or at least on the way. "Yeah." Sam's voice was hoarse, and his answer barely squeaked out.

John must not have heard him because a moment later he walked into Sam's bathroom to see him sitting cross-legged in the middle of the bathroom floor.

"Are you okay, or are you still sick?" John asked, the annoyance in his voice tinged with a hint of concern.

"I thought I was gonna get sick when I first got up, but I think I'm okay now."

"All right, get dressed, then come out to the kitchen. We need to talk. Abbie is making you some toast and coffee."

John stood there as if waiting for a response, but the mention of food made Sam's stomach queasy again. He had to swallow a couple of times before he could answer.

"Be right out," was all he could manage as John left him alone.

Slowly, Sam pulled himself up, went to the sink to wash his face and brush his teeth, then went back to the bedroom and threw on jeans and a hoodie. Not the nice ones that the Graysons had bought him, but the worn out, original clothes he had brought with him. If he was leaving soon, he might as well go ahead and put his shoes on.

He couldn't believe he'd managed to do all that without getting sick, and when he walked into the kitchen, he was surprised Jamie wasn't there yet. Instead, Abbie poured coffee and gave him a gentle smile.

"Good morning. I was going to fix you eggs but decided plain toast might be better." She set the toast and coffee in front of him.

"Yeah, probably. Thanks."

She and John sat at the kitchen island with him and sipped their coffee without saying anything, but he could sense the tension in the room. It was too quiet, with none of the usual morning banter. After a few minutes, John sat his coffee cup down and cleared his throat.

"Well, I guess we'd better talk about what happened last night," John said.

"I know, I'm sorry," Sam said, and he was sorrier than either of them would ever know. He was sorry he'd broken their rules but even sorrier he'd messed up this chance at a good life. There was no one to blame but himself. He took a deep breath. "I'll go pack before Jamie gets here."

Abbie leaned her head to one side and studied him for a long moment. "Did you call Jamie?" Abbie asked Sam.

"Uh, well, no." Sam was confused. "Did you want me to make the call?"

John and Abbie were both bewildered, looking at each other, then at him, and he questioned whether he might still be under the influence of the alcohol from last night.

"What call, Sam?" John asked, and the confusion in his voice matched the look on his face.

"The call to tell Jamie to come get me." Sam cast his eyes down to his plate. He couldn't look at them as he said the words.

John sighed. No one said anything for a moment.

"Sam, look at me. Is that what you think—that we're sending you away?" John asked quietly.

Sam nodded but couldn't look up at John to answer. Of course, that's what he thought because that's what had always happened in the past.

"Oh, honey," Abbie said, on the verge of tears. "We're not sending you away. Yes, you messed up. You broke curfew, lied about who you were with, and drank. There will be a punishment, which means you'll be grounded for a while. But we're definitely not sending you away."

"Why not?" He didn't understand, and all he could do was

stare at them with his mouth hanging open. There must be some catch. This wasn't how things happened in his world.

"Do you want to leave?" John asked hesitantly.

"Well, no. I don't ever want to leave here. I figured you'd want me gone after last night. That's what always happens." Sam slumped his shoulders, his eyes cast down.

"No, son," John spoke gently. "Not here. And I'm so sorry for what you've experienced in the past."

"In our home, we work through our problems," Abbie said. "And believe me, there will always be problems." She put her hand on Sam's shoulder. "None of us is perfect. We all mess up from time to time. You made some bad decisions last night, but every teenager does at one time or another. The key is to learn from those mistakes and not keep making the same ones. But, the bottom line is, messing up doesn't result in being sent away."

Sam didn't know what to say.

"We'll keep telling you that until you believe it. Even if we have to tell you every day," John added, and he sounded as sincere as Abbie did.

How could this be? No one had ever treated him this way. It was always one strike and you're out, and sometimes there wasn't even a strike—he was simply out with no warning whatsoever.

"Thank you." He nodded, trying hard to keep his emotions in check. "And I really am sorry. I'll take any punishment you want to give. Y'all are so good to me, and I never should've lied. When I realized they were drinking, I should've left, or at least not drank."

John nodded his head in agreement. "Leaving would've been the best decision. But we know you're sorry, and like Abbie said, we all make mistakes. The right thing to do is own up to your mistakes, like you just did, and not repeat the same ones."

"By the way, who was the other boy?" Abbie asked.

He had wanted to protect Justin, but Abbie deserved to know since he'd lied to her when he told her he was only hanging out with Tyler. "That was Justin. He lived in a group home with

Tyler and me. He's been in juvie a bunch of times, and that's why he ran. And that's also why I didn't tell you I was hanging out with him too. I'm sorry. I promise I won't lie again." Sam hoped they could tell he was sincere.

"Thank you, Sam," Abbie said. "I appreciate your honesty."

"Well," John said, "as far as your punishment, Abbie and I decided to ground you for a month. I know that might seem a little extreme, but this could've turned out a lot differently. I want you to give some serious thought as to what could've happened if you'd driven and gotten into an accident. You can still do school activities, but that'll be it for now."

"That's fair." He nodded as relief washed over him. "And thank you for not calling social services. I promise I won't mess up again."

Abbie laughed and shook her head. "Oh, kiddo, I promise you will. We all will. But no matter what, just remember that messing up does not result in us sending you away."

John and Abbie chatted throughout the rest of breakfast, but Sam was mostly silent. He sat in awe of what happened this morning. It was the opposite of what he expected, but then the Graysons were the opposite of every foster family he'd been a part of.

sixteen

As he left the university, John breathed in the unseasonably warm fall air and gazed at the trees in their bright autumn hues of red, orange, and yellow. He loved fall more than any season and tried to take in the beauty of it each day and never take it for granted.

Official basketball practices had begun, and he and the other coaches had led the team through some tough endurance drills today. The boys still looked a little rough from a conditioning standpoint, but then again, they always did at this time of year. His experience with prior teams told him they would be in tip-top shape by the time games began in mid-November.

But he had other things to think about in the meantime. He was anxious to get home because it was October twenty-fifth—Sam's seventeenth birthday—and he and Abbie had a special surprise for him.

The idea started a couple of weeks ago when John and Abbie returned home from a university function, and upon finding the upstairs quiet, they went to the basement to check on him. The sound coming from the basement stopped them in their tracks at the top of the stairs. Sam was playing the piano and singing. John and Abbie listened, in awe of his talent.

Sam had told them he played piano "a little," but what they'd heard him play was amazing. They never dreamed he could sing and play like that. They'd sat at the top of the stairs and quietly listened without him knowing. When the song ended, John nodded at Abbie to go downstairs, so they both headed to the basement.

Sam was startled at first and then his face turned red. "I didn't hear you come home."

"That was beautiful. We had no idea you had so much talent." Abbie marveled.

"That was amazing," John said in admiration. "What was that song? I've never heard it before."

"Just something I wrote." Sam shrugged. His face turned an even brighter shade of red.

"You wrote that?" John was stunned. "Did you write the words or the music?"

When he shrugged and said he wrote both, John and Abbie turned to each other and laughed, both at the incredible talent they had accidentally stumbled upon and Sam's complete unawareness of his talent.

So, on the way home today, John stopped to pick up a guitar for Sam's birthday from him and Abbie. A splurge for a birthday gift for sure, but they'd already agreed to make music lessons part of his homeschooling, so they could justify it that way.

Sam was doing amazingly well both at home and in school, and he helped out around the house every chance he got without them having to ask. He'd been overlooked most of his life, so they wanted to do something special for him.

John pulled into the garage and went to the kitchen to find Abbie chopping peppers and onions for the fajitas she was making for dinner.

"Where's Sam?" John asked before even saying hello to his wife.

"Well, hello to you too." Abbie laughed as John gave her a quick peck on the cheek. "Did you get it?"

"I sure did. It's in my office. I'll bring it out when we finish dinner," John said. Abbie agreed with the plan, and they talked about how they couldn't wait to give it to him.

Dinner couldn't get over with fast enough. Sam had requested fajitas when Abbie asked him what he wanted for his birthday dinner, and he told them he'd never had a birthday dinner before.

It hit John like things often did during conversations with Sam. He realized there were many kids out there who didn't know what it was like to have their birthday celebrated or even have a special meal "just because."

As soon as they finished dinner, Sam jumped up to clear the table the way he often did.

"Wait just a second." John got up from the table and motioned for him to sit back down. "Abbie and I have a birthday surprise for you."

"And besides," Abbie said, her eyes dancing, "you don't have to do any chores on your birthday. Now, close your eyes."

He closed his eyes, and John could hear the two of them laughing as he hurried to his office to grab the gift.

"Okay, stand up Sam, but keep your eyes closed," John commanded as he returned to the kitchen.

Sam did as he was told, and Abbie laughed.

"You can open your eyes now," John said. When Sam opened them, John handed the guitar to him. "It's all yours," John said.

Sam gasped, his eyes wide. "What? Are you kidding me?" he exclaimed, half shouting, half laughing.

"You," John said, "are already enormously talented. We're going to arrange guitar lessons for you, and we'll include it as part of your music theory elective."

Sam just stood there, still looking stunned, and then he put the guitar strap around his shoulder. At first it seemed he might cry, but instead he laughed and then he hugged both John and Abbie. "Thank you so much. I never dreamed I'd have my own guitar."

The smile on Sam's face meant everything. He'd come such a long way since his first night in their home. He was grateful and happy, and so were they.

seventeen

Things were better at home than they'd been since Sam had arrived. He had settled in now and opened up to them a little at a time. In a call last week, Abbie had told Jamie that Sam appeared to be doing better than at any time since she'd known him. He also flourished in his homeschool studies with Abbie. At the academy, he excelled in his schoolwork and got along well with all his classmates. It was almost too good to be true.

Abbie thanked God that Sam was happy and adjusting well to their family. He initiated conversations with both her and John a little bit more each day—nothing too personal, but enough for them to get a glimpse of his past.

He acted astounded that they wanted to have dinner with him every night and said he'd never been part of a family who ate together. And he acted surprised when they wanted to know about his day. Last night, Sam had laughed when John had asked him how his day had been. "Your first scrimmage of the year was today, and you want to know how my day at school went?" Sam had laughed and shook his head. It was disheartening to think until now, no adult had ever been interested in his everyday activities.

Abbie was lost in thought when John come in through the garage and tossed his keys on his desk.

"Is that a roast in the oven I smell?" John asked as he made his way to the kitchen where Abbie sat at a bar stool with a cup of coffee, music streaming in the background. Mercy Me's "I Can Only Imagine" was playing, one of their favorites.

"Oh, hi, hon. I didn't even realize what time it was." Abbie forced a quick smile. "How was practice?" she asked as John gave her a quick kiss.

"A little rough today. But that's expected. It'll come together in time." John studied her. "How about you; is something wrong? Where's Sam?" he asked as he looked around for a clue as to what might be wrong.

Abbie sighed and crossed her arms on the countertop in front of her. "I sent him to the basement to watch a webinar so we could talk in private."

"Did something happen with him today?" John asked. "Other than the drinking incident, he's been doing so well."

Abbie shook her head and bit her lower lip. She hated having to tell John. "No, nothing happened directly with him," she said. "But Jamie called today. She said his father has been released from jail, and he has already petitioned for custody of Sam."

The color drained from John's face as he dropped to the stool next to Abbie's. They didn't know a lot about the man, only that he'd been arrested for drugs. And they'd been told the Department of Child Services had removed him from the home previous times due to complaints or incidents involving his father.

Sam never revealed anything, and if someone brought up his father, he became quiet. They'd never pressed him for details, but Jamie once told them she suspected abuse. Whenever she questioned him about the possibility of his father abusing him, however, Sam denied it. Jamie didn't believe him, but without any proof, it was only a suspicion. And now both Abbie and John shared that suspicion. Sam had no desire to reunite with his father.

"You know," John mused, "he clearly doesn't want to be with his father; whether there's been abuse or not, he just doesn't want to be with him. There's something there."

"I know." Abbie nodded slowly. "Jamie and I discussed that, but unless there's some sort of proof of abuse or Sam speaks up, the state of Tennessee pushes for unification with the biological parent. There's not much anyone can do."

John hesitated, and they'd been married so long that Abbie predicted what he was about to ask. "How long until he leaves? And does he have any idea about this?"

"Jamie said they don't know exactly. His father filed the request today. She said once a judge receives it, the court will assign parenting classes for him to complete, and then he'll have to appear before a judge in family court. She said it could be anywhere from a few weeks to a few months, depending on how motivated his father is. And no, Sam doesn't know. Jamie said she'll come talk to him when the time comes and for us not to say anything for now."

Abbie's stomach sank. This was the devastating part of being a foster parent they'd been warned about. Although they hadn't said it out loud, Abbie recognized from his words and actions that John felt the same way she did. Sam had found his way into their hearts, and they'd begun to care deeply for him in the few short months he'd been in their home.

The prospect of losing him and maybe never seeing him again was tough enough, but even worse was the possibility that there were details and incidents involving his father that Sam hadn't revealed to anyone. He could possibly be sent back to live with a biological parent who didn't want him. Or even worse.

* * *

Sam sat on the sofa in the basement family room with the laptop, trying to focus on the webinar, something about the War of 1812. He was supposed to be taking notes for his history lesson, but he couldn't concentrate on it.

He'd overheard Abbie's side of a phone conversation today and figured she sent him down here so she and John could talk. From what he could gather, he concluded he'd be leaving soon. But not to a new foster home—he'd reunite with his father. Both anger and queasiness hit him at the same time.

He'd been through this before. The part where he found out he was about to be shipped off to yet another foster home, or worse, to his father. Normally Sam would go numb at this point. He'd detach from his foster family, if there'd been any attachment at all, which was rare.

This time was different though. He had connected with the Graysons, and he hated to admit it, but he'd become attached to them. They were the first family Sam had ever lived with who treated him with respect and like a family member instead of merely a boarder. They genuinely cared about him. He was beginning to heal, and there were moments when he even felt like a normal teenager. Or at least what he thought a normal teenager would feel like.

There were new friends in his life now, and lately, he'd even dared to dream about going to college. Until now he'd never dreamed about anything other than survival. But life with the Graysons made him feel safe, secure, and normal. He didn't have to fight for survival or fear people traipsing in and out of the home, so the dreams he'd always suppressed could come to the surface. Not only that but there was something else he'd never experienced before—he didn't want to give up this family and this new life that was worth living.

He clicked through the screens on the computer mindlessly so at least Abbie would think he watched the webinar like she'd asked him, but he certainly couldn't concentrate on the War of 1812 when his own war was waging.

What if he talked to John and told him the things his father was involved in and the people he associated with? John was easy to talk to, and more importantly, he might even believe Sam. It would be difficult to talk about those things, but if he couldn't tell John, he would never be able to tell anyone.

Sam decided to wait until the time was right, and then he'd tell John everything. Hopefully, he'd be allowed to stay here with the Graysons and never have to leave.

eighteen

Sam pulled his hoodie over his head, ran his fingers through his hair, then checked himself in the mirror one more time and frowned. His new, shorter haircut made him look more like his father, and that wasn't a reflection he wanted to see. He'd be sure to let his hair grow out again.

"C'mon Sam. You'll be late to school," Abbie shouted from the kitchen. "I'll meet you in the car."

"Coming!" He shouted back. He picked up his books and then grabbed a bottle of water and a granola bar from the kitchen on his way out to the car.

He hadn't found out anymore about the man, so maybe he'd given up his quest for custody, or possibly he'd already applied and had been denied. Sam wanted to ask, but since no one had officially told him about the conversation, he decided not to. But he was prepared to talk to John about his father when and if the time came.

"You know, basketball games are getting ready to start, which means John will be traveling a lot." Abbie glanced over at him as she drove him to school.

"Yeah, I've heard you all talk about how much he's away."

Sam frowned. He enjoyed hanging out with John and would miss him.

"Yes, he's gone a lot during the season." Abbie didn't seem happy or sad as she said it. She just seemed accustomed to it. "We have a tradition each year where we all spend the weekend together right before the first game of the season. Since games start next week, we'll do it this weekend."

His stomach twisted and turned, and he hoped he was wrong about what was coming.

"When Kyle and Hannah were living at home," Abbie continued, "it meant no friends that weekend, just our family having a weekend together. And now that they're out on their own, they come home and stay for the weekend, and we hang out, watch movies, play games—stuff like that. And this year I'm so happy you'll be a part of it, Sam."

The blood drained from his face. Abbie smiled at him, and he forced a smile back, but his mind could only focus on one thing. Kyle would be around for the entire weekend.

"Also, since John will be away over Thanksgiving for a tournament, we'll celebrate Thanksgiving this weekend also. I know it's a couple of weeks early, but it's the only time we'll all be together." Abbie smiled to herself.

Sam studied Abbie as she drove. She smiled and sang along with the radio, and she clearly looked forward to the weekend. He'd never been part of a family this close, who liked spending time together, so this was foreign to him. It was all good except for the fact that Kyle would be present for the entire weekend.

Since that awful dinner a few months ago, the two hadn't been together for more than a few minutes here and there. In those brief encounters, Kyle completely ignored Sam, which was fine. It was better than the interrogation and attack he'd aimed at Sam the first time they met. Now Kyle would be here for a whole weekend, and Sam didn't expect it to turn out well.

"Do you feel okay, hon?" Abbie asked him as they sat at a red light. "You look a little pale."

Sam shrugged. "Just a little tired, I guess." He took a deep breath and stared out the passenger window so his face wouldn't give away his anxiousness.

Abbie continued to talk, but Sam had trouble focusing. She said Kyle's fiancée, Cassie, would be here for the weekend, as well as Hannah, of course. He was thankful for Hannah. She'd been nothing but kind to him, and he was relieved she'd be there for the entire weekend.

He figured John would be as thrilled as Abbie about the whole family getting together, so Sam would do his part to get along with Kyle. If Kyle didn't reciprocate, then Sam would avoid him and do whatever necessary to get through the weekend. That was the least he could do for John and Abbie.

* * *

Friday came faster than Sam had hoped, and he'd grown more anxious and worried each day. Abbie had been excited all week, of course, and he'd helped her shop, clean the house, and get everything ready. Staying busy helped keep his mind off the situation with Kyle. The sleeping arrangements were set. Kyle would sleep in one of the basement bedrooms, and Hannah and Cassie would share the other. Sam was relieved to know he'd still have his main floor bedroom to retreat to if it all got to be too much for him.

He glanced at the clock in the kitchen. Hannah would be here soon, and he couldn't wait to see her. He'd texted her earlier in the week and confided that he was anxious about spending so much time with Kyle. She'd told him not to worry. "I've got your back," she'd replied. He was grateful. She had become what he imagined a sister might be.

She told him she'd prayed every day for Kyle, for his heart to soften concerning Sam. The best he could dare hope for was that Kyle wouldn't be confrontational like he'd been at that dinner when they first met.

Hannah's cheerful, sudden entrance stopped his thoughts from spiraling out of control. Abbie and Hannah hugged, and he went to help her with her bags, and she turned and gave him a huge hug.

"Sammy! I'm so excited we get to spend the whole weekend together. We're gonna have so much fun," Hannah exclaimed with a huge smile.

He didn't know about that, but he was certainly glad to see her. And he was also certain she'd be the only one who'd get away with calling him "Sammy" this weekend. Or ever.

"Who wants coffee?" Abbie asked as she reached for the coffee cups from the cupboard.

Hannah had introduced Sam to coffee, and now he loved it. The three of them sat in the kitchen and drank their coffee. He smiled while Hannah and Abbie talked about all the things they were going to do together this weekend—play games, watch movies, eat, and catch up with each other. If not for Kyle, Sam would have been excited, too, but as each hour passed, he became increasingly uneasy about Kyle's arrival.

John came home, and as they prepared dinner, he pulled Sam aside. "Hey, I want you to know I'm not going to let what happened with Kyle last time happen again this weekend. I don't want you to worry, okay? It's going to be fine."

"Thank you," Sam blushed. He was incredibly thankful for John and Abbie's kindheartedness. They had done so much to make his life easier, and he was once again grateful.

"Kyle and Cass are here!" Hannah exclaimed, and her energetic voice startled him, while John shook his head and laughed at her giddiness.

John patted Sam on the shoulder and moved toward the door, but Sam stood in the background and worked to steady his breathing. Cassie entered first and hugged John, Abbie, and then Hannah. She talked about the heavy traffic coming through Nashville. Then she spotted Sam and smiled and walked toward him. "Hi, Sam, it's so good to meet you. I'm Cassie," she said.

Her friendliness and the way she smiled at him were comforting. "Thanks. It's nice to meet you too," Sam said.

Cassie hugged him lightly, and it was a little awkward, but if she thought so, she didn't let on. She had a natural prettiness that contrasted with the image he'd formed in his head of what Kyle's fiancée would look like. He'd pictured a tall, aloof, supermodel type, but Cassie was pretty and petite with shoulder-length blonde hair. She had an approachable, laid-back appearance that differed from Kyle's.

As Sam and Cassie talked, Kyle walked in, set their bags down, and greeted his parents and sister with hugs and laughter. This was a side of Kyle that Sam hadn't seen before, so he slipped into the background once again to watch. After a few minutes, he went to pour himself some more coffee when he realized Kyle was approaching him.

"How are you, Sam?" Kyle asked quietly.

Kyle's words caught him off guard. He'd figured Kyle would come in and ignore him completely.

"*Umm* ...good, thanks," was all Sam could come up with. He had trouble making eye contact with the guy.

"Why don't we go downstairs and get you all settled in your rooms?" Abbie popped in between them suddenly.

Kyle, Cassie, and Hannah followed Abbie to the basement and left Sam and John in the kitchen.

"You two watch the turkey in the oven please," Abbie yelled back over her shoulder as she and the kids headed down the stairs to the basement.

"Everything okay?" John asked in a low voice.

"Yeah, everything's good." Sam stretched the truth a little. The exchange wasn't long enough to know whether it was good or not, but John was relieved, and happy, and that's what mattered. Even if it wasn't okay, he wouldn't let it ruin John's weekend. He'd pretend things were fine even if they weren't.

As the evening wore on, they sat down to a huge, elaborate dinner. It was exactly like the Thanksgiving dinners Sam had seen on TV but had never experienced in real life. They had a huge turkey, stuffing, real mashed potatoes, homemade rolls he had helped Abbie make, and pumpkin and apple pies for dessert. They even ate from fancy plates Sam hadn't seen before. Abbie called them her special-occasion plates.

Most of the dinner talk centered around the team and John's hopes for the season. They discussed the upcoming schedule, the travel involved, and a couple of injuries the team had already incurred.

The conversation then moved to Hannah and her new job as a second-grade teacher at a Christian school outside of Nashville. They all laughed at some funny stories she told about the little kids she taught. She loved her job.

Kyle talked about his job as an attorney for a law firm in Nashville. He'd graduated from law school in May, and this was his first real job. He said he was low on the ladder, but he enjoyed his work as an associate attorney. And Cassie passed her CPA exam. She accepted an offer from an accounting firm and was scheduled to start in a couple of weeks.

Sam liked hearing about what their family was up to. It helped him get to know them better. The best part was, so far, he didn't have to talk much. He could just listen and nod or laugh where appropriate.

That all changed, though, when Hannah asked him about school, and suddenly all eyes were upon him. He was nervous talking in front of them but relieved to see they were all still eating so they didn't just sit and stare at him. He told them about his homeschooling and the academy, and Abbie jumped in a couple of times to say how well he was doing, and Sam appreciated her comments.

Kyle didn't say anything, but he politely listened and nodded, much like Sam had been doing. Cassie asked him some questions about how the homeschool academy functioned, and Hannah, being a teacher herself, was interested in knowing all the subjects he studied. Overall, the conversation at dinner went better than he'd predicted.

Since it was Friday and everyone was a little tired from the work week and the big dinner, they decided tonight would be a low-key movie night. That was fantastic news for Sam because it meant he wouldn't have to talk anymore.

The girls had decided on a Christmas movie, so everyone gathered in the cozy family room and ate pie while they watched *Elf*. Sam situated himself at the opposite end of the large sectional sofa from Kyle. He ended up between Abbie and Hannah, which suited him fine. They laughed their way through the movie, and other than that, there wasn't much conversation. He'd cleared a major hurdle for sure.

When the movie ended, and it was time to turn in for the night, Sam nearly ran to his room in relief. The fact he'd made it through day one was extremely comforting.

He took a shower and settled into his bed to read when someone knocked lightly on his bedroom door, probably John or Abbie stopping in to tell him goodnight as they often did.

"Come on in," he said. He bookmarked his book, sat up in his bed, and tried to hide his shock as the door opened. It wasn't John or Abbie, but Kyle. Sam's expression must have given him away because Kyle laughed slightly and hung his head.

"I guess I'm the last person you expected, or wanted, to see come through your door."

"No, it's okay." He shrugged as he lied through his teeth.

"You care if I sit down?" Kyle pointed to the chair at Sam's desk. He waited for him to nod his okay and then pulled the chair out. He faced the bed where Sam sat with his back to the wall.

Sam's mouth was dry, and his heart beat a little faster than normal as he waited to see what this was about. This could be worse than any scenario he'd conjured up in his mind. He'd already decided if Kyle wanted to tell him how much he hated him, he would endure it for John's sake.

Kyle sat with his hands together for a long while, staring at the floor, and Sam wondered if he would ever speak. When he looked up, Sam didn't see the harsh, contempt-filled facial expressions he'd seen at that dinner months ago. Kyle's face was softer now, and he gave Sam a sheepish half-smile.

"Well," Kyle finally broke the silence, "I'm not good at this at all, so I'm just going to say what's on my mind."

Sam braced for what was surely coming.

"So, here goes." Kyle sighed. "Dad and I have always been close, and the older I get, the more I appreciate that. When he and mom first said they were going to become foster parents, well, I thought they were a little bit crazy." Kyle laughed half-heartedly and shrugged. "I mean, Hannah and I were finally out of the house, so I figured they'd travel, take vacations, and do more of what they hadn't been able to while we were home."

"Then when they said they'd only foster little kids, I thought, okay. I can see mom with a little kid to take care of, and Dad talked like he was fine with whatever she wanted, so it was okay. But when they got their very first foster placement, a teenager—you—I was shocked and confused. And a little hurt."

Sam listened intently to Kyle, but in the back of his mind, he made a note of what he'd said about Sam being not only the first foster child they ever had but also a teenager they didn't want. He hadn't known either of these things and didn't know quite what to make of them.

"The day I met you, Dad's protectiveness of you took me by surprise, and to be honest, I resented it. I didn't even realize at that moment why, but the more Cassie and I discussed it, the more obvious it became that I was jealous." Kyle shook his head, and Sam remained silent, anxious to see where this was going.

"Anyway, I want to apologize for the way I acted." Kyle looked straight into Sam's eyes. "I mean, when I think back on it, my behavior toward you was, well, horrible, and I want you to know I'm so sorry. I never meant to make your life harder than it already was, and I hope you can accept my apology. I've realized that for you to be in the situation you're in, you've probably had a lot of tough times, and I contributed to that. From now on, I just want to be supportive."

Sam was stunned. He was glad to be sitting on the bed, otherwise he might have fallen over. And at that moment, he noticed a resemblance between Kyle and John that hadn't been there before. Not only in looks—Kyle had dark hair like John used to have in pictures before his hair turned mostly gray—but he could see it in the honesty in his eyes and the sincerity in his voice as he apologized.

"Sure, it's okay. I mean, yeah, I accept your apology," Sam stuttered all over himself and blushed. "This close family thing is all new to me, and it's taking some getting used to for me too."

Sam didn't know what he should do now, shake Kyle's hand or what, but Kyle reached out and bumped Sam's shoulder lightly with his fist and smiled.

"Thanks, Sam. It means a lot. But it's not okay. I know that, and I plan to make it up to you. I want to get to know you this weekend. And not by interrogation." They both laughed, and Kyle said goodnight and got up to go downstairs to bed.

Sam settled back into his bed and thought about the apology, the new start with Kyle, and the way this weekend began. Relief washed over him, and now he couldn't wait to spend the rest of the weekend with this family who included him as their own.

nineteen

John boarded the plane at the Nashville Airport with his team, headed to Los Angeles for the Thanksgiving weekend tournament. The first tournament of the year always brought excitement, but he had mixed feelings. He was a born competitor and looked forward to the challenge of every game, but he was also a family man who hated being away from his family on holidays.

Normally, his family traveled with him for Thanksgiving tournaments, but this year was more complicated. Kyle and Cassie had her parents to think of as well and taking Sam across the country required special permission. Given the circumstances, they decided this year Abbie and Sam would stay home, and Hannah would come stay with them for the weekend. Abbie planned to decorate the house for Christmas with Hannah and Sam's help, and she was excited.

Once the plane was in the air, it didn't take long for his players and coaches to settle in for the long flight. Most everyone had their earbuds in or napped, so John sat by himself in a window seat and thumbed through his notes and scouting reports for the tourney. He'd already memorized them, of course, so after a while, he decided to close his eyes. But as he attempted to sleep, memories of that former player, Andy Quinn, invaded his thoughts as they had more frequently lately, and today he was particularly bothered.

"Hey, Wes," John called out to his long-time friend and assistant coach, who sat two rows in front of John on the other side of the aisle. "Come back here for a minute."

"What's up, Coach?" Wes yawned and stretched as he got up, walked back to John's row, and settled into the empty seat next to John. "I was enjoying naptime."

"Sorry," John said to his friend who'd also served as his lead assistant for many years. Wes had been his best friend since college, and John could count on his honesty, in matters both on and off the court. "I've been thinking about Andy Quinn,"

Wes moaned in frustration and scratched the back of his head. "And just why are we going there again? John, we have dissected that kid's situation until there's nothing left."

"He's been on my mind a lot lately. I guess because we're fostering Sam, and that's just made me think a lot about Andy." John stared out the oval window at the clouds hovering just below them.

Although it had been many years since Andy had played at TU, John still thought he'd failed the young man. His assistant coaches, athletic director and others who were privy to the situation, including Abbie and Wes, had told him repeatedly he'd done everything possible. In fact, he'd gone over and above the scope of what most coaches would've done. But nevertheless, John still felt as though he failed the kid.

Andy hadn't been highly recruited, but he'd been an above-average high school player, and when John watched him play, he saw a diamond in the rough. He most likely wouldn't have been the star of the team or an NBA player, but John had seen the potential for him to have a solid, important role on his team if he worked hard. More importantly, he would get a college education in return.

If he were honest, Andy had reminded John of himself at

that age. John had also been an above-average high school player who hadn't had many breaks and was by no means a superstar. He'd been raised in northeastern Tennessee by his mom after his dad died in a mining accident when John was young. Even though his dad had been a supervisor, the family still lived barely above the poverty line.

"I wonder whatever happened to Andy?" Wes mused.

"He's probably either in prison or dead if he continued on the path he was on. If he'd just stayed out of trouble, basketball could've made a real difference in his life, just like it did in mine," John said. "He could've gotten a free college education and done whatever he wanted after that."

"He was a gamble to begin with, John. You know that. And, as gambles sometimes go, that one didn't pay off." Wes shrugged and laid his head back against the headrest. "I remember at first it'd been subtle things, like reports of him falling asleep in class. We chalked it up to the arduous schedule that goes along with being a student-athlete—keeping up with classes, workouts, practices, having a social life and still getting a good night's sleep."

"Yeah, and when he didn't show up for practice, that was the beginning of the end," John remembered. "Wasn't it you who found him passed out in his dorm room?"

"Sure was. The place reeked of alcohol. Nothing like a good ol' late-morning drinking binge," Wes said sarcastically.

John shook his head as he recalled conversations with Andy and his mother. He had assigned special mentors to him, and the coaching staff conducted daily check-ins. Everything John could think of, he did. Then grades came out. Andy's grades were bad enough that the administration placed him on academic probation. One more semester like that, and he'd not only be off the team but expelled from the university.

At the beginning of Christmas break Andy's freshman year, John and Abbie had invited him over to their house for dinner one evening, and John presented him with a plan for the next semester. It would be hard work, but with the help of tutors, mandatory study time, and a shortened practice here and there, he could pull through this. That night when Andy left John and Abbie's home, he'd said with confidence, "Thank you, Coach, I won't let you down." He'd looked John in the eye and shook his hand. Not only had John believed him, but he had believed *in* him.

"Was it Christmas day when you got the call?" Wes asked, apparently trying to remember the details from all those years ago.

"Day after. I was home with Abbie and the kids when our former athletic director called me to say Andy had been arrested early that morning for possession of drugs and drug trafficking. Just like that." John snapped his fingers. "In jail, off the team, and expelled from the university."

In the weeks that followed, they'd learned Andy's girlfriend was pregnant and still in high school. What a mess the young man had made of his life.

John had gone to see Andy in jail a couple of times, but he always refused the visit. John never knew whether it was because he didn't care or was ashamed. Whatever the case, he never saw or talked to Andy Quinn again.

"There was nothing more you could've done," Wes said, just as he'd said a number of times before. "I don't understand why you still blame yourself. You know nothing in your power—no number of tutors or shortened practices—could've fixed that situation because he didn't want to fix it."

"Deep down, I do know. I just had never felt so powerless before," John recalled. "And I don't think I have since."

"You wanted him to succeed more than he did. There's nothing you can do in a situation like that. He had to want it as badly as you did, and he didn't. I don't think he wanted it at all." Wes yawned and stretched.

"I know, I know. Thanks for letting me vent. You can go back to your nap now." John smiled at his friend.

Wes tapped John's knee with the rolled-up magazine he'd gotten from the seat pocket and went back to his own seat.

John tried to nap again, but he had too much on his mind. Thinking about that mess from yesteryear made him glad he'd let Abbie talk him into fostering Sam. Although there were similarities between the two situations, they were also worlds apart. Sam was trying hard and wanted a different life for himself, whereas Andy didn't.

Back in the spring, Sam had arrived at their home a fearful and traumatized kid, who would quickly push his sleeves down when he realized a scar or cigarette burn was visible. John shook his head and stared out the window. It had taken a while and was still an ongoing process, but Sam felt safe with them, and they were building trust. Slowly but surely.

In the last few weeks, Sam had confided in John about a few things he'd gone through. There were no huge revelations into his past, just small insights, and he always stopped short of saying too much. Yet as John pieced it all together, he came to the realization that Sam had suffered a lot of neglect and trauma in his sixteen-plus years.

John shivered as the hair on his arms stood up. His heart broke for the kids out there who endured abuse, neglect, and trauma at the hands of the adults who were supposed to nurture and protect them.

Yes, Sam was doing well with him and Abbie. But it had been good for John too. He couldn't believe how much he enjoyed having a kid in the house again.

* * *

Drew zipped his coat and pulled the collar up around his neck in an effort to block out the air from the unseasonable cold snap, but he wouldn't let this gray, blustery day get him down. He exited the social services building and walked briskly to the bus stop. The bus pulled up ahead of schedule, and he broke into a jog to get to the next block.

He made it just in time, found a seat at the back of the bus, and unzipped his coat. He took out the yellow envelope, slowly opened it, and removed the document as a smile took over his face. It was a signed and notarized certificate stating he'd completed his court-mandated parenting classes. This is what he needed for his appointment with a family court judge in mid-December.

It'd been a long time coming.

Drew had messed up badly back in the spring. Several drug runners had been working for him, and things were going well. He'd been raking in piles of cash. But then things got messy, and the kid got in the way. From what he'd learned from his lawyer, the kid said something to a friend at school about Drew's lifestyle which caused a visit from DCS.

He certainly didn't want to lose his business. Normally he wouldn't have cared whether the kid got taken away from him or not, but while in jail, he found out he could use him to make some serious cash. Seems there were a lot of perverted men out there who'd love to spend time with a young teen girl and would pay anything for the chance. His son would be the one to reel these girls in. But one thing was for certain. Drew would have to be much more careful going forward.

The only thing that could mess up his plan was if he couldn't convince the judge he was a suitable parent, that he'd rid his life of drugs and drug dealing. Drew needed to be convincing so he could get the kid back and start making real money. More money than he'd ever need.

Drew would indeed do whatever it took to convince the judge.

He had to get Sam back.

It was the first day of winter break, and Sam woke up excited about Christmas coming up in a few days and for time away from school. As he jumped out of bed and rummaged through his closet to find his favorite gray jeans, he realized something. For the first time in his entire life that he could remember, he was happy.

To begin with, when had he ever had clothes to rummage through? His wardrobe had always been just a few things from Goodwill he may have picked out, or maybe a social worker or a foster parent gave to him. Here he had actual store-bought clothes. John and Abbie had been more than generous, and he was thankful.

But even deeper than that, he'd always been so busy worrying and surviving that Christmas never mattered to him before. There were never celebrations or fancy trees or colored lights. Certainly no gifts. For the first time ever, he appreciated all the festive decorations at school and in downtown Franklin. He and Abbie had been decorating the house for Christmas. Everything about the holiday that used to make him sad now made him smile.

This was all so new. Sure, he'd been with other foster families at Christmastime, but not until now had he ever been included as if he were a part of a family.

He liked his new school and the friends he'd made there, and living with the Graysons was beyond anything he'd ever imagined. He'd never known a family like this, who openly loved each other. Sure, they had disagreements here and there, but at the end of the day, they all got along and liked spending time together.

He was beginning to get close to John and Abbie, and he was safe here, like he never had been in any other foster home. Or in his own home for that matter.

There'd been homes where the parents were nice enough, but still, there was always that nagging thought in the back of his mind that a social worker would show up unexpectedly to move him. The Graysons had made it clear to him that as far as they had any control, he could remain with them indefinitely.

"Sam, are you up yet?" Abbie shouted from the hallway. "Kyle will be here in just a few minutes."

"Getting dressed now," he shouted as he pulled out a navy long-sleeve T-shirt and his favorite gray TU hoodie. Abbie had told him last night to dress warmly. The high temperature today would only be thirty degrees, which was very cold for middle Tennessee in December.

He let his mind drift again as he looked for his shoes. Thanksgiving had been great. He wished John could've been there, but the rest of the family was together, and they watched all the team's games on TV and FaceTimed with John. Everything had gone surprisingly great between him and Kyle. They hung out, played basketball in the driveway, and watched games on TV. He imagined having a real brother must be like that.

And Abbie had become more like a mother to him than even his own mother had been during his first five years. He finally admitted to himself that maybe he didn't really remember his own mom, only the memories brought about by the picture of her he carried. But were those even his memories? Or were they things he'd conjured up in his imagination?

Whenever he thought about how his real mother must've been, he imagined someone just like Abbie—kind-hearted, a good listener, and someone who put her family before everything else. Deep down, he didn't truly know if his own mom had been that kind of person. But he was certain Abbie was.

He was lucky enough to get to see Lauren several times lately as well. She'd known him longer than anyone else in his life, and the other day she commented that he seemed happier than he'd ever been since she'd known him, and he admitted to her that he was.

"Kyle's here," Abbie yelled.

Sam grabbed his coat and gloves and ran out to the driveway with Abbie, where Kyle, Cassie, and Hannah were waiting. He and Abbie climbed into the backseat of Kyle's SUV with Hannah. John would meet them there. He had a home game tonight but said he'd be able to get away for a while to meet them at the festival later.

Kyle had Christmas music streaming from the speakers, and Hannah rubbed her red gloves together, seemingly more from excitement than being cold.

"I can't wait for you to see the Dickens' Festival, Sam. I can't believe you've never been," she chatted.

He shrugged. A festival had always been the furthest thing from his mind, but he didn't want to say that and spoil the mood.

"The first thing we need to do is grab coffee to keep us warm," Kyle added.

Sam couldn't quite believe he was in a car with Kyle, going to a festival. A few months ago, he wouldn't have thought it even remotely possible.

They pulled onto Main Street in Franklin, and Sam was in awe of the decorated storefronts. The day was cloudy, but snow flurries made it all the more festive. Christmas lights connected the streetlamps, and lights, tinsel, and snow paint framed every store window. It was like a scene from the Christmas movie channel Abbie kept on in the background at home.

They parked in one of the town's parking garages and walked to the coffee shop to meet John and get their coffee. Then the group set out for the town square, where all the booths were set up.

Holly and green garland adorned the porch columns of his favorite bookstore, Landmark. The shop had originally been a two-story house, and today there were candles in every window. He smiled as it reminded him of the images from Dickens' *A Christmas Carol*.

Being an avid reader, he'd read *A Christmas Carol* more than once, and here before him it played out in the streets of Franklin. He was fascinated. Carolers dressed like characters from the book—men with tailcoats and tall hats and women with long, full dresses—as they sang "God Rest Ye Merry Gentleman." He held his steaming cup of coffee with both hands to keep warm and stared at the mesmerizing scene.

As they walked a little farther down Main Street, Marley and old Scrooge himself were bellowing, "Bah, humbug". They even pulled off the English accents, with a slight Southern drawl, of course.

"Hey, guys, come see the Christmas tree!" Cassie yelled. She, Abbie, and Hannah had gotten ahead of the guys, who'd stopped to look at a wood-carving booth. They jogged up to where the girls were, and the sight took Sam's breath away.

Light, fluffy snowflakes drifted and swirled all around them, and in front of him towered a twenty-five-foot Christmas tree with hundreds of brightly colored lights, ornaments, and tinsel. The sight of it, mixed with the scent of evergreen and snow, overwhelmed Sam's senses.

A stranger offered to take a picture of their "beautiful family" as she put it, so John, Abbie, Kyle, Cassie, Hannah, and Sam all huddled before the giant Christmas tree while the kind stranger took pictures with Abbie's phone. They all laughed and smiled and made faces, and afterward, they headed inside a warm pizzeria for lunch.

No matter what the future held, he'd always remember this day. For once, he allowed his dreams to be bigger than he ever dared imagine. Dreams of college, a career, friends, and his biggest dream of all seemed to already be unfolding—to become an unofficial part of the Grayson family.

twenty-one

Abbie smiled as she and Sam brought groceries in from her car and unloaded them in the kitchen. It was fun to watch his excitement over winter break. She wasn't accustomed to a teenager wanting to spend time with the family, and she laughed at the irony.

Kyle and Hannah were great kids, and she loved every moment of being their mom, but their lives were very typical of a teenager compared to Sam's. They'd wanted to spend all their school break with friends, or at Sam's age, girlfriends and boyfriends. But not Sam. His life had been different, and all he'd ever wanted was a family. She realized for the first time in his life, he had one he could depend on, and he wanted to spend time with them.

She'd told him they wouldn't be doing any homeschooling until after the first of the year, so he played his guitar and piano and wrote, which he was good at.

They'd picked up dinner from one of their favorite eateries, Newk's, and she and Sam chatted about the upcoming Christmas week while they put the food in the refrigerator to heat up later when John got home. They heard a car door close, and Abbie glanced at her watch.

"Wow, he's really early. Practice was either so good that he cut it short or so bad that he walked out." Abbie shrugged.

Sam laughed. "Hopefully, it was a good practice," he said as he walked over to the front door and peeked through the side panel. "Oh, it's not John, its Jamie. Must be one of those surprise visits," he said, without a care in the world.

The blood drained from Abbie's face, and she quickly turned around so he wouldn't notice. She hoped he was right, but she prayed this wasn't the visit she and John had feared for the last couple of months. Sam opened the door to let Jamie in, and when Abbie's eyes met the social worker's, she understood.

"Hi, Jamie," Sam greeted her, happily, oblivious to why she was here, which made it all the worse.

"Hi, Sam. Hi, Abbie, how are you both?" Jamie said, but her smile didn't reach her eyes.

Sam told her about winter break while Jamie glanced at Abbie, and once again, Sam apparently hadn't noticed anything was wrong.

"Sam, I need to talk to you in private for a moment," Jamie said after he'd finished telling her about all his plans for the upcoming week.

"Sure, we can go to my room," he said, seemingly still unworried.

Abbie told them she'd be in the kitchen. Sam's calm demeanor suggested he thought this was nothing more than a routine surprise check-in. Abbie was just glad they left the kitchen before Sam could see the tears fill her eyes.

* * *

The air left Sam's lungs, and he was certain he'd pass out. Black spots invaded the edges of his vision, and that old familiar, terrible sensation of not being able to breathe overwhelmed him, as if someone had punched him in the chest. It was the same feeling he had the last time Jamie told him he was going back to his father, except this time was worse. Much worse.

He'd endured some horrible events last time, which made it even more awful to have to go back. But even more than that, he loved it here with the Graysons. In his entire life, he'd never belonged anywhere until he came here. And he was safe here with them.

His mind raced, and he remembered what he'd promised himself before—at some point, he'd tell John the truth about his father. Well, if ever there was a time to do that, it was now, but John wasn't here. He could never tell those things to Abbie. Would Jamie let him call John? But what if John didn't believe him? Or what if he did but DCS and Jamie didn't believe John? His head spun, and he needed more time to think. He panicked.

"*Uh*, can you, *um*, give me a few minutes to get my stuff together?" Sam asked.

"Sure, I'll go wait in the kitchen with Abbie." Jamie stood and turned to leave the room. "Just come in there when you're ready."

He nodded and took a deep breath as she left the room. He only had a few minutes and wasn't exactly sure how he'd do this. Going to his father's was not a possibility, that much was certain, and he could only think of one alternative. He stuffed some clothes in his backpack and made sure he had his cell phone, his journal, and his picture of his mom.

But how would he get out without Abbie and Jamie seeing him? He couldn't go out the front or the back door because both were in clear view of where Abbie and Jamie sat in the kitchen. The garage door wasn't a possibility either because he'd have to pass through the kitchen to get there.

Then he remembered the double doors in John and Abbie's bedroom that opened to the back deck. There wasn't a gate at that end of the deck, but he didn't think it was too high off the ground, so he could climb over the rail and jump without anyone seeing him.

He threw on a hoodie, slung his old backpack over his shoulder, stuck his cell phone in his back pocket, and then walked as softly as he could across the hall to John and Abbie's bedroom. Very gently, he opened the double doors and walked onto the deck and to the right. There was a house up the road on that side, but those people usually weren't home during the day, and with it being a cold December day, any neighbors that were home weren't likely to be outside.

Sam walked to the rail at the farthest point from the kitchen windows and paused to survey the scene. He shook his head. The deck was quite a bit higher off the ground than he'd estimated. But it was the only way. Hopefully, if he rolled when he hit the ground and didn't land on an arm or leg, he wouldn't get hurt.

It suddenly occurred to him he only had a few dollars in his pocket, the change left from a twenty-dollar bill he'd used to get coffee that morning. He wouldn't be able to get far on less than fifteen dollars.

John had told him once that he kept a little cash in a drawer in their bedroom for emergencies, like if Sam ever needed lunch money or something and he and Abbie weren't home. He'd never taken him up on it, but now would be the time.

But possibly ten minutes had passed since Jamie left him to pack his stuff. Surely, she'd look for him soon. Should he risk it to go back in? He had to think quickly. No, he needed to make his move right now. The money would have to last until he could get to ... where? He had no plan whatsoever, but he'd have to worry about that later. For now, he just needed to make a run for it.

Sam threw his backpack over the deck and then climbed over the top rail and held on. He hung there for a second and stared at the ground. He guessed he'd have to drop more than ten feet, and he hoped it wouldn't be too bad. He closed his eyes and let himself drop, hitting the ground hard on his left hip.

Ugh, he hadn't managed to roll like he wanted, but he didn't land feet first either, thank goodness, because he probably would've broken something. His hip stung, and he'd surely have a big bruise, but he didn't think any part of him was seriously injured. He made a thudding sound when he landed. Hopefully, they couldn't hear that from where they sat in the kitchen. He couldn't take any chances though, so he got up quickly and brushed himself off.

He took off, limping at first, then running, with no plan still and no idea which direction to go. It occurred to him that running might draw attention to him, so he slowed down and walked past a couple of neighbors' houses before crossing the street. He arrived at the golf course down the street without anyone seeing him that he was aware of. By now Jamie and Abbie surely realized he was gone. The woods on the far side of the golf course caught his eye. That's where he needed to be. He could disappear easily there.

"Hey, Sam," a man's voice called out from behind him, startling him. The voice was familiar, but he couldn't quite place it. He was trying to decide whether or not to run when a golf cart pulled up right beside him. Sam's heart rate sped up when he realized it was a neighbor he'd met, a friend of John.

"Oh, hi, Mr. Patel." Sam attempted to steady his voice and act normal, but he feared he appeared anything but normal.

"Going to study?" Mr. Patel asked.

"*Uh*, what?" Sam picked up his pace. In the back of his mind, he could hear Abbie telling him not to say 'what' but to say, 'I'm sorry?' instead.

"Your backpack looks like it's loaded down." Mr. Patel pointed out.

"Oh yeah, I'm, *uh*, returning books to a friend I borrowed them from. I'm going to keep moving, Mr. Patel. It's really cold out." Sam broke into a jog.

"You want a ride?" Mr. Patel offered.

How am I going to get rid of this guy? "Thanks anyway, but I'm almost there." He waved and picked up his pace to leave the man behind. He wanted to run but that might seem suspicious, so he jogged off and hoped Mr. Patel would think he was just trying to keep warm in this cold, blustery weather.

Great. Mr. Patel was one of the neighbors John and Abbie were friends with, and he lived just a few houses down from the Graysons. They would certainly ask him if he'd seen Sam. He'd have to change plans and not go into the woods near the golf course where he encountered Mr. Patel, but instead, get back to the other side of the road again and into the wooded area on that side.

He turned and jogged up to a house on the edge of the golf course, crossed back over the road, and slipped into the woods. As far as he could tell, only Mr. Patel had seen him and would hopefully tell anyone who asked that Sam had either gone into the golf course woods or into the house he headed up to.

Sam jogged through the woods as far away from the Graysons' house as possible. Without a plan, he just had to keep running until he could think of one.

twenty-two

Abbie dabbed her eyes with a tissue as she and Jamie finished their conversation and sipped the last of their coffee. "We were warned about the letting go part of fostering, but it's so much harder than I expected." She tried her hardest to keep the tears at bay. "If you ever need placement for him again, please call us, okay? We would take him back anytime."

"I will. The two of you were so good for him. He really thrived here." Jamie patted Abbie's hand and glanced at her watch. "Well, it's been over fifteen minutes since I left Sam to pack. I'm going to check on him," she said.

Abbie nodded and let her mind drift to John and wondered if he'd take this as hard as she had. Of course, he would, John had—

"Oh, no!" Jamie shouted and ran back toward the kitchen. "He's gone, along with all his things!"

Abbie was confused. "Are you sure he's not in the family room down the hall from his room?"

"I looked. He's not there," Jamie answered.

"Sam?" Abbie called for him throughout the house and checked the basement, with Jamie close behind. Abbie couldn't imagine where he'd gone. "I don't see how he could've gone anywhere. We would've seen him any way he chose to go out, unless ... oh, no."

Her heart sank, as she ran to her and John's bedroom. Sure enough, the French doors were unlocked and slightly opened. Abbie flung them open the rest of the way and ran out onto the deck.

"There's no sign of him, but, other than a window, this is the only way he could've gotten out without us noticing," Abbie said.

"Do you think he would've gone over this railing to get to the yard?" Jamie was out of breath from chasing Abbie through the house. "It's pretty high."

The two peered over the railing closest to the bedroom. "What's that laying down there in the grass?" Jamie pointed at a small, shiny object below.

They ran to the gate at the middle of the deck, down the steps and through the backyard to where the object lay.

Abbie panicked as she realized what it was and picked it up. "Sam's cell phone."

"Great, I wonder if he even knows he dropped it." Jamie took out her own cell phone and scrolled the contacts. "I'm going to get in the car and go look for him and call a couple of people to help look."

"I'll take my car too." Abbie tried to catch her breath.

"No, you need to stay here in case he comes back or tries to call or text you from another phone," Jamie insisted.

Abbie didn't like the idea, but she was right. If he was nearby and didn't see Jamie's car in the driveway, he might come back. So, she went back into the kitchen and waited. Helplessly.

* * *

Jamie was concerned. It was unlike Sam to run these days. In his younger years, he'd run away a lot, but the last time was several years ago. Ever since then, he'd always been cooperative when she came to pick him up, and although today he appeared shocked and disappointed, he had gotten into the routine pretty quickly.

The routine. How sad. Jamie hated it for kids like Sam, who wanted a forever family so badly but never got one. He hated going back to his father because the man couldn't stay on the straight and narrow path. For Sam, being with his biological parent was no more permanent than a foster home. No wonder he wanted to stay with the Graysons. They offered him the stability he'd never had. And they were genuinely good and caring people.

Jamie slowly drove the streets of the Graysons' neighborhood but there was no sign of him. She didn't want to call the police, but she needed to. He couldn't get too far with no cell phone and little money, but she didn't want to take the chance of losing him into the abyss some foster teens end up in. The longer he remained gone, the greater the danger of that happening.

She had no choice but to call the local police. Now they, along with some coworkers and a couple of off-duty police officers who'd helped her out in these situations before, would have his description.

Then Jamie did something she didn't do very often but needed to do more of—she prayed.

* * *

Abbie thought about texting John, but he should already be on his way home, so instead she waited for him. She felt helpless, but more than that, she was distraught and consumed with worry alternating with heartbreak. This was not the way she'd pictured Sam leaving them. She suddenly realized she hadn't pictured him leaving them at all.

"Abbie, Sam, where are you guys?"

Abbie jumped at the sound of John's voice and his keys hitting the bottom of the bowl on the kitchen counter. He rounded the corner into their great room, and she could tell by the way he looked back at her that she must be a mess. Her eyes were swollen from the tears, and she held a fistful of tissues. Before he could ask anything, she simply shrugged. "He's gone."

"Gone? Honey, what happened?" John dropped to the sofa beside her and stared into her eyes.

"Jamie came to get Sam, but he ran away while he was supposed to be packing. We have no idea where he is." Abbie stifled a sob.

"What do you mean he ran away?" John's eyes were wide with a mixture of confusion and panic. "Tell me what happened, Abbie."

Abbie explained how Jamie told him he was going back to his father, and she recounted the events to him—how Sam had slipped out their bedroom doors and over the deck and had dropped his cell phone.

Back to his father. The words cut through her like a dagger when she said them aloud. She and John had their suspicions that Sam's father was abusive, but Sam had always denied it. They'd learned in their foster parent training classes that kids often try to protect themselves by running. But if Sam denied his father was abusive, why would he run from him?

In those classes, the social workers warned them about the heartbreak most foster parents eventually experienced, but Abbie never expected this. Especially not with their first foster placement, a teenager who was supposed to only be here for a weekend but had stayed for seven months. She and John had recently decided they would continue to let him live here and support him after he turned eighteen. Without a doubt, Sam had woven his way into their family and into their hearts.

Abbie and John sat on the sofa next to each other and let the tears fall. Fostering was so much harder than they'd imagined. And now, not only were they left to deal with Sam's removal from their home and family, but they also had no idea where he was right now, or if he was safe. All they could do was stay here at home and wait by the phone. And pray.

# twenty-three

Sam wished he knew what time it was. December sunsets occurred incredibly early in middle Tennessee, so even though it had been completely dark for a good while now, he figured it probably wasn't much later than 7:00 p.m. The air had already turned sharply colder, the wind picked up, and although it didn't snow often in middle Tennessee, the air smelled clean, like snow. He couldn't believe he didn't think to put on a coat instead of a hoodie or grab his gloves, but even more unbelievable was the fact that he'd lost his cell phone somewhere along the way.

He hadn't realized he'd lost it until he was deep into the woods, and once it got dark, he'd reached for it to turn on the flashlight. If he could figure out where he'd dropped it, he'd backtrack, but he had no idea when or where he'd lost it. Plus, he'd been gone at least a couple of hours now, so he couldn't afford to backtrack that far.

Before he realized he'd lost his phone, he'd developed a plan to call his friend Justin from the group home they'd both lived in. Their mutual friend Tyler had told Sam that Justin still lived there. Justin was a little younger than Sam, but much more street-smart. He'd be able to help him somehow or tell him where to go to hide out for a little while. His fifteen dollars wouldn't last long, and he needed his friend's help.

His plan B was to call Lauren, but she would undoubtedly tell her parents. That's the honest person she was. But it didn't matter anyway; he couldn't call anyone without his phone.

Sam kept stumbling along in the pitch-black woods, and it gradually started getting a little lighter. Still dark, but not quite as black as it had been. Finally, he was at the end of the woods and relieved to have made it out of there. He found himself on the edge of a rural road, but once his eyes readjusted, he realized it wasn't that much lighter than it had been in the woods.

There weren't any streetlights in this rural area or even any house lights. A dense fog set in as well, and the dampness made the air feel colder by the minute. His teeth chattered, and he stuck his hands in his pockets in an attempt to keep warm. He walked for a while to try to get his bearings, but nothing looked the least bit familiar.

Headlights approached from behind him. They were far enough back he didn't think they could see him, especially with the fog, but he stepped farther off the road anyway and walked toward the woods. The car passed by, and he was relieved that he didn't recognize it since he had no idea how close or far away he might be from the Graysons' house.

Oh, no. Red brake lights lit up the darkness ahead, and the car slowly backed up. The driver must've seen him after all.

He froze for a second and didn't know whether he should turn around or head back into the woods. The idea of going back into the cold, black darkness of the woods made him shudder, and he stood motionless in indecision as the car backed up close to where he stood.

"Hey, young man, do you need a ride somewhere?" A lady who appeared to be alone shouted out the car window. "I'm on my way to Nashville but can drop you anywhere between here and there."

"Uh, no thanks," Sam said, but then second-guessed whether

or not he should take her up on it. She sounded friendly and didn't look familiar. This would without a doubt be the fastest way out of the area. If he made it to Nashville, it would be a lot harder for anyone to find him.

"You sure? It's awfully cold out tonight, and you're kind of out in the middle of nowhere without a warm coat." The lady made a warm car ride to Nashville sound very appealing.

Sam normally trusted no one, and his instincts told him not to trust her either, but the cold, damp wind, the dark cover of night, and his lack of a plan made him more vulnerable than he would've been otherwise. The lady appeared to be a little older than the Graysons, and she seemed harmless. Maybe she had a son his age and was just being friendly.

"Okay, I guess ... I mean, if you're sure you don't mind." Sam tentatively approached the car.

"No. I don't mind at all. Hop in." The lady smiled, and he imagined her car was very warm.

He opened the car door but hesitated before he got in. With the car's interior lights on, he could see the lady clearly, and he was positive he'd never seen her before tonight. A scan of the back seat told him she was alone, so he hopped in.

The lady's eyes were on him while he buckled his seat belt, and then she glanced at her cell phone before she started driving. When she got the car up to speed, the automatic door locks clicked. A thud in his chest took his breath away, and he snapped his head toward her.

"Hi, Sam," the lady said in the same friendly voice. "You're okay. My name is Kathy. I'm a social worker and friend of Jamie Richards. I'm just taking you somewhere safe."

Then she picked up her cell phone and hit a button. "Hey, Jamie, I've got him, safe and sound."

* * *

How could I have been so stupid? The cold and the fog combined with losing his cell phone had rattled him. Otherwise, he never would've accepted a ride this close to where he ran away from. He knew better than that.

The lady made conversation, but he wasn't up for talking, so he stared out the window without answering her while she went on and on about all the people looking for him. She said she worked in another DCS office and had just gotten off work when Jamie called her and then texted her his picture.

He tried to tune her out, but she got his attention when she said Jamie and his foster parents were all relieved he was safe. Oh, no, the Graysons. Why hadn't he stopped to think about how worried they'd be about him? He sighed deeply and hoped this wouldn't keep him from going back there if there was ever an opportunity. But if an opportunity to go back did arise, that would mean things would have to go badly with his father first, so he pushed the thought from his mind.

"Here we are." The lady pulled into the DCS office parking lot. He looked out the passenger window in time to see Jamie running toward the car, her eyes wide and a frown on her face. The lady hit the unlock button, Jamie opened Sam's door, and the tirade began.

"Sam Keller, don't you ever do that again. Where were you going, and what were you going to do? Abbie didn't think you had any money on you, and you dropped your cell phone before you even got out of their yard. What on earth were you thinking?" Her voice rose with every word.

So that's where my cell phone went. Ugh.

"I don't know," he said, with his head down.

He didn't want to talk to Jamie, and he certainly didn't owe her an explanation. If she hadn't figured out by now what his father was all about, she never would. He'd go with her to his father's house as planned and try to hang in there until his eighteenth birthday. And if things got bad, he would run away again. But next time, he'd plan it out.

If only he had the courage to speak up the last time his father regained custody of him. At the time, Sam had been in a foster home. Things were good enough there, but Jamie had come over one day unexpectedly to tell him his father was out of jail and had been granted custody of him again. For a fleeting moment back then, he'd considered telling her everything his father was involved in and the revolving door of criminals in their house, but he didn't. He was afraid if she didn't believe him, his father would find out what Sam said, and there would be consequences, so he kept quiet.

Jamie must have sensed it at the time because she'd asked him if there was anything he wanted or needed to tell her. "No, it's fine," he'd answered because he'd convinced himself it would be fine. He'd decided he could endure anything for a few months, because thankfully, a few months was the longest he'd ever been with his father.

* * *

Abbie had called her best friend, and Wendy had rushed over to be with them while they waited. John and Abbie stayed off their cell phones in case Sam called one of them while Wendy called their neighbors to see if anyone had seen him leave.

No one had seen anything, until she called John's golf buddy down the street, Tom Patel. Tom had seen Sam with his backpack earlier, walking along the golf course. He'd told Tom he was heading to a friend's house, and when Tom offered to give him a ride he said, "No, thanks," and jogged off in the direction of the Janson's house. Wendy thanked the man and hung up. She'd already called all the other neighbors in that row of houses, and none of them had seen Sam. Neither had any of Sam's friends she'd called from his dropped cell phone.

Abbie couldn't take it a minute more, so she picked up her cell phone and called Jamie's number, and she answered before the phone even rang. "Jamie? It's—".

"Abbie, I just picked up my phone to call you. We have Sam! A coworker of mine found him, safe and sound. She picked him up out on Williamson County Road. Another social worker is taking him to his father now," Jamie said.

"Oh, thank God he's okay." Abbie nodded at John and Wendy and then collapsed onto the couch with her head in her hands. "Why on earth did he run. Did he say?"

"No, he wouldn't talk. I lit into him pretty hard about running, but he wouldn't talk to me." Jamie sighed. "Unfortunately, this happens sometimes with kids who've been in the system for a long time. Sometimes it doesn't even matter if it's a good or familiar move, there's simply trauma in moving."

Abbie let that sink in. "We're so thankful he's been found, and he's safe," she said softly. "Thank you for all you did to help us. And we'd still take him back if the opportunity arises."

"Of course. I'll call you first if he needs care again. But I'm holding out hope it'll work out with his father this time," she said.

"I sincerely hope it does, for Sam's sake." Abbie meant it. She did hope things would work out for Sam and his father.

But she had a sinking suspicion that Sam running away was more than just a result of trauma from moving again. She prayed she was wrong, but in reality, she couldn't shake the troubling suspicion that Sam's reunion with his father wasn't the best thing for him.

twenty-four

"Should we take the Christmas trees down today?" John stood in the middle of their great room and sipped his morning coffee while studying the twelve-foot Christmas tree. It was one of three trees they'd put up this Christmas. Abbie had wanted to go all out for Sam like she'd done when Kyle and Hannah lived at home.

"Oh, I don't know. Do you want to take it down today? I mean it's not even New Year's Day yet." Abbie laughed at him but then became serious. "It was a good Christmas, wasn't it? I mean, in spite of the circumstances."

"Yeah, it was." John reflected as he took a seat on the sofa next to Abbie and set his mug on the coffee table. "It turned out better than I expected, but man, I miss that kid." With only a few days between Sam's leaving and Christmas day, they hadn't had much time to process what had happened before the Christmas festivities hit.

"I'm glad we told Jamie we'd take him back if things with his father didn't work out," John said as an afterthought.

Abbie nodded but hesitated for a moment before she spoke. "I should have told you this. You were at practice a couple of days ago when it happened, and I just didn't think the timing was right."

John sucked in a deep breath. Surely Abbie wouldn't decide on her own to turn away Sam. It had to be something else. "What happened? Did someone call about Sam?"

"No, hon, of course not. I would've told you in an instant. A different DCS worker called and asked if we'd like to foster a seven-year-old girl. I almost laughed," she said.

Sarcasm wasn't Abbie's style, but she gave a sarcastic laugh as she told John about the call. "I mean, how funny is that? Back in the spring that would've been our perfect scenario."

"You're right, we would've jumped at the chance." John chuckled and shook his head. "What'd you tell her?"

"Well, I told her about Sam, and how we needed some time. I asked her to please pause us from their list for a little while until we felt ready again. Except for Sam, of course. I told her we'd always be available for him. She said she understood completely," Abbie said softly.

John reached for Abbie's hand, and they were both quiet for a moment. He'd be lying to himself if he said the past couple of weeks hadn't been tough, not only for him and Abbie but for their kids also. Hannah had taken the news extremely hard. She'd become attached to Sam, and Sam to her. They'd texted a lot and had a lot of silly inside jokes. They were quickly becoming like brother and sister.

Kyle surprised John and Abbie the most. When they'd called him the day after Sam left to let him know, he took it okay and had even asked if they planned to foster again. But on Christmas day, Kyle wasn't his usual self, and when John asked him if everything was okay, he said it didn't seem right that Sam wasn't there with them, because he had become family.

"He affected our whole family, didn't he?" Abbie asked, reading his mind the way she always did.

"I was thinking the same thing," he smiled at her. "Yesterday,

Kyle told me how much he regretted how he'd treated Sam early on and wished he could do it over."

John picked up his coffee mug again and stared at it in an attempt to ground his thoughts. "We need to try to move on as we discussed, and who knows, maybe in the future there will be other foster children, or maybe even Sam."

"I know, you're right," Abbie said. "I'm glad I decided to accept that new position at church. It'll help take my mind off things."

On the day before Sam's Christmas break, she'd been offered a different job at their church, similar to what she had done before, only a few more hours a week. At first, she turned it down, but after he left, she decided she should take it. She called the church administrator the day after Christmas to see if the spot was still open, and it was.

"I'm glad too." John stared at the Christmas tree. "I think it will help you. We're going to be all right."

And John prayed a silent prayer Sam would be all right also.

twenty-five

Sam hated living in Memphis. Maybe it was a nice enough city, but the part he lived in definitely was not. His street consisted of mostly drug houses, and he lived with his father in an old, dilapidated apartment complex. How did his father ever get that past social services? But for all he knew, no one from social services had shown up since they'd been in Memphis.

He walked through the cold rain to his new school and followed the stream of students into the main entrance. It was the first day for students after Christmas break, and today, he was the new kid. He didn't even feel anxious like he normally would when starting a new school. He was just glad to be out of his father's house for a while.

He wandered around until he found the school administration offices and took his place in line to get his class schedule. So far, he'd seen a drug deal in the parking lot, a fight in the hallway, and two boys dragged into the principal's office. And it was only 7:45 a.m.

As he inched his way to the front of the line, he wished he were still being homeschooled by Abbie Grayson and attending the academy where he'd made some nice friends. Or even attending Franklin High again, just because Lauren was there.

"Name, please," the black-haired, severe-faced woman barked, startling him back to the present. She didn't even bother to look up from the stacks of files on her desk. So much for welcoming new students.

"Keller. Sam Keller," he replied.

She never even acknowledged his reply but rummaged through her stack of files. "Sam Keller. Here it is." The lady pulled some paperwork out of a file, set it in front of him, and rushed through the information without taking a breath.

"This is your class schedule, a map of the school, your locker number, and your combination. Don't lose these. Take the schedule to the bookstore near the main entrance and they'll get your books for you. Then take your books and this note to your first-period teacher. Welcome to East Memphis High. Next!" She managed to give him the papers and all that information without ever looking at him.

"Thanks," he mumbled, feeling like he should apologize, but he had no idea why.

Sam made his way through the maze of hallways, found the bookstore, waited while they pulled his books, and then located his locker. The school was so big that no one noticed him or realized he was new. He preferred it that way. He'd rather disappear into the crowd of students and big classes without anyone paying him any attention. The day proceeded unremarkably, and Sam was good with that. He found all his classes, his teachers were all okay, and he sat by himself at lunch.

Once the final bell rang, he swung his backpack over his shoulder, zipped his coat and pulled the hood up, and shoved his hands deep into his pockets. Cold raindrops were still falling, and the morning dreariness had lasted into the afternoon. They lived close enough that he could either walk to school or take the bus. Even though it was a cold, rainy January day, he chose to walk. He didn't want to arrive home too quickly.

It was difficult to think of this new place as home because it sure didn't feel like it. The Graysons' house, now that was a home. Not because of their enormous, comfortable house. That was certainly a plus, but to Sam, home was all about what John and Abbie did to make it feel like home. They actually paid attention to him, something he'd never experienced before. They wanted to know how his day went, what happened at school, and if he needed help with anything. Who else in his life had ever treated him that way? Absolutely no one.

He shook his head as he walked on. The faded, run-down apartment complex where he lived with his father came into view all too soon, and he studied the building. The gray paint, weathered and chipped, matched the dismal sky, and some of the shudders were crooked or even missing. Even though he was freezing, and the wind and rain had picked up, he slowed his pace. That building was the last place he wanted to be.

He still kicked himself for running away on his last day with John and Abbie. What had he been thinking? He ran on impulse and was sorry he did because he never even got to say goodbye.

John wasn't home to say goodbye to, but Abbie was. He could've told her goodbye, thanked her for all they'd done for him, and she could've relayed the message to John.

Instead, he ran, and not only did he not get to say goodbye to them, he was also sure he worried them to death. What did they even think of him now? If he ever needed to be in foster care again, he probably ruined any chance of going back to their home.

He slowly walked up the steps to their second-floor apartment and couldn't delay going in any longer because of the cold. He took a deep breath and opened the door. His father sat at a table in the combination kitchen-living room area with a man and woman Sam hadn't seen before. Their heads all snapped toward the door when he walked in, but no one acknowledged him.

They went back to their business, and he went straight to his room, where he'd stay until time to go to school tomorrow. He'd stay there while his father and his friends smoked and drank, and while people came in and out buying drugs. He double-checked his bedroom door to make sure it was locked. Experience had taught him people who were high would do about anything, and his father would let them.

For once, his father had given him a little money for food, so Sam had bought bread, peanut butter, cereal, and apples and kept those, along with a case of bottled water, in his room. He also had paper plates, paper towels, and plastic utensils. With a connected bathroom, he was pretty much self-sufficient and never had to leave his room. His safe place. That's how he preferred it.

Just nine more months—that's how long he had to hold on. Then he'd turn eighteen and could get out of here, away from this man forever. He had no clue how he'd support himself. That used to worry him, but he didn't think about it anymore. He wanted out and away from his father. The rest, he'd figure out later.

* * *

Day number 3580. This journal is the last bit of sanity I have left. When I put the pen to paper, it's almost like I am writing about someone else's life rather than being caught up in my own nightmare. Or a piece of fiction. But this is real life. My real life. I don't have anyone to talk to anymore, so my journal is my only outlet. Not that I would say these things out loud to another person anyway. And I won't even write them here because I don't want to ever go back and read the words.

When I lived with the Graysons, I started to think God did exist. But now that I'm back here, I know that's not true. How could a god let these things happen to a kid? I know I'm not the best person, I've done my share of bad things. Like lately, stealing and shoplifting. But is it my fault if I have to do those things just to be able to eat? How could God let a kid go through what I'm going through? If you exist, God, please show me. I'm screaming on the inside, but no one hears me, and it seems no one can see me. I feel invisible.

I haven't gone to school all week because he beat me up, and I have two black eyes. I was hoping for social services to come because I didn't show up at school, but no such luck. No one knows me here, and no one cares. Actually, no one anywhere cares. By now, Lauren has probably forgotten about me, and the Graysons probably have a new foster child. A cute little kid like they originally wanted.

I wish I could go to the Graysons and tell them how bad things are here, and the things my so-called father has done and is planning to do. Why didn't I tell them when I had the chance? Maybe I could sneak out and see John? I don't know any other way out of this. No one sees me. If I died, no one on earth would know or care.

But no, I can't go to the Graysons. That would be a huge risk. What if they didn't believe me? Or what if they called social services, and they didn't believe me? I can't imagine what he would do to me then. Or worse, to them. No, I'll do my best to keep hanging on until my eighteenth birthday. Eight more months, that's all. One day at a time...

twenty-six

John believed late February practices were some of the most important of the season. His team was playing well going into the last week of the month. They were getting ready for senior night, followed by the conference tournament.

It had not been the stellar season John expected following the national championship win last year. His team hadn't played to their potential, but it wasn't too late. If they worked hard and did well in the conference tourney, they could still get into the national tournament in a decent seed.

But when it came to basketball, John hated to lose more than anything, so he worked his team even harder than before. He demanded a lot out of his players, but they respected him for it. He wasn't perfect though.

Last night's game had been a close one, and even though they won by two points, John's team had played terribly, especially his two veteran players, who should be leading by example at this point. As a result, practice today hadn't been fun. John took his frustrations out on them. When one player made a mistake, he made them all run. And while they were running, John yelled at them about their mistakes from last night's game. He kept hammering them, kept reminding them, kept running them.

Wes asked him if he remembered his team had won last night. Yes, John remembered, but they were capable of doing more and being much better than what they showed last night. And they'd have to be exponentially better than last night to win in the tournament.

John didn't enjoy practices like this. He realized he'd pushed the limits with a couple of his players, but his assistants would smooth things over. They were good at that, and John would let them do their job.

His frustration boiled over as he approached his office. He was frustrated with himself as their coach and unhappy with his team, and he kept his head down as he walked past his administrative assistant, Lisa. He just didn't feel like chatting.

She was new and had only worked for John for a couple of weeks. So far it had gone well, but Lisa had big shoes to fill as his last administrative assistant had worked for him for thirteen years and retired. She could predict his every move, and he'd dreaded having a new assistant, but Lisa was working out well so far.

John had been trying his best to make a good impression, so he normally attempted to hide his sour moods from her when they had a bad practice, but he just couldn't today. He chose to bypass her instead and had almost reached his office door when Lisa stopped him.

"Oh, Coach, *um*, excuse me, sir, but there's a young man here to see you," Lisa stammered nervously. "He said he knows you. I've never seen him before, but Coach Wes walked by and recognized him, and he told me it'd be okay to let him wait in your office."

John was annoyed at first and didn't do a great job of hiding it. He wasn't in the mood for a visitor, but if Wes said it was okay then it was most likely an administrator or someone he needed to see.

"Thanks, Lisa." He forced a smile so she wouldn't think he

was mad at her. It wasn't her fault he was in a foul mood. "Did you happen to get the person's name?"

"*Um*, yes." Lisa clumsily fumbled through a stack of Post-it notes on her desk before picking up a bright blue one.

"His name is Sam Keller."

A mixture of emotions raced through John's mind. He was excited to see him but also worried about why he might be here. He opened his office door, and sure enough, there he sat on the black leather sofa in John's office. Sam stood and smiled as soon as John met his eyes.

"Sam, wow, I can't believe you're here." John practically ran to him and the two hugged for a long time. At last, they let go and sat on the couch.

"I hope it's okay that I came here." Sam wrung his hands together and bit his lower lip.

"Of course, it is! Man, it's so good to see you." John beamed. He couldn't quite wrap his head around the fact that Sam was here, sitting in his office. If he were being honest, he thought he'd never see the boy again.

"It's good to see you too." Sam smiled but it wasn't the smile John had become accustomed to. His smile was weak and didn't reach his eyes. And he was fidgety. The sparkle John and Abbie had become accustomed to was absent. "I never got to tell you goodbye or thanks for all you did for me. Today I had the chance to come up here with a friend, so, I figured I'd try to catch you."

As Sam spoke, John noticed he was much thinner than when he'd lived with them, and he had deep, gray circles under his eyes. His hair was longer and unkempt, and he didn't look at all like he did the last day John had seen him. Instead, he looked almost exactly like the boy Jamie had brought to their doorstep when he and Abbie first met him almost a year ago. John silently prayed for whatever was going on with him, but he kept smiling for Sam's sake.

John had to know so he came right out and asked, "How are

things going with your dad? Where are you living?" *Please, God, if things aren't good, let Sam tell me. Please show me.*

"We're living in Memphis, and it's fine." His response landed flat, without emotion. He stared at the floor when he said it, and before John could ask any other questions, Sam changed the subject. "How's the team? I haven't been able to watch any games."

John told him about the lackluster season, the rough practice this afternoon, and how tough he'd been on them. Sam chuckled and shook his head at that part. When John asked him more about himself, he once again deflected the questions and asked about Abbie and each of the kids.

John told him what the family was up to. He emphasized how much they all missed him, and Christmas hadn't been the same without him there. Sam didn't say anything and once again stared at the floor and struggled to find the words. He nodded. "Good. I'm glad everyone is good."

"Hey, do you have time to get coffee or something to eat?" John didn't want this time with Sam to end, and he desperately wanted to keep this dying conversation going.

"I wish I could, but I have to meet my friend in a few minutes for the ride back," Sam answered without making eye contact. "I miss all of you a lot, and I wanted to say thanks for all you did for me. You seriously did more for me than anyone else in my whole life, and I'll never forget it," Sam choked out the words and was near tears, as was John.

"We'll always be here for you." John put his hands on Sam's shoulders forcing the boy to look him in the eyes. "Always, no matter how old you are or what you need. I want you to remember that, okay? Promise me you will always remember that."

"I will, thank you." Sam nodded, his mouth opened slightly as if he wanted to say something else, but he didn't. Instead, he stood, picked up his coat and his backpack, and then took a couple of steps toward the door. "I've gotta go."

"Take care of yourself, and remember what I said." John walked the boy out of his office, and once again Sam paused like he might say something, but instead, he simply said goodbye. Just like that, he was gone once again.

* * *

Sam managed to keep his composure and soon he was back outside in the cold, and he walked briskly to try to keep warm. He needed to catch a bus soon before he froze out here. It was colder here in Nashville than it'd been in Memphis, and he wasn't prepared.

He shoved his hands in his pockets and shook his head. Of course, there was no friend he came here with. He'd made that up. The truth was, he'd skipped school, bought a bus ticket, and made the trip here to tell John all the things he'd kept hidden for so long. John had been his only hope of getting out of the horrible situation he was in, but Sam had totally blown it. He was so angry at himself right now. He stood at the bus stop shivering and wondered how he'd completely lost his nerve.

The bus headed for Memphis finally arrived. Sam boarded and found a seat by the window, and even though the bus was barely warm, it was warmer than outside. He blew on his hands while thinking about what he'd done, and he wanted to kick himself. It had been foolish of him to come all the way here and honestly think he'd tell John everything.

What's worse, he could tell John suspected something was wrong. John had given him every opportunity to speak up, but when it came right down to it, Sam froze.

What was he afraid of? Possibly that John wouldn't believe Sam's crazy allegations against his father? Then maybe the door John told him would always be open to him wouldn't be anymore. Or what if he told John everything, and it was too much for John and Abbie, causing them to not want him?

No, what scared him most was the worst-case scenario he

could imagine. That his father would follow through on his threats to hurt anyone Sam ever talked to about him, his business, the things he did, and the people he was involved with. Indeed, that was the worst thing that could happen.

* * *

John couldn't stop thinking about Sam as he drove home. He was convinced the boy hadn't come all the way to Nashville just to tell him goodbye and thanks. The pauses where Sam struggled for words hinted at something more. But what could it be?

Then it occurred to him, and John gasped at the realization—Sam had his old backpack with him. He only took that particular backpack with him when he moved to a new home, because he kept his most treasured belongings in it. Otherwise, it stayed under his bed. He had that very backpack with him today. There was no plan to go back to his father.

How did I miss that, God?

He pulled into the garage and ran into the house to tell Abbie. He replayed their whole conversation to her, and the fact he had the worn, brown backpack with him. She had the same foreboding sense John did.

"John, I think we should call Jamie and tell her about this visit. Maybe she can send someone from DCS in Memphis to check on Sam and his dad. I'd hate to think this was his attempt at a cry for help, and we missed it."

She was right. Together they called Jamie, but their twenty-minute conversation with the social worker didn't leave them relieved at all about the situation. She said they didn't have enough to go on to warrant a DCS visit, but knowing Sam and his case like she did, she could make a call to his father masked as a courtesy call, just to ask how things were going. She would gauge his response and go from there.

John and Abbie agreed that her plan sounded better than

nothing, though barely. If something bad was going on in that home, his father surely wouldn't admit to it over the phone. But it was all they could do at the moment, so they prayed Sam was okay, and that if anything was wrong Jamie would pick up on it. And most of all, they prayed God would protect him.

nothing, though barely. If something bad was going on in that home, his father surely wouldn't admit to it over the phone. But it was all they could do at the moment, so they prayed Sam was okay, and that if anything was wrong Jamie would pick up on it. And most of all, they prayed God would protect him.

165

twenty-seven

Sam returned to his father's apartment in the seedy part of Memphis more sad, angry, and depressed than ever. Not only had he spent all his money on bus tickets to and from Nashville, he'd also totally failed at what he'd set out to do today. Now that he was back here among all the junkies and drug dealers and illicit activity, he was upset at himself for not telling John what he'd planned to tell him.

He was back where he started, except worse off. Out of cash and out of options, he couldn't even run away because he didn't have money to get anywhere. If he did try to leave, he could wind up someplace even worse than this. That is, if such a place even existed.

He barely slept that night, and the next morning, he didn't feel like going to school. He considered skipping again, but the idea of staying here in this apartment with his father and his shady friends made him sick to his stomach, so he got up and went to school anyway. He hadn't made any friends at his new school, but at least it was a diversion.

The school had sent a letter home to his father about Sam's prior school records, but Sam had no idea what had happened with that. They'd placed him in much lower-level classes than he should've been in, so his classes were a breeze. He didn't care, though.

Abbie had made learning fun and challenging for him, the Graysons were always proud of him for doing well. They encouraged him every day. Here no one cared, so what was the point? He continued to go to his simple, boring classes just to get away from his father and his father's companions.

The day dragged on and on until school finally let out. The failed trip to Nashville yesterday had drained him to the point of exhaustion, and as he walked home, he hoped the apartment was quiet so he could sleep.

When he opened the old, faded door, the apartment was oddly silent, all the lights were off, and no one was there, which was unusual. In his father's business, people came and went twenty-four hours a day. Relieved, Sam dropped his books on the floor of his bedroom, collapsed onto the bed, and closed his eyes.

"Sam!" The sound of his name woke him with a start. It was his father, cursing, slamming doors, and yelling his name. How long had he slept and why was the man screaming at him? As he sat up and reached for his cell phone on the bedside table to check the time, his father came bursting through the door. Before Sam could even make a move, Drew punched him right in the jaw.

"Why did you go to Nashville and talk to that coach, *huh*?" His father kept screaming, his eyes bulging, angrier than Sam had ever seen him. Then he saw it; his father held a shotgun.

"You stupid brat, you're gonna ruin my life yet. You know how much I hate that coach and his pretty wife and their fancy house. One way or another, I'll make sure you never see them again as long as you live!"

Sam got up to defend himself, but his father struck him again, this time in the gut with the end of his shotgun. He doubled over in pain and fell sideways back onto the bed, but his father hit him again, this time on his right side under his ribs, and the man just kept punching. One after another after another, and Sam couldn't get his bearings to try to defend himself. Surely the man would shoot him any moment now.

Black dots seeped into his vision and got bigger and took over, and his father's voice sounded farther and farther away, but he remained right there because Sam felt the blows. One after another.

"You had to go whining, and now I've got social services and my probation officer on my tail. You'll pay. You just wait, you have no idea what you're in for. This right here is a piece of cake compared to what's going to happen to you next ..."

Those were the last words Sam heard before, mercifully, everything faded to black.

* * *

Drew was angrier than he'd ever been in his life, and it took everything in him to pull himself away from the kid. He didn't want to kill him, and he wasn't even going to shoot him. He only wanted to teach him a lesson he'd never forget.

Drew had worked hard to keep his identity hidden from that coach. If it weren't for John Grayson kicking him off his team all those years ago, his life would be totally different right now. He'd be living the good life, filled with money and prestige. But no, that holier-than-thou coach booted him from the team and the university expelled him. No scholarship, no basketball, no school.

Since Sam's mother had given him her last name at birth, coupled with the fact that Drew's legal name was Andrew and he went by Andy back then, John Grayson had no idea Sam was the son of his former player. And Drew had no intention of letting him in on his secret.

But now, with that social worker in contact with both him and John Grayson at the same time, the chances were good that he'd find out. So be it. Serves him right anyway to have to take care of his obnoxious kid.

Drew wouldn't even put up with that kid of his except for the plans to use him to make lots of money. This wasn't the timing he'd planned on, but now he had no other choice than to put the plan in motion.

He called his business partners, Blaze and Paulette, and told them they needed to make the move now because of the kid. They said they'd gather all the supplies they'd need and be over right away to help him move the kid. Drew needed to get out immediately before social services or his probation officer showed up.

His partners got there a couple of hours later just as Sam woke up. He moaned in pain, so Paulette injected the kid with something so he wouldn't wake up, and Drew packed up the last of his belongings because he sure couldn't come back here again, now that they might be on to him.

It was pitch dark outside as the two men lugged Sam out of the apartment, down a flight of stairs, and into the back of a van. Drew piled the rest of his belongings and supplies into the van. Around midnight, the trio plus Sam took off, headed for the Alabama beaches.

About five hours later, a bleary-eyed Drew pulled the van into a dimly lit parking lot, which housed a squalid-looking motel right off Highway 90, near the white sand beaches not far from Mobile. The area was desolate and run-down, but a lot of truckers came through here to get around all the traffic on I-10. With Blaze's connections to the trafficking world, this location should work out fine. If cops started snooping around or they just didn't have a good feeling about the area, there were a couple of other places they'd scouted out like this they could move to.

The trio ran through their plans to make sure everyone was on the same page. They would use Sam to lure the girls in. However, the kid was too much of a goody-two-shoes to do this alone, so they were prepared to threaten him with specific people and places. Drew had done his homework, and he laughed to himself. He knew who they all were: Abbie, John, Kyle, and Hannah. And, of course, Lauren. He couldn't leave her out. No doubt the kid would obey then.

But even with the threats, he figured that once out of earshot, the kid couldn't be trusted to do something like this. Blaze, who was in his thirties but had a boyish look about him, would pose as Sam's friend to make sure he did what he was supposed to do. Not only did that mean double the number of girls hauled in, but eyes and ears would be on Sam at all times. One way or another, the kid would be useful to him. It was about time.

twenty-eight

Sam woke up in a stuffy, dark room, completely disoriented. He struggled to sit up, but his body hurt all over. He vaguely remembered his father beating him, but he couldn't recall why. His memory wasn't working. The more he strained to focus and remember, the more his thoughts jumbled up.

His eyes adjusted to the dark, and he realized this wasn't his father's apartment. It looked like some kind of motel. And not a nice one. A thick, dark curtain covered the window, and the radiator underneath it rattled loudly. The room was much too warm, it smelled smoky and musty, and he was lying on a bed with a heavy, dark, ugly bedspread that matched the curtain.

The heat, combined with the smells, were making him sick. He was sweating, thirsty, and his body ached badly. As he tried again to get up, something pulled him back down onto the bed, and he realized he had been tied somehow to the bed. The more he struggled, the tighter the ties around his wrists and ankles became.

He panicked and tried to pray, but it'd been so long since he'd prayed he couldn't find the words. Finally, he uttered, *"Please God, if You're there, help me."* He was too weak and groggy to do anything else but pray those words over and over.

It seemed he'd been lying there forever when the door to his room swung open. The bright light streaming in from outside made his head hurt even worse. His eyes watered as he squinted to see who was there. As the person approached him, he realized it was the lady he'd seen at their apartment recently.

"C'mon kid, time to get up." The gravelly voiced lady grabbed a handful of hair from the back of his head, lifted it roughly, and held a cup of water to his mouth. She reeked of alcohol and cigarettes, which made him even more nauseous. He didn't want her anywhere near him except his lips and throat were parched. Sam gulped the water and then asked her where he was, but she ignored him.

"Let's go darlin', your actin' debut starts today. We gotta get you cleaned up."

Acting debut? Confusion and pain gripped him, and as he gulped some more water, he noticed some kind of powder floating around in the bottom of the cup. Had she drugged him? But before he had time to dwell on it, the door opened again, and his father walked in and got right in his face.

"Let's get going. Today's the day you're gonna make your old man proud." Drew's whiskey breath made Sam's stomach lurch. His father pulled him up by the collar, and he and the lady cut the ties from his wrists and ankles and dressed him. Sam resisted as long as he could until numbness overtook his mind and body. He had no strength left in him, and he couldn't understand the words the two were saying.

He wanted to ask questions, but his mouth refused to form the words. "Where?" was the only word Sam could manage to get out, and it took all his effort.

"On the beach kid, that's where. You're going to walk the beach, talk to pretty girls, and invite them to a coffee shop, and that's when we swoop in and grab 'em. Then you'll go back out and do it all over again." His father laughed, and Sam couldn't figure out what was funny. He didn't understand what he was supposed to do or why. "Fun and easy for you, and lucrative for me," his father added.

Sam listened to the words, but they didn't make sense to him. In no time, they had him up, and his father walked him to the door and shoved him outside. He stumbled, and a guy his father called Blaze grabbed his arm and forcibly walked him across the street to the beach. He was shocked that his legs worked, but without the guy grabbing his arm, he'd likely lose his balance. Sam decided to break away from him anyway.

"Let go." Sam yanked his arm away from the guy, and within a second, Blaze pulled out a gun and poked it into his side.

"You will do exactly as you're told, or you'll be dead, just like that. And if you don't care about your own life, then just think about that pretty little girlfriend of yours. I believe Lauren is her name. And that coach and his family who took care of you. Because they're all next." Blaze snarled and shoved Sam to the ground, waving his gun over him, before finally looking around and taking a step back.

"Now, get up! Get with it, kid, and get your head on straight. See those girls coming toward us? You need to turn on the charm," Blaze sneered through his fake smile, pretending to be horsing around with Sam.

He was still nauseous, but the haziness in his mind wore off a little and understanding dawned on him at last. No way was this going to happen. He couldn't be a part of this. He wouldn't.

"Here they come, follow my lead, and make your move," Blaze barked at Sam.

Then he steered Sam toward the two young girls heading their way. Suddenly Blaze acted like a gentleman.

"Excuse me, pretty ladies, I was wondering if you've seen a green frisbee around anywhere?" Blaze smiled sickeningly at the young girls.

"Nope, sure haven't." The girl in blue shorts smiled. She had long dark hair and appeared to be no more than fourteen or fifteen. Her friend looked even younger. The two paused and didn't appear to be in a hurry to move on. They were definitely interested.

"Where did y'all see it last?" the blonde girl in the yellow tank top asked. She appeared to be the younger of the two, and her eyes were locked on Sam.

Blaze smiled at the girls and turned to Sam, glaring at him through clenched teeth and a fake smile, in a way that said he'd better start talking. "How far down the beach were we?"

Sam's mouth was dry, and it wasn't just from whatever drug that lady had forced him to drink. "*Um*, I don't know," he answered vaguely, looking at the ground.

Blaze elbowed Sam hard in his already injured ribs. He bent forward and coughed.

"Sorry, my cousin Charlie here is sort of shy." Blaze laughed in the girls' direction and then stared menacingly at him.

"You want us to help you find it?" the girl in blue asked.

"Nah, I think we're about to give up," Blaze said in his sickeningly sweet, fake Southern drawl. "But maybe you ladies would like to go with us to get a frozen coffee across the street?"

"*Uh*, well, we should probably get back to our families." The young blonde in yellow glanced expectantly at her friend.

"Ah, c'mon, it's just across the street. You can almost see it from here. Promise we'll have you back here in an hour. Right, Charlie?" Blaze outwardly glared at him this time. This whole situation was more than Sam could deal with. There was no way he could take part in this.

"Hold on." Blaze pulled his phone out of his pocket and stared at it. "I got a text from my mom. Let me text her back real quick and tell her we'll be back in an hour."

Blaze texted something, then handed the phone to him as if to let him see what he'd texted his mom. Sam focused on the words on the screen, but they weren't to or from anyone's mom. In fact, it wasn't even a real text message. It was simply a message Blaze had typed for Sam:

PLAY ALONG OR THE GRAYSONS ARE DEAD. THAT'S A PROMISE.

Sam didn't care about his own life, but he had no doubt they would kill John and Abbie, and maybe even Hannah, Kyle, and Lauren. He had no choice but to play along.

* * *

The walk down the beach and across the street was painful. The girls introduced themselves as Amanda and Ava. They said they were sixteen, but Sam doubted they were anywhere near that old.

Sam was sick. He didn't know exactly what was going to happen, but he had a fairly good idea. Ava, the blonde, stuck close to his side, asking him questions but he could barely get the words out to answer her. She said she was from Troy, Alabama, here with her family on vacation.

She asked him where he was from just as they stepped into the coffee shop. Sam was about to answer her with something made up when he noticed his father and Paulette sitting at one of the tables, sipping coffee, pretending to be patrons.

His heart pounded harder than before. It was a trap, and he couldn't see a way out of it. Thoughts of the horror these girls likely faced flooded his mind, but they were competing with the threats made against the Graysons and Lauren. There had to be a way out of this. Sam swallowed hard and studied the coffee shop to see if there was anyone here who could help.

That's when it hit him that everything was all wrong. The coffee shop was dirty and dingy, and it sure didn't look like any coffee shop he'd ever been to. Instead, it looked like an abandoned convenience store with a coffee pot behind the counter, and Sam realized he'd seen everyone in here before. At his father's apartment in Memphis. These were the faces of men he'd seen regularly when he came home from school.

He turned toward Ava, and her face suddenly paled as if she, too, realized something wasn't right. Without thinking, Sam shouted at both girls. "Run! Now! They're going to kidnap you. Run and don't stop!"

Amanda grabbed Ava's arm and pulled her away from Sam, and they ran before Blaze realized what was happening.

"What did you do, you idiot? They'll tell their parents what happened!" Blaze screamed at Sam as he turned and chased after the girls.

Sam watched in horror as Blaze closed in on them, then out of nowhere, excruciating pain at the back of his head and a blinding, white light overwhelmed him before blackness took over.

* * *

"Well, well, well. Where's your rich basketball coach friend and his family now?" His father hovered over him, dripping with sarcasm. "Nobody's coming to save you, Sammy boy. What's more, no one's ever going to believe you, either. You know why? Because you're not going to live to talk about it."

He wanted to yell and scream at the man, but he was too groggy to get the words or even noises out.

"Yeah, that's what I thought. You don't have a lot to say now, do you, kid? From now on, you will do what I say, when I say, and there's not a thing you can do about it." With that statement, his father, Paulette, and Blaze all laughed like that was the funniest thing they'd ever heard.

"Oh, and we got the girls, no thanks to you," Blaze whispered in Sam's ear, his breath reeking of whiskey and cigarettes.

Even with his blurry vision, the smell and surroundings told him he was back at the run-down motel. Paulette approached him with a syringe and needle, and Sam fought her the best he could in his weakened tied-up state, but his father and Blaze held him while she injected something in his arm. Once again, he couldn't fight off the darkness that crept in.

The next time he awoke, there was no light coming in around the curtains. He was a little more clear-headed and heard voices in the next room, talking about money and what they could charge for the girls.

A sickening awareness came over him as he listened. Panic overwhelmed him, and he yelled out as he struggled. If this were a motel someone would have to hear him, wouldn't they? But as soon as they heard him, his father, Paulette, and Blaze ran into his room. This time, Blaze slapped Sam hard across the face, and the two men held him down while the woman injected him yet again.

"Not as much this time," his father commanded. "We need him to at least be coherent and follow commands when we send him out again. Gag him instead." His worst thoughts and fears were confirmed. If ever there was a time to pray, it was now. The only problem was, he still no longer believed in God.

twenty-nine

Abbie and the kids were in Atlanta for the national basketball tournament supporting John and his team. She was so proud of her husband. This was always such an exciting time of year, and Abbie enjoyed every bit of it. John spent every waking moment with the team and coaches while she hung out with her family and friends, seeing the local sights. Wendy and her family had even come along. They all spent a lot of time together.

Occasionally, Abbie had to push aside thoughts of Sam that crept in. And at their hotel on Saturday morning as she and John enjoyed a quiet breakfast together, John asked her if she'd heard anything new about Sam.

She stared down at her hands. "I'm sorry, honey." She sighed and placed her napkin on her plate. "I've talked to Jamie a couple of times, but I didn't want to tell you about it during the tourney because there's nothing we can do anyway. I knew you'd worry, and it would be one more thing in the back of your mind."

"Abbie," John said pointedly, "you know you can tell me anything, basketball tournament or not." He stopped eating too and sat back for a moment. "What've you heard?"

"Well, last week Jamie contacted his father, and she said the man couldn't have been nicer. In fact, his niceness bothered her. He seemed very fake, as if he were hiding something. He told her they were fine, Sam was doing well, and he thanked her for calling, in a way Jamie described as him saying, 'Thanks, now mind your own business.' There wasn't any more she could do at that point, so she decided she'd call again in a few days." Abbie paused and saw the look of concern in John's eyes, but she needed to tell him everything. Tournament or no tournament, just like he said.

"A couple of days ago, she called his father again, but this time she got a recording saying the number had been disconnected. Knowing Drew was on probation, she tracked down his probation officer, told him she needed to follow up on Sam, and asked if she could have the man's new number. The probation officer said he didn't have another number, which is a probation violation. So, at this point the man became concerned and told her he'd look into the situation."

"Well, that doesn't sound good." John appeared every bit as worried as Abbie was.

"It gets worse." Abbie took a deep breath and continued. "Earlier this morning, Jamie texted me to say the probation officer has been searching for Drew for two days with no luck. So now there's a warrant for his arrest for violating his probation. Jamie asked him if he thought Sam could be in danger, and he said it was possible." Abbie paused, her eyes wide. "He's had a several day head start and could be anywhere with Sam by now."

"I just knew something wasn't right when Sam came to see me." John jumped up, paced the room, and finally stopped in front of where Abbie sat. "He wanted to tell me something. I saw it on his face. I should have pushed him to tell me. And then the backpack—why didn't it register with me before he left that day? I certainly wouldn't have let him leave."

"Honey, hindsight is everything." Abbie stood up and faced

him. "Of course, if you had known then what you know now, you would've pressed him and done everything in your power to find out what was going on. Besides, we both know from experience if Sam doesn't want to talk, he's not going to. You couldn't have made him talk," Abbie said.

John sighed and plopped back down in the hotel chair. "You're right, I just hate that this kid has no one to fight for him. I sensed something wasn't right, but I didn't do anything to try to help him. So, what are we supposed to do now? And if he did come all that way to talk to me, why didn't he? What stopped him?"

"I don't know the answers," Abbie said. "We have to pray Sam is okay, and that God will watch over him."

* * *

Sam relived the nightmare over and over. He would begin to get his bearings, and they would drug him again. He wished they would knock him out, but instead they drugged him to the point where he could barely speak, had no reflexes, and couldn't scream or fight. He was still tied up, so he wouldn't have been able to move much anyway.

He could hear the girls screaming, and he'd try to make his mind go to other places. Sometimes it worked, but mostly it didn't. He alternated between trying to pray to God for rescue and wishing the men would kill him instead.

In his more coherent moments, when he could compel his mind to go to another place, he imagined he was a different person, in a different place. It didn't matter who he was or where, as long as he was away from here.

He'd focus on the fun times he'd shared with Lauren, but then his current reality came crashing into his thoughts, and he was ashamed. Surely Lauren could never be with someone who'd been part of something this horrible. Afterall, these girls wouldn't be here if not for his part in it.

The same with the Grayson family. They were so nice and faithful to God. They wouldn't want anything to do with him after this, either. He didn't know how he'd live with himself when this was all over. If he even lived through it, that is.

Gradually things quieted down, but Sam could still hear muffled cries through the wall. "Hey, is anyone over there?" He yelled, but his voice was hoarse and his throat parched, so he didn't know if they could even hear him. He waited a few moments, but there was no answer, so he managed to push himself up against the wall and hit it slightly with his head, enough to make a light sound.

"Is anyone there?" Sam asked again, his voice only slightly stronger.

"Yes, help me please," a quiet, weak, female voice finally answered.

"I'm tied up and can't move. Are you tied up too?" Sam asked gently.

There was no answer at first, but then the girl cried out.

"Hey, it's going to be okay, we're going to get out of here." Only that was a lie. If he couldn't help himself, how could he possibly help her? "Are both of you over there?"

"No, it's just me, my name's Ava. Are you Charlie?" The girl sounded like she was struggling to speak as much as he was.

"Yes, *uh*, I mean no. I'm the one you met on the beach, but my name's not Charlie, it's Sam. How old are you, Ava?" He figured it was better to keep her talking.

"I'm thirteen." Ava's reply was barely audible.

Thirteen. Sam wanted to throw up. Before he had time to answer her, he heard what sounded like a door being kicked down in the distance, and then Ava screamed. She screamed over and over, and she didn't let up. *Oh, God, please don't let me have caused that by talking to her. Please let her be okay.*

Panic rose in him and before he even realized it, he was screaming also. "Ava, Ava! Are you okay?"

Immediately, Paulette and Blaze were in his room, and Blaze

came at him with a large knife. "Shut up, do you hear me? I'm going to make you shut up if it's the last thing I do!" He tightened the gag in Sam's mouth and plunged the knife into his left shoulder. The pain was unbearable. *This must be what it's like to die.* And darkness engulfed him a final time.

thirty

Abbie sighed as she left the media conference. "From the highest high to the lowest low". That's how John had just described his situation to reporters this morning, the day after his team lost in the national tournament. His defending national champions had lost in the first round of the tourney. The first round. He was bitterly disappointed, convinced he'd let his team down.

She'd told him what he already knew deep down. Much of it was beyond his control—injuries, illnesses, and the loss of his two stars from last year who left to play professional basketball. But it didn't matter. Her husband was the head coach, and ultimately, winning and losing fell squarely on his shoulders. He was inconsolable.

John always took losses hard. Abbie and the kids were supportive and said all the right things, but John had a fiercely competitive spirit. At the end of the day, it didn't matter what anyone said, these kinds of losses were unbearable for him. But experience told her he'd get over it with time.

Kyle and Cassie had caught an early flight home, as did Wendy, Roger and their daughter. John and the rest of the coaching staff met with the team that morning to rehash some things. They would all head home in a few hours. Abbie had convinced John to have an early lunch at the hotel with her and Hannah before going to the airport.

"Dad, I wish we could make you feel better," Hannah said sweetly.

Abbie shook her head at Hannah as if to say, 'You're wasting your time,' but Hannah continued anyway.

"Sorry, Daddy, this stinks. You all worked so hard."

"You'll never know how much the two of you, and Kyle, and Cassie, mean to me." John leaned over and kissed his daughter on the cheek. "No matter how disappointing this is, it's okay because I have you all."

Abbie smiled. It didn't matter that John's smile was noticeably forced, he honestly meant what he said. No matter what else happened, there was no doubt in Abbie's mind that she and their kids meant more to him than anything else in the world.

The three ate their food in silence when Hannah's voice broke the quietness. "I miss Sam. I wonder how he is."

John's eyes reflected the sadness in her own eyes. They hadn't told the kids about Sam's visit to John or how worried they'd been ever since.

"I wish we knew." Abbie pushed her plate away. "And I wish we'd been more prepared for how hard it would be to let him go. I mean, we learned about it in foster-care training, but I never would've dreamed we'd become so attached to a sixteen-year-old who was only with us for seven months."

"Not me, for sure." John stirred his soup but made no attempt to eat it.

In the beginning, her husband had merely gone along with the whole foster parent thing to make her happy. Something was missing from her life, and fostering was her idea. John had thought the idea was crazy, and he certainly never planned to have a teenager because the plan was to foster a small child. But neither of them had expected to become so attached. Sam had turned their world upside down.

In the past couple of months, social services had contacted them a couple of times about foster opportunities, but they passed. They weren't ready yet and couldn't imagine having their hearts broken again. It would take some time before they could even consider fostering another child, but they weren't ready to give up on the idea entirely either.

They'd spent a lot of time wondering how Sam was faring and decided they had to come to terms with the fact they may never know how things turned out for him. That's just how it was much of the time in the foster care system. But that didn't lessen the ache in their hearts.

John quit playing with his soup, pushed his bowl aside, and sighed. "Well, I guess we'd better get ready to head to the airport," he abruptly changed the subject. "All I want to do right now is get home."

The three slowly got up and went to their suite to finish packing, and thirty minutes later they all gathered in the hotel lobby while the assistant coaches made sure the team and staff were all accounted for. The players and assistant coaches all boarded a bus headed for the airport, while John, Abbie and Hannah took a car. The three were quiet during their Uber ride to the airport when Abbie's cell phone rang and startled them.

"*Ugh*, probably more friends calling with their condolences on the game." Abbie groaned. She pulled the phone out of her purse, checked the caller ID, and glanced at John. "It's Jamie calling. Maybe the update on Sam we were hoping for?"

But as Abbie listened to Jamie, it was clearly more than an update. She brought her hand to her mouth and her eyes filled with tears. "Yes, of course, we can," Abbie said to Jamie. "We're in Atlanta, heading to the airport right now. We'll see about getting our flight switched, and if not we'll take a car. I'll text you with an update." Abbie ended the call and she looked from John to Hannah in disbelief.

"She asked if we could provide emergency care for Sam, and I told her yes. We can, right?" Abbie asked as an afterthought, and she realized her hands were shaking.

"Of course, we can," John offered quickly. "Where is he; what's going on?"

Tears streamed down Abbie's cheeks as she struggled to get the words out.

* * *

John and Abbie were beside themselves. The hospital only allowed one person at a time to be with Sam in the post-surgery unit, so they alternated staying with him while the other sat with Hannah in a waiting room down the hall. They didn't want him to wake up alone.

Abbie sat in a chair next to his bed when he started to wake up. He barely regained consciousness and was distressed and incoherent. Abbie's attempts to calm him were futile and only made things worse, but the nurse monitoring him was quickly at his side.

She told Abbie the doctor didn't want him to wake up yet. After his surgery that morning, they wanted to keep him sedated for a while to give his shoulder and other internal injuries time to heal, so she added medicine to his IV to put him back under. All was calm again and as the nurse left, she told Abbie she would update the doctor. They'd move him soon to a regular room.

Jamie had met them at the hospital as soon as they arrived from the airport that afternoon. She had the paperwork they needed to sign to be able to make medical decisions and obtain care for Sam. The poor boy was lucky to be alive. He was in the city's top trauma hospital, and the best pediatric trauma doctor in the region was treating him. But that didn't make any of this any easier to hear. What Sam had gone through was unimaginable. And Abbie couldn't begin to fathom how he'd ever fully recover from what he'd been through and what he'd witnessed.

The doctors explained he'd been stabbed in his left shoulder and had lost a lot of blood. He'd been given a transfusion, and the surgeon was able to repair the damage. He was extremely dehydrated, had several broken ribs, a bruised kidney, and a lot of cuts that required stitches. But despite all this, his vital signs were improving. Barring infection or any other complications, his medical team said he'd make a full recovery.

Physically, that is. Mentally and emotionally—that was a different matter altogether.

* * *

For the first time in a long while, when Sam opened his eyes, his body and mind weren't fighting him so badly. He was able to focus on his surroundings. Everything was white and sterile looking. He was in a hospital room. Abbie Grayson sat in a chair next to his bed, and on the other side of his bed was another chair where John sat, both asleep. Sam was glad to see them but didn't want to wake them up.

The hall was quiet except for some faint beeping noises coming from outside his room. Sam guessed it must be the middle of the night. He had no idea how long he'd been asleep, but he was more alert and clearer headed than he'd been in quite a while.

His shoulder and his chest ached terribly, and a few pieces of what happened came back to him. He remembered being locked in a room, in the dark, with his hands tied. How long was he there, and what had happened to him? He remembered screaming and thinking he would surely die in that place.

The memories were hazy, other than one: Sam had asked God repeatedly to help him, to rescue him, but there was no answer. God never showed up. Instead, He left him to suffer and die there alone.

thirty-one

Sam was released from the hospital four days after he'd been admitted. Abbie was astonished at how much his physical condition improved in that short amount of time. That had to be attributed to his youth. He would need a lot of rest to fully recover, which he could do at their home. It would be a hard road ahead, especially emotionally and mentally.

They flew home, since he'd been hospitalized in Alabama, and the flight was uneventful. Sam was quiet and still on pain medication, so he slept on and off.

John and Abbie had talked to him in the hospital about staying with them. Yes, it was considered emergency placement, but it would be much more than that—it would be long term. Jamie was working to get them guardianship until Sam's eighteenth birthday, and she said she didn't foresee a problem. He appeared grateful and relieved.

When they finally arrived home, John walked around to Sam's side of the car to help him out. "We'll take this slow and easy," John reassured him as he helped him into the house.

Sam was still considerably weak and unsteady. Physically, he'd be fine in a couple of weeks. He'd lost weight during his time with his father, weight he didn't need to lose. And he'd been severely dehydrated to the point the doctors had been worried about his kidney function when he was in the hospital. Thankfully, that was normal now.

His shoulder and ribs still caused him a lot of pain, and he had some awful-looking bruises. But his stitched-up cuts were starting to heal. Despite all this, the worst part had been the panic attacks that usually hit just as he drifted off to sleep.

The doctors were concerned about his mental state not only because of the panic attacks, but also because Sam asked repeatedly about two girls, Ava, who he insisted was in the room next to him at the motel, and another girl, Amanda. Police who were at the scene scoured the surroundings very carefully, and said the room next to him had been undisturbed. There were no signs anyone had been there. But since his father and one of his friends were still at-large, they would be on the lookout for females they might be harboring.

For now, Sam was decidedly calm. He breathed an audible sigh of relief when they made it into the house. He asked if he would be staying in the same room. Abbie smiled and said he would.

"I want to lie down for a while, if that's okay," Sam asked.

"Of course, honey. Get some rest, and we'll check on you in a little bit," Abbie said.

They decided John would run out and get some things Sam needed as well as a few groceries, since they didn't have any food in the house. He left, and Abbie retreated to the family room. She needed some sense of normalcy after all they'd gone through the past few days. Abbie turned on the TV and tried to find something mindless and silly to watch.

They'd had tough conversations with Sam as he remembered more bits and pieces of what he'd gone through. He was in a terrible emotional state and couldn't understand why his father had done the things he'd done to him. But neither she nor John had any answers. This whole situation was beyond their comprehension.

"Abbie, did you hear me?" John stepped into the family room.

Abbie nearly came out of her chair. "Oh, you startled me. No, I didn't even hear you come back."

"Sorry about that. It didn't take long. I just got the necessities for now. And Jamie pulled in right behind me. She's here with the local detective who's working with the Alabama police on the case. Meet us in the kitchen? I'll start some coffee."

"Thanks." Abbie gave her husband a weak smile.

"Is Sam okay?" John asked as an afterthought.

"I haven't heard a peep out of him. Hopefully, he will sleep for a while."

John nodded. "Jamie said they have information about his father. Maybe that means they caught him."

"I certainly hope so. I won't rest easy until they do." Abbie shivered, but it wasn't because it was cold.

"I know, me either." John left the family room and headed to the kitchen.

Abbie paused before getting up from her chair in the family room and lifted a silent prayer as she smelled coffee brewing and heard John welcoming them. *Please God, help us all through this trying time. Especially Sam. And please let them catch his father and everyone who participated in this.* There was no audible answer, but out of nowhere, Isaiah 55:8 flashed in her mind. *"For my thoughts are not your thoughts, neither are your ways my ways," declares the Lord.*

Why would that verse pop into her head now? It didn't make any sense, but she brushed it off as she walked into the kitchen and said hello to Jamie and the gentleman with her.

"Mrs. Grayson, hi. I'm Detective Lacey. I'm the local liaison working on Sam's case."

"Nice to meet you." She shook hands with the man and greeted Jamie.

"Well, first off—some good news—Sam's father has been arrested in Florida and is currently in the custody of the Tallahassee Police Department. We're working to get him back to Tennessee," the detective said.

"Thank you, Lord," John said, and Abbie nodded and breathed a sigh of relief.

The detective nodded but was silent as he stared at Jamie with raised eyebrows, as if waiting for her to speak.

"*Um*, there's something you need to know about Sam's father." Jamie shifted in her seat and hesitated as if she didn't want to tell them whatever was coming next.

Both of their behaviors made Abbie nervous.

"I didn't know this until this morning when I met with the detectives," Jamie began, then thumbed through her notes, set her elbows on the table, and took a deep breath. "I found out that Sam's father was in prison when Sam was born, and since his mother and father were never married, his mother gave him her last name, Keller, the name that's on his birth certificate. The name we knew his father by, Drew Keller, was actually an alias and not his real name."

Abbie was confused. She shrugged her shoulders and made eye contact with John. What could she be getting at?

Jamie paused once again and avoided eye contact with John. "His legal name is Andrew Quinn. And as I looked through Andrew Quinn's records today, I discovered he'd been a student at Tennessee University about eighteen years ago, under the name of Andy Quinn, and he, *um*, well ... he played for you, John, on the basketball team before the university released him from his scholarship and expelled him from school. I'm so sorry we didn't know this until today."

John gasped, as he and Abbie stared at each other with eyes and mouths wide open.

How could this be? Abbie thought, then out of nowhere, "*My thoughts are not your thoughts, neither are your ways my ways...*"

"What? Are you sure? Surely not ..." John's voice was unsteady as he spoke, and he was white as a sheet.

"Oh, John, no ... I mean ... How?" Abbie asked. This couldn't be possible. The room shifted, and she wondered if she was as pale as John. "Mr. and Mrs. Grayson, are you all right?" Detective Lacey asked.

John and Abbie stared at each other in disbelief. How could this be true? How could this have happened? And what's more, how could no one have known until now? Abbie prayed that her husband would get his bearings and speak because she certainly couldn't.

"*Uh*, I don't know if we're all right or not." John paused. "The last we heard about Andy Quinn, he was in prison for drug dealing. I tried to contact him a few times over the years, but he refused any contact."

Snce Abbie had known John, he'd never looked as disoriented as he did right now. Was this actually happening? What were the chances they'd been fostering the son of the former player John had spent so much time worrying about throughout the years? Abbie remembered dinners she had fixed at their home for Andy. She'd even met his girlfriend—

"John!" Abbie's hand flew to her mouth. "I remember his girlfriend was pregnant," She turned her attention to Jamie. "That had to be Sam, right? I mean ... " Abbie stopped and did the math in her head. "The timeline fits."

John's mouth flew open. He appeared to be calculating for himself. "Is that possible?" he asked.

Jamie's eyes grew wide as she quickly thumbed through papers in her file. She stopped at one particular document and stared at it for a long time.

"Yes," she said quietly, "the dates coincide. She would have been pregnant with Sam at the time Drew, er Andy, was sent to prison to serve a five-year drug sentence."

They all sat and stared at each other in silence until

Detective Lacey finally spoke up. "Well, *uh*, this is unusual, to say the least. I don't know that I've ever come across this crazy of a coincidence."

Abbie met John's gaze. Neither of them believed in coincidence. Things people often labeled as coincidence were in reality the work of God or his angels. But why this? "*My thoughts are not your thoughts, neither are your ways my ways ...*"

Once everyone had steadied themselves from the shock, Detective Lacey explained what Sam's father had done—he'd used his son in a scheme to obtain girls to sell. When Sam refused, he was beaten and held captive. At some point, the group received a tip that the motel owner had become suspicious and called the police. Sam's father and his associates fled, leaving his son there. When the police arrived, they found Sam, beaten, drugged, tied up, and stabbed.

Her blood rushed through her. Abbie was angrier than she'd ever been in her life. She couldn't begin to comprehend how a human could treat another human this way, let alone a father treating his child this way. But that was probably the answer. The man was his biological father only—he never formed any other connection to Sam. Thank the Lord Andy had been captured and sat in a jail cell now. She hoped he'd be sent to prison for the rest of his life. There was quite a list of charges against him.

In addition, police had caught two other people who participated in the scheme, possibly the woman who drugged him, and the man who pretended to be his friend on the beach. The one who later stabbed Sam in the shoulder. They had reason to believe there were others who participated in the scheme, but these three had been traveling together.

"Sam has been asking about two girls. Did you find them?" John asked the detective.

Detective Lacey shook his head. "No, and I don't know what to tell you about that. We'll keep investigating, of course, but none of them have admitted to having any minors, other than

Sam. Police have searched the rooms that surrounded his for any kind of clue or DNA, anything that might indicate a person was in the room, but so far they haven't come up with anything."

Abbie and John both nodded. A doctor suggested it could have been a hallucination since Sam was under extreme duress, but Abbie wasn't convinced. He was adamant that at least one girl had been held in a room next to his.

They finished their conversation and thanked Jamie and the detective. Although they wondered about the girls and were extremely shocked about the identity of Sam's father, the good news was the main three were in police custody. But things were going to be difficult for Sam for a while. He would have to identify the two who were with his father, possibly testify in court, and—

"Should we tell Sam we knew his father?" John asked.

* * *

Sam was relieved to be staying with the Graysons for an indefinite amount of time. From what they'd told him, his father was in jail and would stay there until his trial or sentencing, and he'd likely serve a lengthy prison sentence after that.

John said there was practically no chance Sam would have to see him or be in his custody again. Ever. He also said he and Abbie would fight for him if it came down to being faced with seeing the man again. He thought there was more John wanted to tell him, but he didn't, and Sam didn't have the strength to worry about what it might have been.

He didn't dare think beyond now, but with the Graysons' commitment to him, it sounded like he would get to stay here until he turned eighteen. He would age out of the foster care system and be on his own in the world. He could get grants to go to college, if he wanted, but how would he live? He would have to get a full-time job for sure, just to survive.

The statistics on foster kids aging out of the system weren't good, and Sam knew them all. High percentages of aged-out teens ended up homeless or in jail, and the stats were even higher for them becoming drug addicts. The bleakness of the future was more than he could manage to think about right now. He would have to take it all one day at a time.

thirty-two

Physically, Sam's condition improved each day. It no longer hurt to breathe due to the broken ribs, his shoulder was healing and less painful each day, and his doctor in Franklin removed the stitches from all his other wounds. He still had to sleep on the opposite side of his injured shoulder, but that would get better with time.

More than a week had passed since Sam's release from the hospital. A detective was coming today with pictures of some suspects for him to view. The idea of looking at pictures of his abusers turned his stomach and made his head hurt. He feared what kind of reaction he might have if their pictures were in front of him.

Would he be scared? Angry? He didn't want to think about it. John and Abbie offered to be with him during the process and, thankfully, the detective said they could be present. Kyle was also coming, not because Sam needed an attorney, but, according to John, Kyle could protect Sam just in case there was some reason for him to step in on his behalf.

Kyle had been exceptionally nice to Sam lately and had even stayed with him some to give John and Abbie a break. He'd been surprisingly caring and was another person Sam could lean on if he needed to. Lately, he needed all the support he could get.

Kyle's voice startled him out of his thoughts as he entered the kitchen.

"Hey, how are you feeling?" Kyle gave Sam a smile and a quick side hug, avoiding his hurt left shoulder.

"Not bad. A little better every day. I'm kinda nervous about this, though," Sam said.

Kyle went straight to the coffee cart, pulled a blue stoneware mug from the bottom shelf, and popped a coffee pod into the Keurig. "Want some?" Kyle asked.

Sam shook his head. He rarely turned down coffee, but today he was too nervous to drink or eat, too afraid he might get sick.

"Hey, try not to be nervous. The detective is going to show you pictures of several people. If you recognize any of them, let him know. He'll ask you how sure you are, and if you're positive, say that, but if you're not positive, let him know that too." Kyle stirred sugar into his coffee, but his eyes were on Sam the whole time.

"From there, he may ask a few more questions to see how certain you are of the identification. Just answer truthfully. I promise, it's gonna be okay."

"Thanks, I just want this to be over." Sam's throat was dry, so he decided on some water after all and got up to get a bottle out of the refrigerator as John and Abbie came into the room.

"Hi, honey." Abbie hugged Kyle as he stood up, and his dad followed suit.

"I told Sam what I told you guys on the phone last night. I don't think they're going to pressure him. After all, they're on our side, but I'm here to make sure. I'll take care of him, don't worry," Kyle said.

They sat around and talked for a few minutes until the doorbell rang. Sam exhaled. John patted his good shoulder as he got up to get the door. He returned a moment later with a tall man whom John introduced as Detective Lacey.

"Hi, Sam." The man smiled warmly and something about him made Sam feel at ease. "I'm Detective Lacey, and I investigate crimes against children. I know at almost eighteen, you probably don't consider yourself a child, but my unit investigates crimes against kids and teens under the age of nineteen. I'm the liaison for the Alabama detectives. That way you don't have to go there for anything," the detective explained. "First of all, I'm sorry for all you've gone through."

Sam was grateful he wouldn't have to go anywhere near that motel in Alabama ever again. He could see compassion in the man's eyes. He didn't trust him completely, of course, but he was relieved the detective at least seemed like he cared. Sam simply told the man, "Thank you."

After coffee and soda were offered, Detective Lacey explained the process of showing Sam the pictures of potential suspects. "I want you to take your time and examine each one carefully. Even if you think the first one I place on the table is the one, please look at all of them and take your time before singling out one. And if you've never seen any of them, that's fine too. Try to be as sure as you can of your answer."

Sam's hands were shaking, and his breathing sped up. He didn't want to see the pictures of his attackers, but he understood he had to identify them in order for a case to be built against them. Everyone else in the room must have been as nervous as he was because the room was silent.

The detective methodically placed six pictures of female suspects on the kitchen table, directly in front of him.

Breathe, Sam told himself as he tried unsuccessfully to steady his shaking hands. He didn't look at the pictures until they were all in place.

"Okay, Sam, take your time, look them over closely, and let me know if any of these looks familiar," the detective said.

Sam fought the urge to look at all of them at once and forced himself to start with the picture on the left and worked his way to the right, one picture at a time. He'd never seen the first one before or the second one. He'd held his breath and let it out finally, in hopes he'd get to the end without recognizing any of them.

But then the fourth one—dizziness crept in as he tapped her picture.

"This is her. This one right here. I think they called her Paula or Paulette or something." Sam's voice was barely above a whisper and his hands shook.

He'd seen her face up close. She had frizzy, orangey-red hair and a lot of wrinkles, especially around her mouth. And she had bony arms. He'd never forget her raspy voice, and he could actually *smell* her picture—the awful combination of beer, cigarette smoke, and way too much strong perfume. The contents of his stomach inched up toward his throat.

"Okay, Sam, that's good. Did you look at numbers five and six?"

Sam's hand covered his mouth, and he didn't know whether he'd put it there to keep from gasping or throwing up. He lowered his hand and stared at the remaining pictures, but these people were completely unfamiliar to him, and he shook his head. "That's definitely her, number four."

Detective Lacey pushed the picture of suspect number four closer to Sam. "How sure are you, Sam?" the man asked.

"I'm one hundred percent sure." Sam's answer was louder this time, but his voice was still shaky. Everyone was staring at him. He was extremely lightheaded and thought he might pass out.

"I'm playing devil's advocate here," Detective Lacey said, after a moment. "In the transcript of your questioning at the hospital, you said several times the room was dark the whole time you were held at the motel. So, something the defense might wonder is, if it was that dark, how can you be one hundred percent certain this female was one of your captors?"

Kyle nodded in approval of the question, and Sam swallowed the building nausea and regained his bearings. "*Um*, I remember her from being at my father's apartment in Memphis." He tried hard to regain his focus. "She was with him at the coffee shop on the beach, and she was the one who came in over and over and injected stuff into my arm and made me drink water with some kind of powder in it. So, yeah, it was dark, but I could see her because she was only inches away from my face. This is her. I know for sure," he said, his voice stronger than before.

"Thanks, Sam. That makes sense." Detective Lace nodded. "I know you're still recovering, so do you want to take a break before we continue?" The question was more pointed toward John and Abbie than to him.

"No, I'm fine. I'd rather get it over with," Sam spoke up quickly. He didn't want to have to dread another day of this.

Detective Lacey nodded and placed photos of six males in front of Sam. All were suspects who could possibly be the man named Blaze. If that was even his name.

Sam steadied his breathing and studied the pictures, but the identification wasn't as immediate this time. Part of him was relieved that a picture didn't jump right out at him like it had with the woman.

He eliminated four of the suspects right away. The two remaining had similar features and builds, but his memories were still hazy. He stared hard at number six and tapped on it. "I think this is him. His hair is different, though. This one has dark hair, but the man I saw had blond hair. Otherwise, it looks like him."

"If you had to put a percentage on it, how sure do you feel about it?" Detective Lacey pressed.

"I think it needs to be a positive ID or none at all." Kyle glanced from the detective to Sam.

The detective nodded, and then Sam spoke up, "I'm sorry, I think this is him, but I can't say I'm one hundred percent sure. Other than the hair, this one does look like him."

"That's okay, Sam." Detective Lacey reassured him. "You've been more help than you realize, and we're not going to put you through any more today."

Sam was grateful because the room had begun to spin.

* * *

The detective got up to leave, thanked Sam, said goodbye to Abbie, and then John and Kyle walked him out. Once outside, Kyle asked the detective his thoughts about Sam's identifications.

"Well," Detective Lacey said with a smile, "we hit the jackpot with the identification of the female. We had some pretty strong evidence linking her to the scene, and Sam's identification of her sealed it. This is major. We can now charge her with attempted murder since we know from Sam's toxicology what she injected him with and made him drink. It's a wonder he survived, as I'm sure the doctor told you."

John was torn between being happy or angry about this. Happy, of course, because Sam would make a full recovery physically and that justice might be served. At the same time, though, he was beyond angry about what this woman had done and what Sam had endured at her hands.

"Hopefully, she'll be off the streets for a long, long time," Kyle agreed.

"That's the goal," Detective Lacey said. "And we had identified the man Sam picked as the man who was there also. We are still building a case against him. The evidence against him is not as strong, but we're making progress. Sam's identification of him, even though not one hundred percent positive, will help."

They talked some more about the next steps and the plan for Sam to give a deposition behind closed doors. It would be used later in court to keep him from having to appear before his father and his captors. While it wouldn't be easy by any means, at least he wouldn't have to testify in the presence of his attackers.

Since the wheels of the justice system moved slowly, it could be several weeks before Sam would have to worry about the deposition.

thirty-three

It was an unseasonably cool day for late April. The sky was gray, and the forecast called for rain, but Sam didn't care. He had to get out of this house. The walls were closing in on him. He grabbed a book, a blanket, a cup of coffee, and went out to the back deck. He sat at a table far from Abbie's view from where she sat in the family room.

He was thankful for this family, especially John who he'd talked to about his guilt for his part in luring the girls to the coffee shop. Although the police hadn't found any evidence that any girls had been held against their will, Sam was positive he'd talked to Ava there, and positive more than one girl had screamed. What had they done to the girls? Where were they? Thoughts of the two girls and his role in the whole thing consumed him.

His physical recovery was going well. John and Abbie had taken care of him and had been nothing but kind and compassionate. They made him feel safe, which was something he couldn't ever remember feeling before.

But he had one major problem with them—they were devout Christians. Because of all the good they'd done for him, he didn't want to refuse to go to church with them, but legally they couldn't make him go, so he stood his ground. That was their only point of contention.

He was grateful to be in their home and in their care, but he drew the line at attending church. John prayed every night before dinner, and Abbie had prayed for him several times when he was upset or physically in pain. Sam never said anything, but he just didn't get it.

How could a supposedly loving God allow the horrible things that had happened to him? God completely abandoned him and left him to die there. No one would ever be able to convince him otherwise. And what about those poor, innocent girls, Ava and Amanda? What happened to them? Again, he couldn't fathom how a good God could let unspeakable things happen to those girls.

A shiver ran through him, and he tightened the blue plaid blanket around him. He took a sip of his coffee and then shoved the book aside. Who was he kidding? He hadn't been able to concentrate long enough to read more than a couple of pages since this whole ordeal had taken place. He sighed and stared out at the deep green, wooded acreage and let his thoughts consume him. He'd raised his voice and told Abbie in a not-so-nice manner that he would not be going to church now or ever, and she couldn't make him go. He surprised himself at how he'd lashed out at her.

He could tell she was upset about it. After the second week of him not going, she came into his room and asked to talk to him about it. He immediately got defensive, but she didn't fight back. She just let him talk, so he dropped the defensive act, and his tone became more polite.

"You don't understand," Sam had said quietly, but firmly. "I prayed to God to save me, and He not only allowed me to go through all that, but He left me there to die. Why would I want to believe in a God like that? And what about those girls? No one else believes they even existed, but I know they did. Terrible things happened to them, and where are they now? Why would God allow that?"

A tear slid down Abbie's cheek. Sam had prepared himself for an argument. He understood his rights as a teen in the foster care system, and he wasn't going to give in on this. But when Abbie spoke, her face was kind, and her words were gentle. She appeared to choose her words extremely carefully as more tears slid down her cheek.

"I understand, sweetheart. Your questions, your doubt, and your anger. I understand all of it. And you may not believe this, but God does too. Please just consider talking to Him. Question Him. Tell Him you're angry, and you don't understand why He let you go through the things you went through. He can take it," she said.

Sam stared at her and didn't know what to say. In fact, he'd almost laughed. He wasn't about to do any of the things she said because they were completely useless. But he appreciated how kind she was about it and that she didn't push or lecture. Her tears made him feel bad, so he said he might, but that was a lie just for her sake. Sam no longer had any use for God whatsoever.

thirty-four

Sam's physical wounds had healed during the two months after his attack, but emotional healing had been difficult and slow. He didn't like or trust his therapist. John and Abbie watched him constantly, and as relieved and glad as he once was to be here with them, now they smothered him.

It was also impossible for him to concentrate these days. He sat at his favorite spot on the deck and attempted to read a book his therapist had assigned, but it did nothing except make him angry.

"Hey Sam, what are you reading?" Abbie came out on the deck and sat at the table with him, which irked him. This whole huge house and deck, and she had to sit right beside him? At least one of them was always in his space. Why couldn't they just leave him alone?

"A book," he answered without looking up.

"*Hmm.* What's it about?" Abbie asked as if she didn't catch the sarcasm or the fact he was trying to ignore her and didn't want her out here.

"If you must know, it's about a foster kid living with a family who doesn't really want him," Sam snapped. Her constant questions annoyed him. Why was she even out here? She still didn't get the hint. All he wanted was to be left alone.

"That's terrible. Why would she make you read that?" Abbie was still being nice and ignoring his attitude.

"I have no idea." Sam slammed the book shut and stood. "But isn't that how you feel? I know you didn't want me." His words came out louder and meaner than he intended, but it was better than the angry tears that tried to form. There was no way he would let them flow.

"Sam, what are you talking about? Of course, we want you here. Why would you say that?" Abbie asked as if she didn't know what he was talking about. But he didn't believe that—not anymore.

"Because Kyle told me, that's how I know." He lashed at her in earnest now, determined not to let her see his tears.

"You've totally lost me, honey. I honestly don't know what you're talking about." Abbie stared at him with her mouth open.

I guess she never thought I'd find out.

"Kyle told me—at that Thanksgiving dinner we had before John's games started. He told me John never wanted to foster at all and that neither of you wanted a teenager, you only wanted a cute little six or seven-year-old kid who wasn't already tarnished by the system." Sam yelled.

"Sam, you don't understand. What we meant was—"

"So, it is true?"

"Well, not exactly—"

"Is that how you felt or not?" Sam demanded to know, but deep inside he was frightened of where these words were coming from. He hadn't even thought about this conversation with Kyle for a while, but the words kept spilling out, and he had no control over them.

"Yes, but all that changed when we met you," Abbie admitted.

Abbie's eyes filled with tears, but he didn't care. "Well, I guess the joke's on you then, because you got the opposite of everything you wanted," he yelled. "And you know what else? You didn't want a foster child. You wanted a pet, or a possession, something you could show off. You wanted a cute little kid to fill your time, but who wouldn't cause you any problems." Sam threw his book down on the deck and walked away. He wasn't going to give her the satisfaction of seeing his own tears.

"Sam, wait, please, we need to talk about this!"

The patio door slammed behind him on his way into the house. He went straight to his room and picked up his old brown backpack, his journal, and his cell phone. As he headed out the front door, he glanced behind him and saw Abbie still sitting on the deck talking on her phone, probably to John.

Or maybe Jamie, so she could have Sam replaced with a cute little kindergartener.

* * *

"It's okay, Abbie." John attempted to calm her.

He was just leaving campus, and she'd caught him on his cell. Sam had been angry lately, yes, but they'd never seen him aim his anger directly at either one of them until today.

"I don't know what's going on with him, but we will get to the bottom of it as soon as I get home. Just leave him alone and let him cool off until I get there," John said.

She heard his car door close and his engine start. "John, I've never seen him that angry. I know we've had some disagreements about church, but this was much worse than that. And why would Kyle have told him those things? Especially during our Thanksgiving weekend. The two of them were getting along so well then." Abbie's eyes filled with tears again.

"I don't know, but I'm going to call Kyle right now. Just hang tight, I'll be home in a few minutes."

While Abbie sat and waited for John, she replayed the conversation with Sam over and over in her head. What had Kyle said to upset him so much?

"Abbie?" John was home, and she hoped he had answers from his conversation with Kyle.

"I'm so glad you're home." Abbie walked toward him as he came in from the garage toward his office.

"Anything else happen since we talked?" John stepped into his office where he put his backpack down and tossed his keys on his desk, then he and Abbie sat on his office sofa, well out of earshot from Sam's room.

"No." Abbie shook her head. "I haven't heard a peep out of him. Did you get ahold of Kyle?"

"Yeah, I did." John sighed. "Kyle didn't even remember a conversation like that until I told him exactly when Sam said it took place, and then he remembered but said the context was all wrong."

"He said he'd told Sam that although the foster situation wasn't what we'd expected or planned for, we were happy things worked out like they did. He didn't mean any of it in a negative way, and he feels terrible about it. I told him not to worry, he couldn't have known this would all blow up months later."

John stared at the floor and then turned his attention to Abbie. "Let's do this, let's talk to him and clear the air."

"Okay, let's go in the family room; I'll get him." Abbie walked down the hall toward the bedrooms and family room. "Sam, we need to talk to you for a moment, please." She knocked on his bedroom door, but he didn't answer, and she hesitated for a moment before she opened the door and went in. She expected to see him sitting on his bed but instead there was no sign of him.

"Sam, where are you?" She walked back down the hall toward John. "He's not in his room."

"He's probably in the basement." They both headed toward the basement stairs. It was pitch dark, and John turned toward Abbie and shrugged as he switched the light on and headed down the steps.

Why would he be sitting down here in the dark?

"Sam, are you down here?" John asked.

They switched more lights on and checked the spare bedrooms in the basement, but there was no sign of him whatsoever.

"Are you sure he didn't go back outside?" John asked.

"I'm positive," Abbie's pulse sped up, and the panic on her husband's face mirrored her own. They ran back upstairs, and Abbie checked the deck and the library again while John went into Sam's room.

"Abbie, his backpack's gone. Surely he didn't run away." John took out his cell phone and dialed Sam's number. "No answer, it went straight to voicemail."

Not again ...

thirty-five

The storm clouds rolled in as Sam checked his phone and read the text from John.

Without emotion, he turned his phone toward Lauren and showed her the text.

"I believe them, I really do. And I think you do too," Lauren said softly.

They sat side by side at a picnic table in the park. He ran from the house without thinking, and, as usual, he had no plan. It had all happened so fast, he still wasn't sure what had even set him off. He was just ... confused.

He called Lauren as soon as he got away from the Graysons' neighborhood. She picked him up and they drove to Franklin Park. She'd stopped and got a couple of Polar Pops and some chips, and they sat and talked.

"If they call me again, I'm not going to let it go to voicemail this time." Lauren ran her hands through her long, windblown hair. The clouds on the horizon were dark, and they'd seen the storm alerts come through on their phones. "You need to let them know where you are. I'm afraid if you don't, you might end up with consequences you didn't think about. I mean, what if they call DCS?"

They'd been friends long enough that Lauren certainly understood how things worked in his world. It wouldn't be good for him if John and Abbie called DCS. Why didn't he stop to think before he got into it with Abbie and ran? He may have blown it for good with them this time. He sighed and put his head in his hands.

"I'm afraid to call them." He glanced at Lauren. "What if they don't want me back?"

"Sam! You've got to be kidding," Lauren exclaimed. "Did you even read the text John just sent you? Or listen to the voicemail he left me? He clearly said, 'We love you, and we want you.'"

How he wished he could believe as naively as she did. Her innocence was one of the things he loved about her. "What if they're just saying those things so they don't get in trouble for me running away?" It was more of a statement than a question. He'd seen this situation play out with a friend of his.

"Really?" Lauren made a sound that was part cry, part laugh, and she shook her head. "Do you honestly believe that Sam? In the time you've known the Graysons, have you known them to play games?" Her voice rose in frustration.

And rightly so; he was just as frustrated with himself.

"I messed up bad, Lauren. I don't even know why I went off on her like I did. She didn't deserve that." Sam stood up from the table, put his hands in his pockets, and stared at the ground.

"It'll be okay," Lauren's voice softened. "Just tell her that. You've been through so much, and they know that. They seem like great parents. They are, aren't they? I mean, nothing bad has ever happened there, has it?" she asked him gingerly as if the thought just occurred to her that maybe there was something he hadn't told her.

"No, they're great. The best, actually." Sadness overwhelmed him when he thought of how he'd treated Abbie. She was a great mother and had never been anything but kind to him. What made him treat her that way?

They were quiet for a moment, and with the thunder getting closer, Sam pulled out his phone and texted John back.

> I'm sorry I ran off and for how I treated Abbie. I'm at the park with Lauren. She'll bring me home in a few minutes. I'm sorry.

He was about to read to her what he'd texted to John, but before he could, a reply from John came in.

> We're glad you're okay. Don't worry about anything. We'll get through this. Just come back.

* * *

"He said he was sorry, and that was the right thing for him to do. It'll be okay," John said to Abbie while they waited anxiously in the family room, relieved Sam was okay but unsure of what was coming. The most important thing was that Sam was safe, but one thing was for certain, his behavior toward Abbie would not be tolerated.

"I want to believe that John, but I've never seen Sam act the way he did today. It just makes me wonder how much anger he has inside of him."

"Well, let's see how this conversation goes. But either way, we need to let his therapist know what happened. Especially if a book she assigned him to read triggered all this."

"Hey." Sam startled them as he stood in the doorway with his backpack still on. He stood there with his hands in his pockets as if unsure whether or not he should come in.

Instinctively, John and Abbie both got up and went to him. He set his backpack on the floor, and they both hugged him at once. He was tentative at first, but then he hugged them both and hung on like he didn't want to let go.

"Come sit with us," John said.

Sam followed and sat in the space on the sofa where John pointed. Sam turned to Abbie right away. "I'm so sorry. I was wrong to talk to you like I did. I was so disrespectful toward you, and you didn't do anything to deserve that." He appeared on the verge of tears.

"Thank you. I accept your apology, hon. And it's okay." Abbie put her arm around Sam's shoulder.

"No, it's not okay. And I know I shouldn't have run off either. I promise it won't happen again." He bit his lip and stared at the floor.

"Sam," John carefully chose his words. "I just need to ask you —do you believe those things you said to Abbie? Because I'm going to be honest with you—in the beginning, I didn't want a teenager, and we didn't want to do an emergency placement. Jamie talked us into taking you in." John prayed that Sam could handle his brutal honesty. "So, yes, it started out the way you said, but it didn't stay that way for long. We realized the first week you were here that you belonged with us, and we wanted you to stay."

Sam nodded slowly and his eyes met John's. "I guess maybe I did believe it, at least a little, back then. But honestly, I hadn't even thought about that conversation with Kyle for a long time. That stupid book is what got me thinking about it."

"I think we need to shelve that book until we can find out why your therapist wanted you to read it," Abbie said.

John agreed, then asked Sam point blank, "Do you believe we want you here with us?"

"Yes," the boy whispered.

But John wasn't convinced he believed it. At that moment he realized no amount of reassurance would ever be too much for Sam.

thirty-six

Despite reassurance from the Graysons, things just got worse for Sam. The nightmares were relentless. Not a night went by that he didn't wake up screaming or drenched in sweat, and each morning he woke up feeling like he hadn't slept at all. He met with a Christian therapist twice a week, but it was useless. As soon as she said anything about prayer or God, he was done. He'd tune her out. As far as Sam was concerned, therapy was a huge waste of time.

Lauren and his friends from school checked in on him often, but he didn't have much to say to any of them. None of them could begin to understand what he'd been through, and he sure wasn't going to explain it to them. They brought him Christian books, worship music, or asked to pray for him, but he didn't have use for any of it.

He couldn't understand why they kept coming over and kept on trying, despite his lousy attitude toward them. They weren't overly pushy; they were trying to be nice. But they annoyed him all the same. They even came over for a little get-together Abbie had planned to try to boost his spirits. He put up with it because they were the only friends he had, but he wasn't any fun to be around, and he didn't have much to say to them.

He'd also distanced himself from the Graysons and didn't even know why, other than he was tired of people feeling sorry for him and watching his every move like he was on the verge of breaking. Maybe he was. But it was nobody's business but his.

In a few months, he'd turn eighteen. He was biding his time until he could be on his own. Although he didn't know what he'd do or how he'd survive, at least he wouldn't be accountable to anyone. There'd be no one to make him go to therapy or try to make him go to church. And no one for him to disappoint.

The kids his age differed vastly from him. He'd gone through things they could never understand, and he certainly wasn't going to confide in any of them about his past. He didn't fit in anywhere, but he didn't even care anymore. Not about his friends or even the Graysons. Not anything.

* * *

Abbie had tossed and turned most of the night and finally decided to get up and go for a walk as soon as the sun rose. The morning air was more than muggy—it was oppressive, even at 6:00 a.m. But this was summer in Tennessee, and the heavy, sticky air and overly warm nighttime temperatures were part of it.

She smiled as she walked up the sidewalk. If any of the neighbors were looking out their window, they'd think she was crazy. She'd taken three walks yesterday, and she was certainly starting early today. But that's what she always did when she needed to clear her head. And lately, her head needed a lot of clearing.

Sweat already beaded up on her forehead. This wasn't exactly the refreshing walk she had in mind to help focus on the pressing matter at hand—what to do about Sam.

He appeared to be getting worse with each passing day. Not only had he spiraled into a depression, he'd also completely withdrawn from them. Therapy wasn't working either. In fact, a few days ago, Sam's therapist told Abbie he wasn't cooperating. She said she could no longer help him, and they needed to find a different therapist.

Abbie sighed as she rounded the cul-de-sac to head back toward her house. She waved and smiled at Tom Patel pulling out of his driveway, and then her mind went back to the conversation she and John had earlier about whether or not Sam would be better off somewhere else. Perhaps with a family who had a better understanding of what he'd been through, or maybe with one who had more experience with troubled teens. There was no doubt in Abbie's mind that she and John were in way over their heads. They were ill-equipped to deal with this kind of trauma.

And it was apparent the trauma ran deeper than what happened recently. They'd gotten access to some of his DCS records and discovered he'd suffered every kind of abuse possible all the way back to eight years old. She was sick to her stomach just thinking about it. How could she and John ever help him recover?

They'd met with Jamie yesterday afternoon. Abbie asked for the meeting because she and John realized they desperately needed help dealing with Sam. Communication with him had deteriorated to the point it was almost non-existent, and they had no clue how to help him. On top of everything, the prospect of having to find a new therapist completely overwhelmed them.

Abbie realized during the meeting that it was partially their own fault things had deteriorated so much. They should've reached out to Jamie before now, but they hadn't. They thought they could handle things, but they were wrong.

Jamie was compassionate and kind-hearted when they explained the situation to her. She didn't chastise them for not coming to her sooner but instead apologized for not checking in with them more often.

She explained some resources available to teach them how to help Sam. There was an organization that could provide education and counseling for all three of them to better their communication, and there was specific assistance for John and Abbie to help them relate to Sam in a way he could understand, given all he'd been through. The organization and its services sounded much needed. Abbie was hopeful.

But once they discussed all that, Jamie said she needed to have a frank conversation with them. "I realize this has been a difficult transition for all of you since Sam's return," Jamie said. "I know a teenager wasn't what you bargained for, to begin with, let alone someone who needs the specialized care and attention that Sam does. He's a different kid than he was even when you first met him due to the trauma he experienced these past few months."

Jamie paused and looked from John to Abbie. "Having said that, if you want me to find another home for him, there is absolutely no shame in that. Just let me know."

There it was. It was something Abbie had considered, and she was certain John had, too, even though neither one had dared voice it aloud.

For Abbie, it would mean she'd failed, and that her mother was right in saying she shouldn't have taken on a foster child. And John was right in saying they shouldn't have taken in a teenager. For John, it would also signal failure. Another failure, just like Andy "Drew Keller" Quinn.

Abbie wiped the sweat from her forehead with the back of her hand and wondered if her pounding headache was due to the heat or from the burdens on her mind. *So, maybe I can't do this, Lord. Maybe John was right. Together we couldn't help Sam's father all those years ago. What makes us think we can help Sam now?* There was no answer from God, and she focused once more on their meeting with Jamie and the details of the conversation.

She brushed tears from her face and asked Jamie the question she was most afraid to ask, "Do you think that's what we should do? Do you think he'd be better off with a different family?"

"Oh, no, I didn't mean to imply that," Jamie answered. "I just wanted to let you know you have the option, and you shouldn't feel guilty asking. You have provided a great home for Sam, but I also know you need to take care of yourselves and your marriage. This has been rough, I know, and it's not going to get better overnight."

She and John let that sink in for a moment. When Abbie finally spoke up, the tears she'd held back slid from her eyes. "As much as I hate to admit it, this is all so much harder than I ever dreamed."

John nodded. They were on the same page, as usual. "I agree," he added, his voice breaking. There were bags under his eyes that hadn't existed before, and his hair had gone from salt and pepper to nearly all gray. This was hard, and he was just plain tired. They both were.

"It's been more difficult than we could've imagined," John said. "But I think we'd be okay with that if we were helping him. Lately, though, I don't know that we are. In fact, I wonder sometimes if we're hurting him or at the very least, holding him back from healing."

"I understand completely." Jamie nodded. "This is a lot to go through for any family. Go home and have some serious discussions, then let me know what you think. I'll support your decision either way, and I'll continue to do my best for Sam, no matter what."

Abbie completed her walk around the neighborhood, and the cool air conditioning welcomed her as she walked back into the house. Thankfully, all was quiet. Both John and Sam were still asleep. Sam had gone to bed early, and she and John had an honest, productive conversation about how difficult this situation was. As Jamie had pointed out, Sam was no longer the same kid he was when he left them before Christmas. But he also wasn't the same kid Jamie had dropped off to their home the night they first met. The last few months had changed him.

In addition to all the other problems, Sam no longer trusted anyone but John or Abbie. Even with them, the trust barely existed, and he was failing in school. But the thing that bothered them most was his anger—almost hatred—toward God. How would they ever work through all this? It seemed insurmountable.

She and John had talked through every aspect of the situation for hours into the night, and no matter how they approached it, they always wound up in the same place. There really was no other choice. Their decision was mutual, and they agreed no matter what happened, they wouldn't change their minds.

This was the right decision for them, and they hoped and prayed it would be the right one for Sam as well. And they prayed that the conclusion they came to was indeed part of God's plan for each of them.

thirty-seven

Abbie hung up the phone and tried to shake off the sinking feeling of failure. They'd had some rough patches over the years, both in their marriage and with their kids, but nothing like this. She sat at the barstool in the kitchen, put her head in her hands, and replayed the conversation she'd just had with Sheila King from the homeschool academy.

Even though it was summer, school was year-round, and Sheila just told her that Sam had become completely withdrawn. Over the past few weeks, he hadn't turned in any of his work, he'd failed not some, but all of his class assignments and tests, and he'd barely spoken to his friends. It was so bad that Sheila recommended they withdraw Sam from the academy for a while since he wasn't getting anything from it.

Abbie was dragging today, even before the phone call. She let out a sigh as she got up to make a cup of coffee. Maybe the caffeine would help her aching head.

She and John had called Jamie this morning and gave her their decision. It wouldn't be immediate because they wanted to tell their kids first, and they just hadn't had a chance to have that conversation with Kyle and Hannah. But they needed to do it soon because the current situation wasn't working.

She thought about the conversation she'd have tonight with John about withdrawing Sam from the academy for a while. That meant she'd be homeschooling him full time, which, unfortunately, wasn't going much better than the academy.

In fact, she hadn't done much of anything with him school-wise over the past couple of weeks. Just like at the academy, he had barely spoken to her, and efforts to get through to him were exhausting. Even though she shouldn't, she'd let him stay in his room most of the time with the promise that he'd at least read. But honestly, she didn't know if he was even doing that. It was hard to figure out which way to turn.

She'd asked Kyle and Hannah to spend some time at the house, hoping Sam would at least communicate with them—especially Hannah. Sam and Kyle had connected right after he came home to them from the hospital, but now Kyle was busy with work. It was hard for him to come home much, but Hannah said she could. John and Abbie were thankful and hopeful she could connect with him.

They were praying for a miracle.

* * *

Hannah pulled into her parents' driveway, put the car in park and reached for the door handle, but then she paused before getting out of the car. Lately her visits home had been stressful. It was nobody's fault, really. Her mom and dad had become even more worried about Sam over the last few weeks because he'd become so withdrawn.

At least Sam texted her from time to time. A couple of weeks ago, she picked him up and they went to dinner and hung out for a while. Although he wasn't himself, he talked a little while they ate. Kyle told her that Sam had responded to texts from him. Not long responses, but at least it was something.

Her mom had called this morning and invited her for an early dinner. She said it'd been a particularly rough weekend with Sam, and Hannah's presence might help. Hannah sighed. She couldn't help if she didn't go in, so she grabbed her purse and let herself in the front door. She followed the smell of lasagna and garlic bread and found her mom and dad sitting at the kitchen island talking quietly.

"Hi, sweetheart, we're so glad to see you." Her mom smiled, her dad got up, and they all three hugged.

Hannah immediately noticed a little gray in her mom's hair that wasn't there a couple of weeks ago, and her father had a few new lines around his eyes. Had those been there before? They both had dark circles under their eyes, and she wondered if they were sleeping. Recent days had taken more of a toll on them than Hannah had expected. For the first time in her life, she was concerned about her parents' health.

"Rough week, huh?" Hannah put her purse down and took a seat across from her mom and dad. Her mom nodded and looked sadder than Hannah had ever remembered seeing her.

"It seems like he gets more distant from us every day," her mom said, and her dad put his arm around her shoulder.

"Have you told Sam what you decided?" Hannah wasn't going to ask them since they hadn't told her what they'd decided, but she was curious.

"Not yet." Her dad shook his head. "We don't know where his head is right now, and we don't know if he'll even care." And with that, he got up to peak in at the lasagna in the oven.

Hannah nodded. It was apparent her dad didn't want to say any more about it right now, so she put her own curiosity aside and didn't push. They would tell her and Kyle when they were ready. As difficult as things had been, she was pretty certain what their decision was. It was becoming apparent they couldn't keep going like this. The thought made her sad, both for herself and for Sam. How would he fare if he were uprooted again?

She couldn't think about that right now, so instead she got up and set the table while her dad filled glasses with ice and water. Her mom took the lasagna and garlic bread out of the oven and sat the salad on the table. Dad went to tell Sam dinner was ready.

Sam entered the kitchen, and Hannah was surprised by his appearance as well. His clothes hung off of him, his hair was longer, and it was stringy and greasy looking. Dark circles underlined his eyes, too, and he offered her a weak smile as he said hi to her and hugged her.

Surprisingly, he talked a little during dinner, and her mom smiled at Hannah. Clearly Mom was pleased and maybe even surprised. Other than his appearance, he seemed a little better than the last couple of times she'd seen him. But he was nowhere near the person he'd been last fall and winter before he went back to live with his father.

As they finished dinner, Hannah had an idea. "Hey, Sam," she said as she twisted a strand of her long brown hair around her finger, "why don't you go with me to church this evening?"

Her dad stopped mid-bite, and her mom's jaw dropped, but Hannah decided it couldn't hurt to ask. Sam had vehemently objected whenever her parents asked him to go to church with them, so he would need some convincing. Maybe the promise of coffee would help.

Without looking up at her, he shook his head. "No, thanks."

Hannah wouldn't give up easily though. "Oh c'mon, it'll be fun. It's not even a regular church service—it's a night of worship —all music, and I know you love music."

"Nope, don't think so," Sam replied curtly, as if that were the final say.

"We'll stay just long enough for a few songs," Hannah persisted, "and we can even leave before the prayer time if you want. We'll get coffee on the way. And on the way home, too, if you want." She wasn't ashamed to use his love of coffee against him.

Sam shook his head slowly and then smiled, sort of. It was ever so slight, but it was there.

"You're not going to leave me alone until I say yes, are you?"

Sam asked her, the half-smile still on his lips. But his smile still never reached his eyes.

"Nope, you know me better than that." Hannah grinned.

"Okay, but I'm holding you to the coffee. *Two* coffees, one on the way there and one on the way home. And I'm only going for the music. I don't wanna stay for the preaching," Sam said adamantly.

"It's a deal." Hannah clapped her hands like a little kid, and both her parents stared at her with their mouths open.

She agreed to Sam's terms, but if she was the one driving, he wouldn't have much choice if she decided to stay for some of the message, would he?

thirty-eight

Sam said yes to Hannah's plan for the evening because it appeared to mean a lot to her. She'd been nice to him from the beginning, so he'd do this for her. Plus, she offered coffee. Coffee and music, what could it hurt? Maybe he'd feel better and decide not to go through with the plans he'd made for later tonight. He desperately needed something to change his mind. But so far nothing had.

The exhaustion was killing him. He was tired of the nightmares, the images in his mind, and the guilt over the two girls, Ava and Amanda. Not to mention the Graysons were so nice to him, and he was so mean and awful toward them. He couldn't believe they let him continue to live there. Every time someone came to the house, he was certain it was Jamie coming to move him to another foster home, or more likely, a group home.

He was a horrible, scarred, broken person who didn't deserve the Graysons. He didn't deserve anything they offered. With each passing day, he wished a little more he wouldn't have survived his time in Alabama.

That's why he'd made a plan, and tonight he'd go through with it.

The pills he'd siphoned from the Graysons' medicine cabinet were waiting for him when he got home. Most of them were long-expired pain pills from when John had his knee surgery or when Abbie had neck problems from a car wreck, but Sam figured they'd do the trick even though they were old. He had a big bottle full, and he planned to take them all tonight.

Without a doubt, the Graysons would be better off without him. They were such kind, good people. They deserved a kid who wasn't as damaged as he was. And he certainly didn't deserve them. He didn't deserve anyone.

* * *

As soon as they finished dinner, they got in Hannah's car, and she made small talk as they drove. Sam didn't feel like talking so he stared out the passenger window and gave clipped yes-or-no answers and said *"uh-huh"* occasionally, but if Hannah was annoyed with him, she didn't show it.

Sam struggled with what he'd planned. He figured Hannah would be sad, but she'd get over it quickly. Then the Graysons could get that cute little kid they'd originally wanted. One who wasn't damaged yet. Their whole family would be better off, and they'd be happy.

They went through the drive-thru at their favorite coffee shop, got two iced caramel lattes, and arrived at church as the service started outside on the patio. Sam was relieved that they joined the gathering near the back and Hannah didn't try to drag him up toward the front. He didn't want to see any of his friends who might be there. He wasn't up to socializing. It was entirely too exhausting to talk to anyone.

The pastor welcomed the congregation, but Sam tuned him out. Once the music started it was peaceful, but he wasn't into worship music the way he used to be when he and Lauren had gone to church with his friends from school. What was the point? Why should he praise and worship a God who let him suffer like he did and let unspeakable things happen to Ava and Amanda? After about twenty minutes, he'd had enough and asked Hannah if they could leave.

"C'mon Sam, there are only a couple of songs left. Let's hang in there for those, okay?" Hannah turned her attention entirely to the music and away from Sam.

He wasn't happy, but since she was the one who drove, he didn't have much of a choice, so he stood there and sulked.

The worship band finished their scheduled songs, and as the pastor walked back out onto the stage, Sam turned toward Hannah. "Okay, can we please go now?"

"In a minute." She shushed him.

He'd been played, for sure. He took a deep breath to try to keep himself from spouting off at Hannah, but then he realized the music stopped and everything had gotten quiet. The pastor approached the worship leader, but the young man held up his hand and asked the pastor to give him a minute.

The pastor and the band were confused and quiet, until the worship leader, a young man who appeared to be not much older than Sam, began to speak.

"All during this service, God put a specific song on my heart, and I feel He wants me to play it because someone here tonight needs to hear these words. Please bear with us because we've never actually performed this song."

It was quiet again, and the worship leader turned around to talk to the band for a moment. The pastor stepped off the stage, and the crowd watched and waited expectantly. Sam was even paying attention now as this was clearly out of the ordinary.

"This is a song by Lauren Daigle, called 'Rescue,'" the worship leader said. The band played, tentatively at first, and then the young man stepped up to the mic and sang.

Sam listened intently, mesmerized by the words, as if the worship leader sang directly to him and only him. But how could this young man know him or what he'd been through? Or know that God had forgotten all about him? The song gripped him, and he couldn't leave now even if he wanted to.

The song cut straight to Sam's heart. Would God really stop at nothing to rescue him?

The song ended, and Sam couldn't breathe. He was dizzy, shaken, and sick all at once. Tears flowed down his cheeks. He vaguely heard Hannah ask him if he was okay, but she sounded a million miles away even though she was standing right next to him.

He couldn't look at her and couldn't speak to answer her. Instead, he turned away from the stage, the music, and the sound of the pastor talking, and he ran. He ran all the way around the buildings to the opposite side of the campus, where there were no lights except for a couple in the overflow parking lot. There were no cars or people on that side of the church, but he remembered a firepit area next to the woods, with a cross near it. Something inside him compelled him to go there.

His heart thudded hard in his chest and sweat beaded up on his forehead. He ran as hard and as fast as he could until he reached that cross at the edge of the woods. It was almost completely dark there. The grass was a little high and already damp with dew, but Sam didn't care.

At the foot of that simple wooden cross at the edge of the woods, Sam dropped to his knees, bent forward with his head in his hands, and sobs overcame him and racked his body. All at once, the presence of God surrounded him, and God spoke directly to his heart ...

So do not fear, for I am with you; do not be dismayed, for I am your God. I will strengthen you and help you; I will uphold you with my righteous right hand.

The words were audible, and at the same time he sensed them from deep within himself, pouring over his soul and penetrating his heart. He had no idea where they came from, but he was certain who they came from—God.

God had spoken to him.

"I'm sorry, God. I'm so, so sorry for turning away from you," Sam cried out. "Please, I beg you to forgive me for everything bad I've done. Please help me, God, and I will give my life over to you."

Almost immediately, a peace he'd never known before washed over every part of him, and in that moment, he was safe and more loved than he ever had been in his entire life. More words from God came. Not audible this time, but the words burned inside him. God told him he would live, and Sam would spend his life glorifying God.

The words were amazing, and with more conviction than he'd ever had about anything in his life, Sam knew this was no hallucination. Then the realization hit him—the Jesus the worship band sang about had been with him and never left his side during the worst moments of his life. Not only that, he realized that He was with the girls, Ava and Amanda, during their worst moments also.

"I'm sorry I doubted you, Lord. Please forgive me." Again, peace flowed over him, through him and around him.

Tonight, God promised Sam redemption. Somehow, someway, He'd redeem every bad thing that'd happened to him. To think He'd used a young worship leader to orchestrate it all was more than Sam could fathom. He stared at the cross in awe, and he laughed and wiped away tears as he heard footsteps behind him.

"Sam ... are you all right? What's ... wrong with you?" Hannah panted the words. Bent forward, hands on her knees, she struggled to catch her breath.

Sam saw the panic on her face, but he couldn't help it—he laughed, and he couldn't stop. If she didn't already think he'd lost his mind, she surely would once he told her what had just happened.

He didn't spare any details. Through laughter and tears, he told her all of it—the words spoken from God, his realization about those terrible nights, the peace that came over him, and

God telling him he would not only live, but his life would glorify God.

It'd all happened over the course of a few minutes, but Sam suddenly realized God had been working on him all along, all through the years, in the good times as well as the absolute worst moments of his life.

Hannah cried now, too, and she hugged him hard. It seemed she'd never let go, but he didn't care.

"Oh, Sam, I'm so happy. I can't believe this happened. God is so good," Hannah said through happy tears.

They walked to a concrete bench not far from the cross and sat, and they both were quiet for several minutes. Then Hannah turned and stared at him, still without speaking, for an uncomfortable length of time.

"Sam." Hannah's stare bore right through him. "Why did God say you would live?"

He hesitated. It was the question he didn't want to answer. Did he dare tell her about his suicide plan, and that was the reason God told him he would live? He didn't know what to do. Without a doubt, she would tell her parents, and if they told his social worker, he might be taken away from them. Or maybe even committed to a psychiatric hospital. But when he turned toward her, he could tell by the compassion on her face she already knew, or at least had a fairly good idea.

Once again, a peace he'd never experienced before tonight washed over him. Although he couldn't explain why, he was certain things would turn out okay if he told her. He promised God he would trust Him with his life from now on, and it had to begin here.

"Here's the truth, Hannah." Sam sucked in his breath and paused. "I planned to kill myself tonight."

Hannah gasped and her eyes teared up, but Sam kept going.

"I've been taking pills from your mom and dad's medicine cabinet over the past few weeks or so, and tonight I was going to take them all. I was so overwhelmed and couldn't take it anymore." He couldn't look at Hannah as he spoke. She was crying, and it took her several moments to speak.

"I don't know what to say. Why didn't you talk to mom or dad? Or to Kyle or me?" Hannah pleaded.

"You want the truth?" Sam paused before continuing. "I didn't feel worthy of your family—or of living."

"Oh, Sam, how could you think that?" Hanna cried. "Are you telling me God saved you from that? Here? Right now?"

"That's exactly what I'm saying." Sam nodded and smiled through his tears. "I can't explain it, but I feel peaceful and hopeful, and ... I don't know, Hannah. I don't have words to explain it. Some of it was audible—I mean God actually talked to me. Then peace flooded me all at once, and I knew I'd be okay."

"I believe you." Hannah studied him. "I can see it in your eyes, on your face. You look different."

He wondered if he indeed appeared physically different. But then something else occurred to Sam. "Please don't tell your mom and dad what I was going to do," he pleaded.

Hannah shook her head and stared at the ground. "I can't promise you that. I just don't know if I can keep something like this from them."

"I don't want to be taken away from them," he said, his voice no more than a whisper.

"I get that," Hannah said, and she was quiet for a moment. Suddenly, she grabbed Sam's hands. "Let's go home and tell them together. We can start by saying you'll do therapy or whatever you have to do to stay with them, and you'll be open and honest going forward."

He wasn't sure. But on the other hand, didn't he just make the decision to start trusting God? Didn't God say to him, "Do not be afraid?" If he was going to trust God with every situation from now on, for the rest of his life, all of it had to start tonight.

thirty-nine

"It's almost ten o'clock." Abbie glanced at her watch as John picked up the television remote to turn on the news. "I'm surprised Hannah and Sam aren't back yet."

John was a little surprised they weren't home yet, but he wasn't overly worried. "Maybe Hannah talked him into staying for the whole service, and they stopped for coffee after. If so, that's a good thing, right?" John couldn't imagine it was anything but that.

Just as Abbie opened her mouth to respond, they heard the kids enter the kitchen. John smiled at Abbie and winked at her. Of course there hadn't been a reason to worry, and he settled on ESPN News as Sam and Hannah appeared in the family room's doorway. Even though John hadn't been worried before, he absolutely was when he could tell they'd both been crying.

Abbie stood and spoke before he had a chance. "What's wrong? What happened?" Alarm rang in her voice.

"Mom, Dad, we need to talk to you. Can we all sit down?" Hannah plopped into the over-sized recliner, and Sam sat in the leather chair by the fireplace, while John and Abbie settled back into the sofa they'd just risen from.

"What's going on, Hannah?" John asked. He couldn't imagine what this was about.

"Okay, here goes." Hannah smiled at Sam. "Sam is going to tell you what happened to him tonight, something good—but he needs to tell you something else before he can tell you about that."

John didn't understand. Hannah was talking in circles and appeared flustered, but before he could voice his confusion, Sam interrupted.

"I'm sorry," he said, looking from John to Abbie. "You've both been nothing but nice and understanding, and I've acted awful toward you. I've been such a jerk."

John started to interrupt and say something to the effect that it was okay, but Sam waved him off. "I know you're going to say it's okay, but it's not okay. I'm sorry, and I promise I'll never treat you that way again."

"Honey, you've gone through so much," Abbie said. "It really is okay, honestly. We want to help you, but we're not sure how."

"We appreciate the apology, Sam." John nodded his head in agreement. "But more than anything, like Abbie said, we want to help you."

Sam didn't say anything for a long minute. He stared at the floor, and John couldn't imagine what was going on with him. Then Sam turned toward Hannah, and she nodded at him as if to say it was okay.

"There's something I have to tell you, but before I do, I want to ask that you not tell Jamie or anyone else at DCS. I know it's unfair of me to ask anything of you after the way I've acted, but I promise, I'll go to therapy or whatever you want. I'm willing to do whatever it takes to get better."

John's concern was full-blown now, and his wife was wide-eyed and pale, the look of sheer panic on her face. His heart thudded hard in his chest as about a dozen awful scenarios flashed through his mind all at once.

Again, Sam stared at the floor for what seemed like forever

before he started his story. "I don't know a good way to ease into this. I don't think there is one, so I'm going to come right out and say it." He let out a huge sigh as if he'd been holding his breath. "I had planned to kill myself tonight. I picked the lock on your medicine cabinet and snuck pills over the last several weeks. I planned to take them all tonight."

John was grateful he was sitting because the room tilted. Abbie gasped, and after a long pause, Sam kept going. Tears ran down the boy's face, and his voice shook.

"But tonight, at that worship service, something happened." Sam went on to tell them about the worship leader and the "Rescue" song, and how he ran and ran to the cross near the edge of the woods. The cross where Jesus met him.

"I know it all sounds crazy, because it sounds unbelievable to me, and I'm the one who experienced it." His voice pleaded with them to believe him.

They were all crying now, and in sync as always, John and Abbie both got up, walked over to Sam, and hugged him. They held on for a long time, and finally, John let go and went back to his seat on the sofa. Abbie followed.

"Son, I believe every word you said. I believe God spoke to you tonight, and *uh*, well ..." John's voice cracked, and it took a moment to gain his composure so he could continue. "What I'm trying to say is, God has answered our prayers. We've prayed for this for so long." John choked up again, and Abbie was still crying. Only now he could tell they were happy tears.

It dawned on John what might have happened if Hannah hadn't talked Sam into going to church with her tonight, and a deep chill ran through him. When he voiced it aloud, the room fell silent.

"Abbie and I will have to talk about what to do." John leaned forward in his chair, hands clasped, his elbows on his knees. "I think we need to tell Jamie. I'm not saying that's what we're going to do. Abbie and I need to think about it and discuss it. But in the meantime, you need to stay put. You cannot run away again. We'll get through this together. Do you understand?"

"Yes, sir." Sam appeared sincere and told them once again how sorry he was. He promised never to do anything like this again. He said he was exhausted, but at the same time, there was a peace within him that hadn't existed before because he knew God was with him. And he reiterated his promise not to run.

Sam excused himself, hugged them all, and went to bed. Hannah stayed, clearly overwhelmed by all that had happened the past few hours.

"Are you okay, sweetheart?' Abbie asked her.

"Yeah, I think so." Hannah came to the sofa and sat between her parents. She was shaken. "I can't believe what happened tonight. When Sam ran, I had no idea what was going on. When I finally caught up to him, he was on the ground, sobbing, nearly hysterical. It was so scary until he was able to talk to me. Then it all became completely amazing. I mean, the song that triggered this wasn't even planned." She looked at her parents, wide-eyed.

"What do you mean?" Abbie asked.

"Sam didn't tell you this part," she continued, "but the worship songs were supposed to be over with. Pastor Rob walked out to speak, but the worship leader said he wanted to do one more song—one they hadn't even played before, because the Holy Spirit told him someone needed to hear it."

None of the three of them spoke for several minutes.

"That's the God we serve. Only He could make that happen," John said, his voice cracking.

"Thank you, Heavenly Father," Abbie whispered, looking up toward the ceiling.

John took a minute to compose himself. "I don't know the right thing to do. I think we need to report this to DCS, but frankly, I don't want to."

"I know you made your decision on what to do with Sam, and I don't know if this changes that in any way." Hannah stared at the floor. "But he wants to stay here more than anything,

Daddy. He's afraid of being taken away to another foster home or group home. But he said he needed to tell you all this tonight, no matter the consequences, because he owed it to you to tell the truth, and it was the right thing to do."

"I still believe the decision we made is the right one," John said. "But it's late and we're all tired. We'll have a long talk with him tomorrow."

Abbie nodded, and they asked Hannah to spend the night rather than drive back to Nashville at this hour. She agreed. The seriousness of the day and the sheer miracles that had happened were something they all needed to think about, pray about, and thank God for.

Without God's apparent intervention at the cross, tomorrow morning would've dawned tragically different.

forty

John had tossed and turned next to Abbie all night, and she didn't feel like she'd slept at all, so the two got up as soon as a hint of sunlight streamed through the bedroom blinds. Sam and Hannah were both still asleep. Abbie made coffee, and she and John took it out to the deck. The weather forecast predicted a hot, humid day today, but this morning was beautiful with lower humidity and the perfect temperature to sit outside.

They talked about their plan and decided to tell Sam the decision they'd made a couple of weeks ago. He deserved to know that before they discussed anything else. She and John had done a lot of soul-searching since that meeting with Jamie. Both together and separately. No matter how they considered it, their family hadn't been the same since the day Sam arrived. They each came to the same overwhelming realization.

The decision didn't come lightly or without tears. And now they were standing by that decision, one that would change the course of their family forever.

They couldn't pinpoint how, or even exactly when it happened, but Sam had become a part of their family whether any of them intended that to happen or not. He'd become one of their children as much so as Kyle and Hannah. Now, when she and John thought about their kids, they thought of three, not two—Kyle, Hannah, and Sam.

They hadn't realized until their talk with Jamie that the reason things had been so hard with Sam was because they cared so much about him. They loved him.

First, they would ask him what he genuinely wanted. They would do it right away, this morning. They'd put it off because they weren't sure if he even wanted to be here anymore, but after last night, they realized they should've told him at the time they made the decision. What if he'd gone through with his plans last night without ever knowing how much they loved and wanted him? The thought was unbearable.

There were still plenty of things to work through. He needed specialized and intentional therapy, but they'd get him whatever he needed. In the grand scheme of things, they wanted him to be part of their family. Officially and forever. They would ask Sam today if they could adopt him.

"Good morning," Sam stuck his head out the French doors, a cup of coffee in his hands. "Can I join you?" he asked sheepishly.

"Of course." Abbie patted the chair next to her. "Did you sleep well?"

"Not really." He sat next to her and took a deep breath. It was obvious he still struggled this morning. "I kept going over everything in my head, and I wish I could make you see how sorry I am. Not only for what I almost did but for how I've acted and treated you guys." Sam shook his head and stared at the deck boards under the table.

"It's okay," John said, as he leaned across the table. "We haven't known how to help you. On top of that, we made a decision a couple of weeks ago that we should've told you about as soon as we made it. I think it would've changed things." John had his full attention now. Emotion overcame him, and Abbie didn't think he'd even be able to get the words out. He took a sip of his coffee, cleared his throat, and proceeded. "We love you, Sam. And despite the setbacks we've had, we think of you as one of our own kids. Every bit as much as Kyle and Hannah. And we want to ask you," John paused, "if we can adopt you."

At first, Sam stared blankly at John and then Abbie. "What? Are you being serious?"

"Of course, we're serious, Sam." Abbie laughed. "This isn't something we'd joke about."

"You want to adopt me, after all I've put you through? I thought for sure you'd send me away." He shook his head in disbelief, and tears rolled down his cheeks.

"Sweetheart, being part of a family isn't always easy, but we never give up on each other. And no matter what, we'll never give up on you. Not ever. We hope you won't give up on us, either." Abbie hoped with everything in her that he believed it.

"Yes, yes, yes! I would love for you to adopt me," Sam exclaimed, and he put his face in his hands, overcome with emotion. "I never ever dreamed this would happen to me. I never thought I'd have a real family."

Abbie came over to Sam and hugged him, as did John. They all three cried happy tears, and Sam said thank you over and over and over. Abbie would never forget this moment as long as she lived.

* * *

Hannah come out of the house and stared at them. What's going on out here?" Hannah asked. "Am I walking into something good or something bad?"

"I'm upset because I found out you're gonna be my sister," Sam laughed.

"What?" Hannah stopped in her tracks, her mouth open. It was apparent to Abbie that Hannah had not already guessed their decision to adopt Sam.

Sam nodded and smiled. "Your mom and dad are adopting me!"

"Wow! So those are happy tears?" Hannah asked as she

jumped up and down and then ran to where they sat, practically landing on the three of them.

"I don't know yet," Sam laughed, kidding her.

"I'm happy and proud to have you as a brother, Sam," Hannah exclaimed through her own tears.

"Thanks! Me too. I can't believe it." He was half laughing and half crying, as they all were.

"Oh, I can't wait to tell Kyle," Abbie said, taking in the moment. "We'll call him in a little bit."

They talked through the morning, and then Sam handed over the pills he'd taken from them and promised he'd never do anything like that again. Abbie's hand shook as she took the bottle he handed her. She was glad John spoke, because she simply couldn't.

He told Sam again they'd get him through this with the help of the counseling Jamie offered them, a new therapist, and especially help from God. They would need His help now more than ever. They both reassured Sam again that he'd become one of their own kids, a member of their family. Despite the setbacks, they'd come to love him, and they were committed to him. Abbie and John were strong enough in their faith and in their marriage to realize once you love someone, peaks and valleys in the relationship are a given, but love remains.

Sam rode with Hannah to get lunch to bring back for them all while Abbie and John talked some more. After they'd returned and all sat down to lunch, John glanced at Abbie and announced that the two of them had come up with a plan.

"We decided not to tell Jamie about the pills," John started the conversation. "But there will be some new house rules. Medication will be locked up, including your anxiety medication. Abbie or I will dispense it to you every day."

Sam nodded his agreement so far, but the test was yet to come.

Abbie jumped in next. "We'll also look through your room from time to time. And in addition, you'll start with the new therapist right away and keep every appointment. John or I will take you to make sure." She took a deep breath and waited for Sam to react.

"I'm fine with all of that," he said. "I'll do whatever it takes. I promise."

"We're going to do this together," John insisted. "Abbie and I have work to do too. We are going to commit to the family counseling resource Jamie recommended so we can learn how to best communicate with each other and to be able to help you."

Once again, Sam nodded and said it was more than fair. They had a peaceful lunch, and then Hannah left. She had to get back to Nashville at a decent time. She'd taken a personal day today but needed to be back in her classroom in the morning.

Before she left, she hugged Sam for a long time.

"Thanks for everything, especially for making me go to church last night," Sam said.

Hannah hugged him again, even tighter this time. "I can't even think about how different today could've been."

After she left, the three went into the family room. There were still some things to talk about, but the mood was lighter, and Sam was more relaxed and happy than he'd been in a while.

"We talked to Jamie while you and Hannah went to get lunch," John said. "We told her we wanted to adopt you, and she was thrilled. She said she didn't foresee any problems. There are a couple of scenarios where it might take longer, but it will happen."

"So, you don't think my dad will cause any problems?" Sam asked.

Abbie shook her head. "It's all going to work out." She smiled, exuding more confidence than she possessed. To be honest, they didn't know how the man would react. But Sam didn't need to worry about that.

Sam's expression darkened, and he hung his head. "I know him. He'll make things as difficult as he can for me."

"Well, the good news is, you'll be eighteen in a few months,"

John said. "Jamie doesn't exactly know what the situation is with your father, as far as his parental rights are concerned. But that only affects the timing of the adoption—whether it can happen now or once you turn eighteen when he has no say anymore. So, there's no 'if'—only 'when'."

"So, wait ... you mean, you'll still adopt me even if I'm eighteen?" He was puzzled.

"Yes." Abbie smiled and her heart soared. "We found out people adopt kids eighteen and older all the time. We want you to be our son legally. Even if we don't need that to be a family, we want that commitment, for you and for us."

Sam smiled and appeared to be relieved. Then he tilted his head and looked from Abbie to John. "One question. *Uh*, can I change my name to Grayson?"

"Of course," John choked the words out. "Nothing would make us happier."

* * *

After they talked for a while longer, John and Abbie went to make a couple more phone calls. Sam went to his room to grab his journal and headed back out to the deck to get some fresh air and think about the miracles during the past twenty-four hours.

He replayed over and over in his head all that God had spoken in the darkness by the woods last night, and he wrote it all in his journal while it was still fresh in his mind.

As if he could ever forget.

Sam raised his eyes toward the heavens, and at that moment, he thanked God for sending His Son to die on the cross for someone as broken as himself, and he told God he would spend his entire life serving Him, glorifying Him, and doing everything in his power to make Jesus known. He didn't know how or what that would look like, but he was determined to do it.

From here on out, his answer to God no matter the question, would always be "Yes."

forty-one

Sam stood in his big walk-in closet for the longest time before deciding on gray dress pants and a navy, button-down shirt. His hands were sweaty, and although he'd just gotten a haircut, he wished he'd let the lady cut it a little shorter. He wanted to look his best for his future grandparents. They were going to dinner at Abbie's parents' house with the intention of telling them they were adopting Sam.

He sensed Abbie didn't have a good relationship with her parents. The first couple of times Sam met them, he was intimidated because of the way they treated her and John. They weren't always the nicest to Abbie, and it was clear they didn't respect John. Abbie and John were the best people Sam had ever met, so he couldn't understand it.

But he also noted Abbie was always nice and respectful to her parents despite how they treated her. Although she could get some funny, slightly sarcastic jabs in at her parents from time to time. John let it all roll off his back, and he was never disrespectful toward them, either.

On the other hand, the grandparents were always nice to Kyle and Hannah. He could tell they sincerely loved their grandkids.

The couple of times Sam had been around them, they'd been pleasant but a little standoffish toward him. That was fine, though, because he didn't know what he'd do if they treated him like they treated Abbie and John. They were that intimidating.

"Hey, you ready to go?" John came into Sam's room in dress pants and a lightweight sweater. It was so bizarre that they always had to dress up to go there, but then again, Abbie's parents lived in a big, fancy house with pillars, columns, marble floors, and a maid.

John and Abbie's house was bigger, but it was inviting, open, and comfortable. Paul and Sarah's house was cold and sterile. Plus, the maid lived there, cooked all the meals, and did practically everything for them. It all seemed super weird to Sam.

"I think I'm ready. Do I look okay?" Sam was unsure.

"You look great, Sam. What you have on is perfect." John sat on the bed. "Now listen, you know Paul and Sarah can be intimidating. I want you to know that however they decide to act has no bearing on anything. Do you understand?"

"So, you don't think they'll be happy when you tell them you're adopting me?" He desperately needed to know what to expect.

"I wish I could tell how they'll react," John said, "but I just don't know. You've been around them a little, so you know how they are. In their minds, Abbie disappointed them many years ago because she didn't live up to the standards they'd set for her life, and they blame me. That will never change." John shook his head.

Sam hadn't realized that, and it was beyond him how her parents could be disappointed in either of them. Abbie and John both were amazing people.

"All we're asking of you is to get through this evening," John said. "We're doing this because it's the respectful thing to do, but if they aren't respectful to you in return, then you don't have to see them anymore, okay?"

What choice did he have? On the drive to their fancy home in a rich area on the west side of Nashville, Sam tried not to think, and he prayed a lot. The thirty-minute drive was over way too fast. When they arrived, Abbie rang the doorbell. The maid opened the door and let them in.

"We're in here," Sarah called. As they walked into the formal living room, Paul put his *Golf* magazine down, and Sarah motioned for them to sit.

Abbie had told him they were in their mid-seventies but neither appeared that old. Paul's hair was completely gray, he was always tanned, and he usually wore golf pants and golf shirts. Sarah's hair was light brown, and Sam wondered why it wasn't gray.

"Well, hello, Sam. You look good. You're not as pale as the last time you were here. Doesn't he look good, Paul?" Sarah asked.

"He certainly does. How's school Sam? And what can we get you to drink?" Paul asked.

Although they talked to him, they still hadn't addressed John and Abbie. This made Sam uncomfortable, yet it was a little funny at the same time.

"*Um*, school's fine sir, thank you. A Coke would be good," Sam mumbled. Everything about them made him nervous.

"Mom, Dad, hello," Abbie waved from the sofa.

"Oh, hello, you two," Sarah said as she stared at John with pursed lips and lifted her nose. "I almost didn't recognize you without sweatpants on."

John chuckled and shook his head, but Abbie was perturbed. "Mom, when has John *ever* worn sweatpants here?"

Sarah ignored her, and Paul got drinks for them all. They talked about the weather and some general, mundane things before the maid called them into the dining room for dinner. The pleasantries continued over a dinner of pot roast, carrots, salad, and homemade rolls. When the maid cleared the plates and brought dessert out, Abbie stared pointedly at John.

"Sarah, Paul," John cleared his throat. "Abbie and I have something important to tell you." He smiled at Abbie.

Sarah sighed and tossed her napkin onto the table. "You've taken a job across the country."

"Well, *uh*, no," John said. "That's not something we're even considering. I want to finish my career here in Tennessee."

"Well, that's a relief," Sarah blurted, sounding annoyed, while Abbie rolled her eyes. It would have been comical, but Sam was too nervous to laugh.

"What we want to tell you," John started again, "is we've decided to adopt Sam."

The only sound was the ticking of the tall clock in the corner as they all waited for a response. They'd discussed on the way here all the possible responses they could imagine coming from her parents' mouths, with number one being they couldn't understand why John and Abbie would adopt someone who was almost eighteen anyway. Or they hadn't known Sam long enough. Or worse, they would bombard Sam with questions about his past and his biological family, which surprisingly, they'd never done. To Sam, that would be the worst, and he steeled himself for it.

"Well ..." Paul cleared his throat and didn't speak for several moments. Meanwhile, Sarah picked up the napkin she had tossed earlier and used it to dab the corners of her eyes.

"I have to say, I'm surprised. We didn't see this coming, did we dear?" Paul asked.

Sarah shook her head. Paul cleared his throat once more before speaking again.

"Sam, on behalf of Sarah and myself, I want to say we are proud and happy to have you as our grandson," Paul said. At the same time, both he and Sarah got up from their chairs and went to hug Sam.

He mumbled a "Thank you," and Paul and Sarah went back to their seats. John and Abbie both sat with their mouths open.

Finally, Abbie spoke up. "*Aww*, thank you Dad, thank you Mom."

Paul raised his glass. "I propose a toast." They all raised their water glasses, and Sam raised his too. "To the newest member of our family, Sam. We couldn't be happier."

At that moment, Sam realized he had a place in this extended family, because the way he'd seen them treat Kyle and Hannah, their two biological grandchildren, was the way they were treating him too.

forty-two

"That went better than I ever could've imagined." John shook his head in disbelief as he hung his dress clothes in their walk-in closet while Abbie changed out of her skirt and put on shorts.

"I'm still in shock," Abbie replied. "But, as always, I'm thankful that even if I don't have the best relationship with them, at least they love our children. *All* our children," she said to John with a smile.

"I'm very thankful. And now, if the next part of this evening goes half as well, I'll be happy," John said.

For as long as they could, they'd put off telling Sam that John had coached his father. The fact that Jamie or a detective hadn't leaked it by now was nothing short of a miracle, so they had to tell him tonight before he found out from someone else. And with the deposition coming up, he would most likely find out.

"Hey, do you want some pie?" Abbie yelled in the direction of Sam's room as she headed toward the kitchen.

"Sure." His door opened, and he followed her. He'd changed into shorts and a T-shirt too.

Abbie cut the apple pie she'd baked earlier. Each of them grabbed a plate, and they took it into the family room, still talking about what a success the dinner with the grandparents had been.

"Sam, there's something important we need to talk to you about," John said once the conversation about the grandparents died down and they'd finished their pie.

"Oh, no. Something with the adoption?" Sam bit his bottom lip and sat his water glass carefully on the end table.

"No, no, nothing like that. As far as we know, everything is progressing as it should." John paused, drew in a deep breath, and let it out slowly. "It's about your father."

"What about him?" His eyes darkened, and his expression clouded.

"Do you remember me talking awhile back about the player of mine who got involved in drugs, and I had to kick him off the team?" John asked.

"*Um*, yeah, I think so," he nodded his head. "He was the one who went to jail, and you never found out what happened to him?"

"Yes, that's him." John knew full well Sam couldn't begin to imagine how this information affected him, but he continued. "The first time Jamie brought the detective over, we found out they'd uncovered some information about aliases your father used. You know your father as Drew Keller, but, in fact, your mother's last name was Keller. Did you know that?"

Sam shook his head. "I know they weren't married, but I just thought she took his name anyway since they had me. I guess that sounds stupid when I say it out loud," he said, trying to make sense out of this information. "But why would he have gone by her last name?"

"Probably since he'd been in prison and wanted a fresh start," Abbie said.

"I guess that makes sense." Sam seemed to mull it over.

"But it turns out your father's legal name is Andrew Quinn. So that's where the name Drew comes from, short for Andrew, and—

"Wait ... what? I'm really confused," Sam interjected.

"It is confusing, which is why we didn't know," John's voice trailed off.

"Didn't know what?" Sam questioned.

"The player from years ago I told you about—his name was Andy Quinn. And we just found out that Andy Quinn now goes by the alias Drew Keller. Sam, that player from way back then is ... well, he's your father," John finally got the words out as Sam processed for a second before his hand flew to his mouth.

"What? How? I mean, did you know?" he asked, his eyes wide.

John prayed Sam would believe none of them had known. Not himself, not Abbie, and not Jamie. If he didn't believe it, all the trust they'd worked so long and hard for could be gone.

"Honey, we had no clue whatsoever. Like John said, his player was Andy Quinn, and your dad was known to us as Drew Keller." Abbie made an attempt to smooth things over but the look on Sam's face was questioning.

"Did you know me then?" Sam asked, his voice a little shaky.

"No, Sam. When we put the timeline together, all this happened several months before you were born." John once again prayed Sam would believe him. The boy's mouth still hung open, and the color had drained from his face. He shook his head as if trying to make sense of the information.

"We did meet your mom and later learned she was pregnant. When your father went to prison, I went to visit him there several times, but he refused to see me," John said. "We tried to reach out to your mom, but she had moved away, and we weren't able to track her down. As you know, the memories of him have haunted me all these years."

Sam appeared to be soaking it in. "So, you knew my mom," he said softly, more of a statement than a question.

John nodded. "I can't really say we knew her, but we met her. She attended games, and I remember speaking to her once. I just remember her being young, pretty, and nice," he smiled.

"Wow, this is all just, I don't know. Crazy, I guess," If Sam was upset with John and Abbie for any reason, he didn't show it. "And confusing."

"Do you remember us talking about Romans 8:28?" John asked Sam.

"Yes, I've already memorized that one. *And we know that in all things God works for the good of those who love him, who have been called according to his purpose*," Sam quoted, and then it hit him. "Wow," he paused. "That's so amazing. You think God has been working all this out for me all along?"

"Only God knows for sure, but I'd certainly like to think so," John said. He hoped Sam wouldn't ask him why he had to endure so many terrible things in the years in between, because John guessed they'd never know the answer to that question this side of heaven.

"We wanted to tell you as soon as we found out, but we had to process it ourselves," Abbie said. "We hope you're not mad."

Sam was silent for a long moment before answering. "How could I be mad? I mean, what if this was God's plan all along? I'm glad I know Him now so I can see that."

"Amen," John said, and he silently thanked God for His amazing blessings.

forty-three

John pressed the unlock button to his black SUV and loaded his golf clubs in the back. It was sunny and cooler, with the first hint of fall in the air. The golf game with his buddies had energized him.

The adoption process had been stressful and was taking forever to complete. He and Abbie had learned that because Sam's father was still awaiting trial and presumed innocent until proven guilty in a court of law, he still had some say over whether or not his son could be adopted.

The current plan was for social services to present Andy Quinn with a parental termination agreement, and if he signed, they could adopt Sam right away. If Andy refused to cooperate, they could still proceed with the adoption once Sam turned eighteen. It would be up to Sam then, and Quinn would no longer have any say in the matter.

John opened the sunroof and turned the radio to K-Love. Chris Tomlin's classic, "How Great is our God," was playing. Indeed. How many times over the past few weeks had they commented on how great God is? While there were still many details to hammer out, there was no doubt God alone had brought them this far.

He thought about a discussion they'd had with Sam a couple of weeks ago. They'd reassured him once again, that even though he might be eighteen before the adoption is finalized, they wanted him to officially become part of their family. Repeatedly, they'd told him that he'd always be a part of their family, no matter what. But his need for constant reassurance told them it was important for this to be official so he would know the sense of belonging only a family could bring.

For a while now, Sam wasn't just a foster kid, he was their kid. They considered him as much their own as Kyle and Hannah. John chuckled at the thought. Back when the foster journey began, no one could've made him believe it was possible to love a child who wasn't his as much as he loved his biological children. But he certainly loved Sam just as much.

As he pulled into the driveway, his cell phone rang. He checked the caller ID. It was Jamie. This was the day she was supposed to talk to Andy Quinn about the parental termination agreement. John drew a breath and offered a silent prayer as he put his car in park and answered the call.

"Hi, John, it's Jamie, I have some great news for you," she said. She went on to explain Quinn had signed the agreement at once, no questions asked.

"You're free to petition the court. I'd say the adoption could be finalized in as few as thirty days. If you're lucky, you might even be able to get a court date before Sam's birthday at the end of next month."

John was overwhelmed as he thanked her. He couldn't wait to get into the house and tell Abbie. He didn't even pull his car into the garage like he normally did. Instead, he jumped out and ran into the house to look for her and found her on the back deck, reading.

"Honey, I have some great news," John exclaimed, slightly breathless.

Abbie's face lit up as she tilted her head.

"He signed it. No questions asked!" Abbie jumped up and

they hugged each other tightly, both laughing through the happy tears.

"I can't wait to tell Sam when he gets home," Abbie said.

"Hey," John said, his arm around Abbie's shoulder, "what do you say we both pick him up from school and take him for an early dinner and tell him then? He'll be so excited."

Abbie agreed, and they couldn't wait for 2:30 to get there. Sam would be surprised for sure, because they hadn't told him the plan for social services to approach his father today. He would be thrilled. Indeed, how great is our God?

* * *

Sam completed his math test, turned it in, and waited for dismissal. His life was better than ever. He'd aced this test, and a couple of months ago, he probably wouldn't have even turned it in.

Therapy with his new therapist, Dr. Carlisle, was going well. He liked her a lot. He could talk to her easily, and she understood the things he'd been through.

As it turned out, Dr. Carlisle was a Christian, so when she wanted Sam to read or learn about things, she often assigned him biblically based articles and books, which he loved since he was trying to learn as much as he could about God and His plans for Sam's life. Not only was he intent on resolving his trauma issues, but he also wanted to glorify God in everything he did.

John and Abbie told him they could see the difference in him. He wasn't distraught like he'd been so many times after his old therapy appointments. Now, he was making actual progress.

When class was dismissed, he walked out of school with his friends and scanned the parking lot for Abbie's car. Even though he had his driver's license, she still took him to school and picked him up most days. He didn't see her car but spotted John's SUV instead.

"Hey, guys," Sam jumped in the back seat and buckled up.

"What's the occasion that I get both of you to pick me up?" He was happy to see them both.

"Since the weather is so beautiful today, we thought we'd go to our favorite place and eat outside," Abbie said.

Even with her sunglasses on he could see the happiness in her eyes.

On the short drive to their favorite pizza place, they chatted about school and made general small talk.

It was only 2:45, so the restaurant wasn't busy. They got a table in the corner of the patio and ordered. While they waited for their pizza, John and Abbie smiled at each other.

"What's up with you two?" Sam laughed. They were always happy, but they were almost giddy today. "You seem even happier than usual."

John took the lead, and he leaned in toward Sam with his arms crossed on the table in front of him. "Well, today is a special day for our family." He winked at Abbie and continued. "Social services approached your father with the parental termination papers. He's not going to contest it. In fact, he signed the paperwork on the spot. That was our only hurdle, kiddo. We can petition the court, and the adoption could be official in as little as thirty days or so. Possibly even before your birthday next month."

"Seriously?" Sam couldn't believe it. He'd prepared himself for this to drag out well past his eighteenth birthday. "Oh, man, that's the best news ever. I can't believe it's finally gonna happen." After all these years, he was going to have his forever family, and he was overjoyed.

"It's definitely happening," Abbie laughed, "and that's why we're here celebrating. We couldn't wait to tell you. I thought I was going to burst in the car."

Their pizza and breadsticks came out, and as they ate, John and Abbie chatted away happily about what would happen next and how they would have a party once the adoption was final.

Sam was thrilled. He honestly was. So, what was this nagging feeling deep inside him? He smiled and laughed with John and Abbie, but during the meal, the slow, painful realization settled upon him: John said his biological father hadn't hesitated to sign the papers on the spot. He terminated his parental rights. Just. Like. That. With no consideration whatsoever. That was solid proof of what Sam had always thought. His father had never wanted him. Not ever, and today, he simply signed Sam away like someone selling a possession.

He felt sick. He couldn't force a smile and couldn't eat. He lost all focus on what John and Abbie were saying. Sadness overwhelmed him, and he was confused by it. He loved the Graysons and wanted to be part of their family more than anything, so why did he feel this way? Deep inside, he realized that even with all the trauma his father had put him through, the man was still his biological father. And the hard, cold truth was he didn't want Sam. He never had.

That truth was much harder to accept than Sam could've ever imagined.

forty-four

Abbie was aware of Sam's mood change during dinner but chalked it up to him being surprised and maybe a little overwhelmed. By the time they got home, though, it was clear something was very wrong—something more than him simply being overwhelmed.

He'd told them thanks for dinner and how happy he was the adoption was going to work out sooner rather than later. Then he went downstairs to start on schoolwork and his reading for the next week.

Abbie had no doubt his attempt to cover up whatever was wrong was sincere, but it fell flat. Once Sam was out of earshot, Abbie turned to John. "Okay, it's not just me, right? He completely shut down about halfway through dinner, didn't he?"

John agreed. "He sure did, but why? I know he's happy about the adoption, but as dinner went on, it was like he wasn't even there."

Abbie thought about that for a moment, "Do you think it was the talk about having a party? Maybe he doesn't want a party. I mean, we'd never brought it up before, so maybe it's not something he even wants."

John shook his head. "I can't imagine his mood change was about a party, but who knows?"

It wasn't lost on Abbie that there was still a lot they didn't know about Sam. "Let's give him a little while, and then I'll go downstairs and make sure he's okay," Abbie suggested. John agreed, so they went to the family room and watched TV.

A while later, Abbie went to the basement to check on Sam. She expected to see him sitting on the sofa reading or watching TV but was surprised instead to find the basement dark other than the dim light coming from the small lamp on a corner table. Music played softly, and once her eyes adjusted to the low lighting, she saw him sitting on the sofa, silent tears running down his face.

"Hey, are you okay?" Abbie asked. She couldn't imagine what was wrong. He turned away from her and swiped the tears from his face with the back of his hand.

"I'm sorry." Sam was out of breath, and his words came in clusters as he fought back the tears. "It's not you ... and ... it's not the adoption. I definitely ... am happy about it."

Abbie would've laughed at the irony of that except there was nothing funny about the moment. "It's okay, you have nothing to be sorry about. But something is obviously wrong. Whatever it is, you can tell me," she said.

It shook her to the core to see him like this. He'd been through so much, but Abbie couldn't imagine what had come to his mind during dinner when they were happily talking about his adoption.

"Take your time. Tell me when you're ready." Abbie sat next to him and waited.

The tears started falling again, and Abbie put her arm around his shoulders and let him cry. She got up and went to the wet bar to get Sam some water from the refrigerator. He drank a few sips of the water and finally settled down a little bit.

Sam bit his lip and stared straight ahead at the fireplace for what seemed like minutes, obviously willing himself not to cry again. Soon, he gained his composure. "I just want to know what I ever did to make him hate me so much. Why didn't he ever want me?" He managed to get the words out.

Abbie was confused. But slowly, Sam's words registered, and the reality of the moment was a punch in her stomach.

Oh, my. She and John had happily told him over dinner that his father had instantly signed over his parental rights. In their minds that was a great thing, but neither she nor John had stopped to think about how it might affect him. No matter what, Andy Quinn, or Drew Keller, as Sam knew him, was his biological father, and they'd pretty much told him the man cared so little about him that he signed him over—without hesitation, no questions asked.

"Oh, Sam." Abbie reached out to pull him toward her and put her arms around him. "I am so sorry. I can't believe how insensitive we were. We were so excited, we never stopped to think about how that news might affect you. I'm so sorry."

"It's not your fault," he whispered. "I don't even want him to want me. I wouldn't go back to him if I had to, but I just wanna know why he hates me so much. Why hasn't he ever wanted me? Why has no one ever wanted me?"

Abbie had no answers. "Listen, all I know is, it wasn't you, and it certainly wasn't anything you ever did or didn't do. It has everything to do with him and the flawed person he is, and absolutely nothing to do with you. You have to understand that, sweetheart."

Sam nodded but didn't say anything.

"John and I love you, Sam. And *we* want you. We already think of you as our son, and we can't wait to make it official. Please, just remember that, okay?" Abbie pleaded.

He stopped crying and told Abbie thanks and he loved them both also. She sat with him until he fell asleep, and then she covered him with a blanket and went upstairs to John.

"I can't believe I was so insensitive. Why didn't I think about how that might make him feel?" John asked.

"It's not your fault, babe." Abbie shook her head. "I didn't think about it either. It goes to show us, once again, how little we still know about what Sam's life has been like. To live through the trauma he's been through with his father and some of the other foster families, and to be shuffled from one home to another for years ..." Abbie's tears took over, and she was quiet.

John nodded. "You know the other night when we were reading the book that Dr. Carlisle wanted us to read?" he asked. "The one about how trauma like Sam's can last a lifetime, even with therapy? I thought to myself, no, he can overcome all this. But the truth is, we have no idea how deep-seated the trauma is. And we still don't even know everything about him and what he's been through."

They decided tomorrow morning they would both talk to him together and reinforce to him he hadn't done anything wrong, and that his father suffered from profoundly serious problems to put Sam through all the things he had. They'd let Sam know how much they loved him and wanted him here, and they would continue to reinforce those things to him for as long as he needed to hear them, even if it was a lifetime.

forty-five

The first day of fall. Autumn had always been Sam's favorite season, but this year he had so much more to be excited about. Day trips they'd planned to see the fall colors, TU football games with John and Kyle, and his favorite things—coffee and soup. But most of all, he was excited about his birthday, which he hoped and prayed would also be his adoption day.

He just had to get through today's hurdle first—the deposition. He and John sat in Kyle's office at the law firm and waited for the deposition to start, while Kyle ran through last-minute instructions.

Sam attempted to focus, but he was overwhelmed as he stared out Kyle's law office window overlooking the city of Nashville from the twenty-fourth floor of the corporate building. The view was breathtaking, but he'd give anything to be out there somewhere rather than in this building, preparing to be interrogated about things he'd been trying hard to forget.

"Now just remember what we talked about," Kyle said, bringing Sam back to the matter at hand. "Be honest with your answers, and if you don't remember something, it's okay. I'll stop the questioning if they ask anything inappropriate or if you need a break."

Sam took a deep breath. "Okay. Can Dad go in with me?"

Kyle snapped his head up from his paperwork. The heat rose in Sam's cheeks, and he realized maybe Kyle didn't know John and Abbie had told him he could go ahead and start calling them Mom and Dad.

But a huge smile took over Kyle's face, and he nodded. "Yes, Dad can be in there with you."

Kyle's secretary buzzed his phone. "Mr. Grayson, everyone has arrived. They're in the conference room and ready when you are."

"Thanks, Jessica, we'll be right in," Kyle said.

Sam's throat tightened. His heart raced as he focused on keeping his emotions in check. When they entered the conference room, Jessica handed him a ginger ale. He thanked her. Maybe it would calm his queasiness.

He and John took a seat as Jessica set out coffee, and Kyle made all the introductions. The prosecutor, Mr. Burnett, would run the meeting and ask most of the questions, but defense attorneys for his father and his father's two associates-in-crime, Paulette and Blaze, were also present and would be able to ask him questions.

Kyle had explained to Sam that this could go on for many hours and would be emotionally exhausting for him. Especially when the defense attorneys got their chance to ask questions.

Mr. Burnett started the meeting and explained how the process worked. The court reporter would transcribe every word spoken, so it was important for Sam to answer all questions orally and not just nod or shake his head. He began with some basic questions such as name, address, and school status.

"Sam, it's important for you, as well as everyone else in the room, to remember you are a witness here. You are the victim and not the one on trial. So, take a deep breath and simply answer things honestly and to the best of your recollection." Mr. Burnett smiled at Sam and appeared to be on his side.

They spent about an hour talking through his childhood, the foster homes he'd lived in, and the various situations with his father that had landed Sam in the foster care system repeatedly.

It dawned on Sam that this was the first time for John to hear most of this, especially the extent of drug use he had witnessed and was even involved in himself at one time. He hoped and prayed John wouldn't be mad and would forgive him for not sharing with him and Abbie all the gory details of his life before he came to live with them.

After about ninety minutes, they took a break before getting into the crimes they were here to discuss. Mr. Burnett wanted to consult with Kyle, so John asked Sam to walk outside with him for some fresh air. He had no doubt John was mad when they rode the elevator together in silence with John staring straight ahead.

They exited the elevator on the ground floor, walked outside, and rounded a corner to an empty sitting area in a tree-lined courtyard. John still hadn't said a word, so Sam started to explain himself when John abruptly stopped, turned around, and put his hands on Sam's shoulders. Sam was surprised to see nothing but kindness in the man's eyes.

"Sam, no, there's nothing you need to say. I don't even know what to say." John paused, stared at the ground, and then started again. "I'm so sorry for all you had to go through as a child. I never had a clue until today what your life had been like before we met you. I'm so sorry."

John held Sam's gaze for a long moment, and Sam saw sadness in his eyes rather than the anger he'd expected.

"I was afraid you were mad at me because I didn't tell you all that. I'm sorry I didn't, and you had to hear it in there." He looked away, partly sorry and partly embarrassed.

John shook his head and his hands remained on Sam's shoulders, forcing eye contact. "There's nothing at all for you to be sorry about. I understand. It's a lot, and I can imagine you didn't want to talk about it and only wanted to get it behind you."

Sam nodded and took a deep breath that filled his lungs with the autumn air. He was relieved John wasn't mad. His new family was on his side no matter what, and as they rode back up the elevator to finish the deposition, he found a new sense of strength he'd never had before. He could handle whatever the attorneys threw at him.

* * *

John listened to Sam answer question after question. The boy's strength amazed him. He already relived so much of this in the form of flashbacks and nightmares, yet his answers were calm and professional. He was proud of Kyle for preparing Sam so well.

They were about to get into the gut-wrenching details of the days in question. This would be the worst part for Sam. But first, the prosecutor asked him about his visit to John at his office on the Tennessee University campus, and it occurred to John that he and Sam had never discussed that visit.

"What was the purpose of your trip to Nashville to see Coach Grayson on campus that day?"

Sam drew in a breath. "I had planned to tell him everything my father had done and was involved in. Everything I knew about, anyway. I figured he'd know what to do and could figure out a way to help me get out of there."

The floor underneath him gave way—Sam's visit that day had been a cry for help. John would never forgive himself for not seeing it at the time. Never.

"When on your way to visit with Coach Grayson, did you intend to go back to your father afterward?" Mr. Burnett asked.

"No, sir." Sam stared at his hands folded in his lap. "I didn't."

"What did happen during that visit, Sam?" The man continued with the questioning.

"*Um*, well, I didn't tell him anything I planned to." Sam didn't look at anyone.

"Why was that?"

He took a drink of his ginger ale, and he turned paler than before. "Well, when I got there everybody was in basketball mode, preparing for the tournament. It kind of jolted me back to reality. I realized he had a lot of other things and other people to worry about besides me. I decided I didn't want to bother him when he had all that going on."

Sam's words pierced John's soul. It was almost more than he could take. Sam had been in a life-and-death situation, but John had given the appearance that basketball was more important than anything else. John felt sick.

"Also," Sam paused for a moment, "I was afraid maybe he wouldn't believe me. Or if he did believe me, my father would do something to him to retaliate. All of that ran through my mind while I waited for him in his office. Basically, I talked myself out of it before John even came into his office."

"Can you tell us what happened when your father found out about the visit?" Mr. Burnett asked.

"Nothing happened that night. But the next day when I got home from school, I took a nap. I woke up later to him screaming and cursing at me. He screamed at me for going to see 'that coach'." Sam paused for a moment.

"I told him I didn't tell John anything, but he didn't believe me. He said someone tipped off DCS, and he was on their radar again, so we had to move. He told me it was my fault 'the plan' had to be set into motion earlier than expected. I had no idea at the time what he meant by that." Sam stared at the floor and appeared to be in his own world as he spoke, reliving the horrible moments John hadn't known about until now.

"Then he picked up his shotgun, and I was sure he was going to shoot me." Sam's voice broke slightly. "But instead, he swung it around and hit me in the chest with the barrel of the gun and knocked me down. Then he beat me with it until I blacked out."

John couldn't catch his breath as the realization hit him—Andy had almost killed Sam because he and Abbie had decided to call social services. It was almost more than John could bear. He had messed this up for Sam in every way possible.

The questioning went on to the next thing Sam remembered, which was when he woke up in Alabama and was told what he had to do. Sam struggled to get through this portion of the deposition.

They continued to the point after he told the girls to run from the "coffee shop," and Sam awoke at the motel, tied to the bed. The attorneys paused the testimony several times for Sam to compose himself. About halfway through that line of questioning, Kyle asked for a short recess, and they went to Kyles's office.

Once there, Sam slumped back onto the sofa and closed his eyes.

"I'm going to ask for a continuation to tomorrow. This is too much for you for one day," Kyle said.

Sam shook his head and sat up. "No. I don't want to have to come back. I wanna get this over with today."

John nodded slowly at Kyle. It had to be up to Sam at this point.

"Okay, if you want to continue, we will. But I need to tell you, when the questioning is handed over to the defense attorneys, it could get worse," Kyle warned.

John couldn't imagine how it could get any worse than it already was, but Sam was steadfast in his decision.

"I have to get it over with today." Sam's answer was sure and direct.

It was nearing 5:00 p.m., so Jessica brought in soup from a nearby restaurant, and Sam ate a little. He said the soup made him feel better and a little stronger.

John hoped that was the case. He prayed Sam could get through this next part.

* * *

John and Kyle watched Sam like he was going to fall apart. Only he wasn't. He was at peace. God was with him and would carry him through this next part.

He'd prayed nonstop about the two girls, Ava and Amanda. Everyone told him there was no sign that anyone had been held against their will at that motel, and his father and his associates had said there were no girls. They told the police Sam had made them up.

Although the investigators were never able to locate the two girls or their parents, Sam was certain at least Ava was in the room next door to his. It was no hallucination, and he certainly hadn't made her up. She was out there somewhere, and his father most likely knew where.

"Sam?" Kyle's question brought him back to the present—something about him not being okay and postponing.

"I promise, I'm okay. I really am." The glances Kyle and John shared told him they didn't believe him, but he was thankful they let him proceed.

The three walked back to the conference room to finish the questioning. Sam got to say his peace—he was certain beyond a doubt that Ava was in the room next to him. The questioning ended at the point when Sam had been taken to the hospital, his questioning by the detective at home with the Graysons, and his identification of Paulette and Blaze.

They were ready to start the defense questioning, and Kyle asked Sam if he needed another break. It was 7:30 p.m. It was hard to tell how much longer this would last, but he didn't want a break. His determination to get through it all tonight was stronger than ever.

When Sam's father's attorney took over the questioning, Sam

was ready. He would answer whatever questions they threw at him. But the attorney shocked everyone when he stated, "I have no questions at this time."

Mr. Burnett and Kyle, each with mouths wide open, appeared as if they might fall out of their chairs. This is the part Kyle had said he was most worried about. But instead, they passed on questioning. Sam couldn't imagine what this meant.

Next, the questioning went to the attorneys of Paulette and Blaze. The questions weren't anything unexpected. Kyle had prepared him well for these exact questions. They focused on the identification of Paulette and Blaze, and how Sam could be so sure it was the two of them due to the darkness of the room he had described and his physical and mental condition at the time.

After a few questions each, the attorneys were satisfied, and the deposition was finished.

Sam whispered a thank you to God for getting him through this.

forty-six

John's afternoon meetings on campus had gone well. He and his assistant coaches had a good plan for the upcoming season and the new players on their team. Practices would start in a couple of weeks, and John was anxious to get into that routine. He checked his cell phone as he walked out to the parking lot to head home for dinner. Two missed calls from Kyle.

He hoped this wasn't about the trial dates. Even though they all knew it was coming, they dreaded it. John and Abbie had talked a lot about the trial and whether Sam would have to attend. Kyle hoped his deposition testimony would be enough to keep him from testifying in person, but there was no way of knowing.

John threw his bag in the back of his SUV, got in, and dialed Kyle, who answered on the first ring.

"Hey, I forgot you were in meetings today," Kyle said.

"It's okay, sorry I didn't have my phone on. What's going on?" John could hear the tension in his own voice.

Kyle's laugh caught John by surprise. "Dad, you're not even going to believe this. It's over. They've pled guilty—all three of them. They asked for plea deals yesterday, and we said no to all of them. And then today, each pled guilty. There won't be a trial, just sentencing in a few weeks. We'll likely want Sam to write statements, but he won't need to go to court. It's over."

"I don't even know what to say." John laughed, although he was in total shock. "Did you think this might happen?"

"Not for a minute," Kyle exclaimed. "But the prosecutor said Sam's deposition was so compelling, and the social service and medical records backed up everything he said. Apparently, the defense attorneys all went back to their clients and said they didn't have a case unless they could prove Sam is lying. Which of course they can't because the evidence is on Sam's side. This is the absolute best outcome, but I never even dreamed it would happen."

"So, what exactly are they pleading guilty to?" John asked. "Is trafficking still on the table since no one has proven the girls were there?"

"The judge threw out the part about the girls, due to lack of evidence." Kyle sighed. "But the detectives said they will continue to investigate. They pled guilty to kidnapping Sam, which is a federal offense. And the fact they took him across a couple of state lines makes it worse. Add the assault charges, and they should get a pretty hefty sentence," Kyle said.

John was overjoyed. He congratulated Kyle and told him how proud he was of him.

In a couple of weeks, their adoption of Sam would be final. They'd all worried a trial would overshadow it. But not now. No doubt, God had cleared the way. This was indeed the greatest news. He couldn't wait to tell Abbie. And especially Sam.

The drive home took forever, but John finally made it home, found Abbie and Sam sitting out back and told them the good news.

The three went out and celebrated. Later, he and Abbie agreed they'd never seen Sam this happy. It was as though a weight had been lifted from him as the realization hit that his father would likely go to prison for a long time, and he would never be forced to face the man again.

Sure enough, two weeks later Kyle called with news that the judge gave Sam's father the maximum sentence of twenty years. Of course, a life sentence would have been better. Unfortunately, that wasn't an option. He would be eligible for parole at some point, but they'd worry about that when the time came.

His accomplices got similar sentences. The justice system worked in Sam's favor, and after nearly eighteen years, he could put the past behind him, get on with his life, and, at last, begin to heal.

* * *

The adoption process was progressing and had even picked up speed. The Graysons worked with an adoption specialist who helped them with the process and paperwork. They'd had a home visit and a social worker talked to Sam to make sure this was what he wanted. Apparently, the process was much easier with an almost eighteen-year-old than with a younger child.

They'd just learned the adoption would be finalized in late October and could be scheduled on Sam's actual birthday, which was something he had asked about. He was beyond excited that it was becoming a real possibility.

"My birthday has always been a bad day. Either because I was with my father, and he didn't even acknowledge it. Or I was with a foster family, and they didn't acknowledge it. If they did, it only made me wish I had my own family. This will change all that," he had told him.

It made perfect sense to John. "Think of the happy celebration we can have every year on your birthday." He was thrilled it was working out this way.

"Oh, I have another question for you," Sam said sheepishly. "I don't know if it's even possible."

"Shoot." John was curious as to what he was thinking.

"Well, you already said I could change my last name to

283

Grayson. I was wondering," he paused, "if I can change my middle name too."

Abbie nodded. "Your middle name is Joseph, same as your father. I never thought much about it until now. What would you want to change it to?"

"Well, I don't know how you would feel about this, but I was thinking about John. Samuel John Grayson," Sam said.

John didn't know what to say. He'd always been an emotional person, but lately, it was draining. It took a moment for him to compose himself before he could speak.

"Nothing would make me happier," he choked out the words. "I guess I've got another phone call to make," John said, and Sam and Abbie laughed.

"I know I've told you before, but I want to tell you again how thankful I am to you both. I never thought being a permanent part of a family would happen for me. When I came here that first night I figured this was just another home." He shrugged.

John offered up a prayer of thanks to God. Because only God could work out all the details for the three of them to get to this point. God knew all along this wasn't just another home for Sam. It was his forever home, with his forever family.

forty-seven

Sam woke up early on October twenty-fifth, his eighteenth birthday. His alarm was set to go off at 6:00 a.m., but he'd been awake since 5:15, so he could spend some time with God. He read Romans 8:28, the verse John always quoted, "*And we know that in all things God works for the good of those who love him, who have been called according to his purpose.*" As he reflected on all his struggles, he thanked God for all He'd done to set a plan into motion that got him to the Graysons that May night when he was sixteen. That night changed the entire course of his life.

Abbie and John, soon to officially be Mom and Dad, had never fostered before and had been adamant they didn't want a teenager. And he'd been certain this was just another home—no more, no less. Of course, only God could have weaved this story together, and Sam was completely in awe of His power and might.

In a couple of hours, the three of them would get in the car and drive to family court in Nashville, where he would stand before a judge with his new family. His adoption would become final, and he would officially, forever, be part of the Grayson family.

"Happy eighteenth birthday, Sam. And Happy Adoption

Day!" John and Abbie shouted in unison. They were dressed and ready to go. Sam had never seen them happier since he'd known them.

They sat at the kitchen island waiting for him with coffee and his favorite cranberry-orange muffins Abbie picked up from the bakery last night. She poured three mugs of coffee—his favorite fall blend.

"I can't believe today is finally the day. After all you've been through and all we've been through together." Abbie beamed.

John nodded and his eyes glistened already. "I'm so happy, for all of us. When all this started, I was certain I didn't want a teenager. Who would've thought we'd end up here a year and a half later?"

"God stepped in." Abbie reached for John's hand. "He knew Sam needed us, and we needed him."

Sam thought about her words. He'd never considered that they might need him, but they said they did. They told him he'd opened their eyes to so many things, like the importance of every child having a family, and the need for people to feel included, wanted, and loved.

They told him he'd changed how they viewed the world, and they hadn't ruled out fostering other teens in the future. But first, they wanted to have time with him. "Time for you to get all the attention and all the love you deserve," Abbie had said. And he was perfectly fine with that.

* * *

They arrived at the courthouse in Nashville thirty minutes early for their 10:00 a.m. appointment with the judge. They sat in the car and waited, which Sam didn't understand. John said he'd get a text when it was time to enter the courtroom, so they listened to the radio and talked, and Sam told them he was nervous and excited.

John constantly checked his phone until, finally, he received the text they'd all three been waiting for.

"They're ready for us." John turned around and smiled at Sam in the back seat, and the three got out of the car.

John stopped and put his hands on Sam's shoulders.

"Do you realize, when you get back in the car, you will be Sam Grayson?" John asked.

"No, I'll be Samuel John Grayson." He laughed. The three headed into the judicial building and took the elevator to the third floor. They stepped off the elevator and headed to room 301. When they got to the room, the door was closed, and John stepped back and motioned for Sam to take the lead.

"You go in first, son." John smiled.

Sam was confused for a second. It seemed weird John would want him to walk in first, but he did as he was told. He expected to see a judge, their adoption attorney, and probably a court reporter, but when he opened the door, there was a whole room full of people. They all stood and cheered.

Stunned for a moment as the realization of what was happening hit him in full force, Sam was overwhelmed but willed himself not to cry as John and Abbie put their arms around his shoulders. He composed himself and looked around the room in total disbelief. All the people he had come to know and love on this journey were in this room. Kyle, Cassie, and Hannah had rushed up to them and hugged him, and Abbie's parents, Sarah and Paul—his new grandparents—were close behind.

Next he noticed his best friend Lauren and her mom, and his close friends from school, Nate, Tara, and Michael. In the next row was Abbie's best friend Wendy, her husband Roger and their daughter, Isabella, along with John's best friend and assistant coach Wes and his wife Susan. Behind them were several other friends and neighbors who had supported John and Abbie on this journey and had befriended him along the way.

And, of course, with possibly the biggest smile of all, there was Jamie. His long-time social worker. Looking back, Sam could see she'd always done her absolute best and was instrumental in him being fostered by the Graysons.

After several minutes of happy greetings and hugs, everyone in the courtroom took a seat. Sam expected the judge to be mad, bang on the table with his gavel, and tell them to settle down like he'd seen on TV. But this judge was all smiles. He welcomed the Grayson family and all their extended family and friends. Even he clapped and cheered.

Once the courtroom quieted down and Sam, John, and Abbie took their seats at the front, Judge Porter talked about what a happy occasion it was. He was genuinely happy for Sam and the Graysons.

"Sam, I'd like for you to step forward with your adoptive parents please." Judge Porter grinned. "And your future brother and sister too."

The three got up and stood before the judge, along with Kyle and Hannah, with Sam in between John and Abbie.

"Sam," the judge said, "I understand you'd like to take the Graysons' last name and also change your middle name to John, is that correct?"

"Yes, sir, I mean Your Honor, sir. I'm sorry, sir." Sam blushed.

Judge Porter smiled warmly at Sam. "We're a happy court Sam, and decidedly informal here. No worries, young man." Several people in the courtroom chuckled, and Kyle, who was standing behind Sam, patted him on the back.

"First, Mr. and Mrs. Grayson, I would like you to sign the certificate before you, indicating you are now the parents of Samuel John Grayson. Sam, you may step forward and watch," Judge Porter instructed.

John had his arm around Abbie's shoulder as they approached the table in front of the judge's platform. They each read over it and Abbie signed first and then John.

The judge came around the platform, stepped down, and joined them.

"As soon as I sign, it will be official." And then Judge Porter leaned over the table and signed on the dotted line. Next, he turned toward the courtroom as did Sam, his new parents, and new siblings.

"Friends and family, it is with tremendous pleasure that I introduce to you the Grayson family: John, Abbie, and their children, Kyle, Hannah, and last, but not least, Samuel John."

The entire courtroom broke into cheers and tears. They all rushed to the front of the courtroom, where the Grayson family stood and hugged each other tightly. John whispered to Sam that the rush of people reminded him of the fans rushing the court when his team had won the NCAA championship. Except this was even better.

After 3,738 days in the foster care system, Sam's wish for a forever family had been granted, thanks to a series of events dating back to before he was even born that only God, full of mercy and grace, could orchestrate.

Sam still had a long way to go to be free of all the trauma he'd experienced. But God was in control. Jesus had told him at that cross months ago that he would live, and that's exactly what Sam intended to do.

The End

acknowledgments

To my husband, Jeff—I could not have done this without you. You encouraged me every step of the way, and this book would not have been possible without your support. I love you and our life together and wouldn't trade a minute of it.

To my daughter, Nicole—Your love and dedication to writing and to the creative world in general are an inspiration, and your constant support and encouragement kept me going.

To my son, Brandon—Your achievement of completing an English degree, your devotion to editing, and your love of music have taught me not to be afraid to pursue my dreams.

To Derek and Vanessa—Thank you for loving my kids and being part of our family.

To my lifelong, best friend, Dana—You've been right here every step of the way and have always encouraged me, and believed in me, even when I didn't.

To my mom (in Heaven), Martha, and my dad, Jim—Thank you for instilling in me the love of reading and books.

I love you all.

To Scrivenings Press, Linda Fulkerson, and my editors—Thank you for believing in me and in this story. My heart is forever grateful.

Kimberly Banet left the corporate world in 2020, after working in Human Resources for nearly two decades and started her own small hobby business, Starlight Stitches. At first, the business consisted of inspirational and seasonal crafts and home décor, but then she decided to do something she had wanted to do for years—write a Christian fiction novel.

After more than three years of writing and re-writing, learning the craft by reading books, attending webinars, and entering contests to learn from judges' critiques, the dream became a reality with the publishing of her debut novel, *Just Another Home*.

Kimberly received her bachelor's degree from Indiana University where she majored in Business and Psychology. She and her husband of more than thirty-five years, Jeff, have resided in the beautiful rural community of Starlight, Indiana, since 1989 where they raised two wonderful children: Nicole, who lives in Seattle, Washington, and Brandon, who lives in Louisville, Kentucky. Today, they share their home with their dachshund, Daisy Mae, and their yorkie-poo, Winnie.

When they're not working, she and Jeff enjoy weekend road trips and visits to state parks, vacations in the Florida panhandle or the mountains of Tennessee, and college basketball and football. Kimberly's hobbies include reading, Bible journaling, crocheting blankets, making seasonal crafts and mugs, and spending time with good friends.

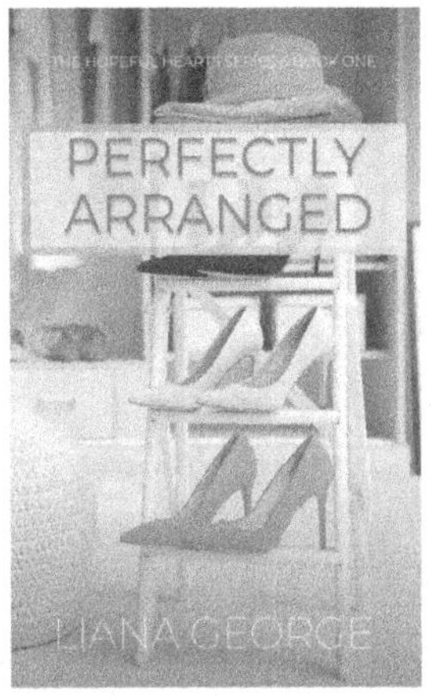

Perfectly Arranged by Liana George

Book One of the Hopeful Hearts series

Short on clients and money, professional organizer Nicki Mayfield is hanging up her label maker. That is until the eccentric socialite Katherine O'Connor offers Nicki one last job.

Working together, the pair discovers an unusual business card among Ms. O'Connor's family belongings that leads them on a journey to China. There the women embark on an adventure of faith and self-discovery as they uncover secrets, truths, and ultimately, God's perfectly arranged plans.

Get your copy here: https://scrivenings.link/perfectlyarranged

* * *

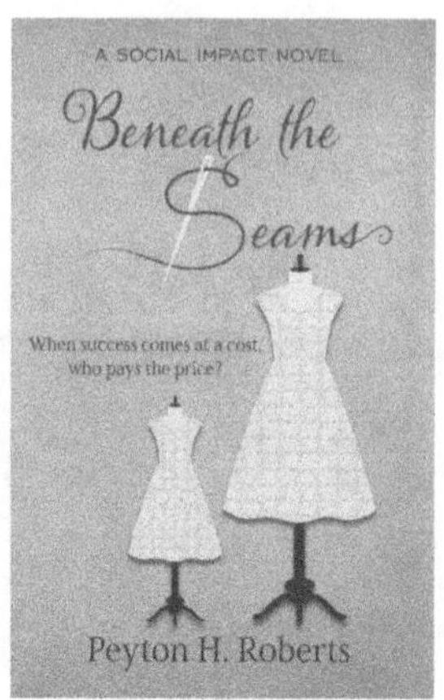

Beneath the Seams

Peyton H. Roberts

Fashion designer Shelby Lawrence is launching her mother-daughter dresses nationwide when she receives a photo of the girl who will change her life forever. Runa, the family's newly sponsored child, is a clever student growing up near Dhaka, Bangladesh. Shelby's daughter Paisley is instantly captivated by their faraway friend. As the girls exchange heartwarming messages, Shelby has no idea that a tragedy in Runa's life is about to upend her own.

Dresses are flying off the racks when a horrifying scene unfolds in Dhaka that threatens to destroy Shelby's pristine reputation. Even worse—it sends Runa's life spiraling down a terrifying path. Shelby must decide how far she's willing to go to right a tragic wrong.

Both a gripping exposé of fashion industry secrets and a heartwarming mother-daughter tale, Beneath the Seams explores love, conscience, hope, and the common threads connecting humanity.

Get your copy here:

https://scrivenings.link/beneaththeseams

* * *